DARKNESS COMES BEFORE THE DAWN

Darkness Comes before the Dawn

Book Four of the Karina Series

TERRY UMPHENOUR

iUniverse LLC
Bloomington

DARKNESS COMES BEFORE THE DAWN
BOOK FOUR OF THE KARINA SERIES

iUniverse books may be ordered through booksellers or by contacting:

iUniverse LLC
1663 Liberty Drive
Bloomington, IN 47403
www.iuniverse.com
1-800-Authors (1-800-288-4677)

ISBN: 978-1-4759-7579-6 (sc)
ISBN: 978-1-4759-7581-9 (hc)
ISBN: 978-1-4759-7580-2 (e)

Library of Congress Control Number: 2013902415

Printed in the United States of America

iUniverse rev. date: 10/11/2013

In memory of Judith Holschen,
fellow teacher, adventurer, and friend.

Contents

CHAPTER 1   The Underworld. 1

CHAPTER 2   Hypothermia 10

CHAPTER 3   Going Vertical 24

CHAPTER 4   Cave Rescue. 39

CHAPTER 5   The Maze 47

CHAPTER 6   Devil's Icebox 64

CHAPTER 7   A Race against Time 72

CHAPTER 8   A Return to the Past 85

CHAPTER 9   Hawaiian Holiday. 99

CHAPTER 10   Make-A-Wish Foundation 113

CHAPTER 11   Volcanoes National Park 123

CHAPTER 12   Earthquake 135

CHAPTER 13   A Hot Time at Sea 148

CHAPTER 14   Eruption. 158

CHAPTER 15   On the Run 169

CHAPTER 16   The Darkness before Dawn 179

CHAPTER 17   The New Dawn 193

CHAPTER I

The Underworld

Bats! Karina froze in place as dozens of dark-winged shapes fluttered past her head. Her heart pounded wildly, but the bats didn't send icy chills up and down her spine. Bats didn't frighten Karina. Her flesh crept from the terrified shriek that still echoed in her ears—the shriek that drove countless little brown bats from daily slumber into frenzied flight, the shriek that dredged up unknown fears, and the shriek that could have only come from one of her friends.

"Hurry!" Karina yelled to Joe.

She ran recklessly down the shadowy passageway—against all rules for cave exploration. The dim light provided by the tiny halogen lamp fastened to her helmet bounced wildly along the wet, slippery cave floor.

"Stop running!" Joe shouted.

A restraining hand firmly gripped Karina's shoulder. Her feet slid forward and threw her off balance. She nearly crashed into the cave wall's sharp rocks. Her helmet slid forward on her forehead and blocked part of her vision. Karina struggled to control her emotions. She turned to face her partner.

"Sorry, I should have known better."

Karina fought against the impulse to race toward the direction of the scream—the direction her friends had traveled. She adjusted the unwieldy, mud-stained helmet that protected her from the jagged rock ceiling only inches above her head.

"There was only one scream," Joe said in a reassuring tone, as one might calm a frightened child. He swiped a strand of curly, black hair away from his brow. "Some bats probably startled Megan or Heather. My guess is that it was Megan. She was awfully nervous about going this deep into the cave without an adult leader."

At seventeen, Joe was two years her senior. Karina took a deep breath and let it out slowly. She shined her helmet light onto Joe's chest. Nearly six feet tall, Joe stood almost six inches taller than Karina. His blue eyes sparkled in the reflected light. "You're right," she conceded. "But let's hurry anyway, just in case."

She remembered how pale Megan had turned at breakfast when Martin, Karina's guardian and headmaster of Blue Horizons, had informed them that he felt the class had learned the necessary skills for safe cave exploration. Blue Horizons, a small alternative school located in the state of New York—far from the Missouri cave she currently explored—taught many courses through real-life experiences that included flying an ultralight airplane and cave exploration. Often these courses were taught off campus and lasted for many weeks. That morning, for the first time without adult supervision, Martin had sent three teams of students into Little Scott's Cave to explore.

Megan was so nervous that she hadn't even eaten breakfast. During the previous five days of exploration, Martin had been her partner. He had worked to help Megan overcome the claustrophobia that terrorized her during each underground excursion.

Continuing at a safer pace, Karina worked through the narrow, winding cave and dodged numerous serrated rock spurs jutting out from the limestone walls. Little Scott's Cave was "dead," meaning that its formations no longer grew larger, so Karina wasn't particularly worried about damaging a cave formation, but Martin had taught her to respect nature. She didn't want to break anything—or get cut. Injuring herself would only make whatever situation awaited her even worse.

"There," Karina said, pointing her light toward a hazy pinpoint glowing in the distance. "I see only one light."

"Don't panic." Joe moved in front of her and led the way. "Stay close."

Trembling and fearing the worst, Karina followed Joe through the dark passageway. She refused to let her imagination run wild. He would handle the situation as he always did. Past experiences gave her confidence that Joe could handle whatever emergency awaited them. In just over a year, he had rescued her three times, twice saving her life. Joe had helped her land an ultralight airplane when she was deathly ill from a rattlesnake bite. Without his timely assistance, she would have crashed. Then he had rescued her from the Amazon rainforest when she had gone off on an ill-fated search for a lost pilot. And only three months earlier, he had helped her survive a shipwreck.

Joe's headlamp suddenly illuminated a slim, dark figure with long blonde hair flowing from beneath her helmet. He asked quietly, "Heather, are you hurt? Where's Megan?"

"I twisted my ankle."

Heather sat on the damp, slippery mud. Grasping her right, boot-enclosed ankle with both hands, she rocked back and forth, obviously in great pain. "Megan, like, lost her balance and put her hand on the ceiling to keep from falling. She touched a bat and freaked. I grabbed her arm and tried to keep her from running, but I slipped and went down. Megan ran down that passageway on your right."

Karina knelt beside the much taller girl. "Take off your boot and let me have a look."

Heather shook her head. "No. I might not be able to get it back on. I can feel my ankle swelling. There is almost half a mile of passageway to navigate to get out of here. Like, I don't intend to walk barefoot on this slippery mud and sharp rocks. Go after Megan. I'll wait here for you."

Karina shook her head. "We can't leave you alone. You're hurt."

Joe grasped Karina's right arm and gently pulled her to her feet. "Heather's right. Paul and Jessica should be along soon. We'd better search for Megan. According to the map Martin showed us last night, that passageway breaks up into many divergent smaller ones, some of which have deep holes filled with water."

She bent over Heather and placed a gloved hand on the taller girl's shoulder. Not long ago Heather and Karina had been something less than friends, but after surviving a shipwreck and other adventures together, they had become close. "Stay put," she instructed. "No heroics. Understand?"

Heather nodded agreement. "Yeah. Like, go. I'll wait here."

"Paul and Jessica are supposed to meet us here within the next ten or fifteen minutes. Break out a light stick and save your batteries," Joe said. Then he pointed his headlamp down a narrow passageway to his right.

"Use your emergency blanket to keep warm," Karina added. "Fifty-four degrees Fahrenheit seems warm when you're moving, but it doesn't take long to get cold when you're sitting on damp ground."

Heather pulled a chemical light stick and a thin emergency blanket from her backpack. "I'll be fine. Like, go already. Find Megan before she does something dumb and hurts herself."

Karina edged past Joe. "I'll lead. You have better eyes in the dark than I do. I'll light up the floor; you concentrate on searching the shadows."

"Good thinking." Joe positioned himself directly behind Karina and a little to her left. "Go slow. If Megan has fallen and is unconscious, we don't want to miss her."

Karina ducked under a rock outcrop, and darkness closed around her. She entered the narrow, winding passageway that led deep into the cave—a passageway that led to more than eight miles of dark shadows and unknown hazards. Martin had instructed them not to enter the wilder sections without adult supervision, but Megan had given her and Joe no choice.

Ankle-deep water reminded her of Martin's lecture on dangers that might be encountered while exploring caves. She realized that Megan faced two immediate dangers: falling and hypothermia. Megan could also get lost or slip into deep water and drown, but falling and hypothermia presented the most likely threats. Falling might lead to fractures or head injuries. Both could lead to serious consequences, possibly even death.

"Take that passageway on the right," Joe instructed, his words breaking the silent darkness and making her jump. She had been so absorbed in thought that she hadn't even seen the new passageway. Karina shined her headlamp first toward the right and then down a much larger passageway on her left.

"Are you sure? The left is bigger, and it's dry."

"Megan would be panicking, not using rational thought." Joe stepped into the right passageway, removed his backpack, and took out a map. "Megan's right-handed. She probably hugged the wall to her right and didn't even notice the other passageway. This one is more dangerous. The map indicates waist-deep water and a long way to go before reaching dry ground. The one on the left is much longer, but it's dry and pretty easy to travel."

Karina sighed deeply and took a final moment to shine her light into both passageways. She wanted to go left, but Joe's logic forced her to accept his decision.

"Let's leave a light stick here and a marker pointing which way is out in case Megan went that way and comes back before we do," Karina suggested.

Joe pulled her close to him and gave her a warm, enduring hug. "Great idea. When it comes to handling a crisis, you've come a long way."

"I've had lots of experience lately," Karina said dryly and returned his hug, burying her head against Joe's chest. *Why is it that every time we have a chance to be truly alone, there is always some emergency?* Karina sighed and gently pulled free from Joe's strong arms. *First things first.*

She stared into the dark void and decided that this situation wasn't as serious as others she and Joe had shared. Still, being lost in a cave had its own dangers, and Megan might be in serious trouble.

Joe broke the inside cylinder of a chemical light stick and shook it to mix the two liquids inside. Immediately, the cave around them filled with a soft, white light. Using the heel of his boot, Joe scraped an arrow in a muddy section of the cave floor that stood above the water level. It pointed down the passageway to where Heather waited for them. Then he etched the word "out" along the shaft of the arrow and placed the light stick next to the drawing.

Karina shivered slightly. Her feet and legs were soaking wet from splashing through the shallow stream. "Let's hurry. I'm getting cold. If Megan came this way, she must be freezing by now."

"She'll be fine as long as she keeps moving. Lead on."

Twenty minutes later Karina and Joe waded through cold, hip-deep water but saw no signs that Megan had traveled through the water-filled passageway. Karina was ready to suggest going back and getting more help when Joe abruptly grabbed her arm and pulled her to a complete stop.

"Look! A flashlight!" Joe pointed his headlamp toward a small plastic object floating in the brown water. He picked up the flashlight and examined it closely. "It's one of ours. Megan must have come this way."

"Megan!" Karina shouted and then listened as her own voice echoed down the seemingly endless passageway. Only silence greeted her effort. The dark cave swallowed her voice, leaving an uneasy silence.

"Walk slowly. We might find more signs," Joe said.

Trembling from cold and fear of what she might find, Karina strained her eyes, seeking out any clue that might lead the way to her friend. She sloshed forward; the water's depth increased, inching above her waist and coming to rest halfway up her chest. Karina's teeth chattered slightly; her exhaled breath produced wispy clouds that her headlamp illuminated.

Karina thought, *Poor Megan must be terrified and cold. Maybe she's injured and all alone in this eternal darkness.*

Joe swung his headlamp to their right and switched on a backup flashlight, interrupting her worried thoughts. Increased brightness from the combined light sources exposed a dark object half submerged in the murky water. He carefully lifted a nylon backpack from the water by a broken strap and then opened it.

"That's Megan's backpack," Karina stammered, trying to control her shivering.

Joe rummaged through the soggy bag. "This isn't good. Her extra flashlight, batteries, water, emergency blanket, and light sticks are all here. Megan has only her headlamp and what she's wearing. If she hasn't changed batteries, she may already be without light."

Karina shined her light in every direction. "Then she can't be far. She wouldn't try moving in total darkness. Even if she's still panicked, she'd grab onto something and stay put."

"Megan!" Joe's voice echoed. "Shout if you can hear us."

Only silence answered from the darkness beyond. Karina shined her light onto Joe's chest to get his attention. "I'll look to the right.

You look to the left. We've got to find her quickly. How long did Martin say a person could survive in fifty-degree water?"

"About two hours if a person is in the water and isn't able to move and generate heat," Joe responded. "If Megan's out of the water, she should be able to last five or six hours. But she's tiny and doesn't have much body fat."

Karina increased her pace, determined to find her friend as quickly as possible. At least thirty minutes had passed since Megan had broken away from Heather. Megan would be turning fifteen the next day, and the class had planned a surprise birthday party. Karina feared tragedy might annul the celebration unless she and Joe acted quickly.

For the next hour, she waded through cold, muddy water, stopping to shout every twenty yards. She and Joe searched two short side passageways that they found on the right side of the cave, but they found nothing and had to continue down the long, wet main passageway.

Shivering from being cold and wet, Karina stopped. "Do you think we should turn back? Did we miss something on the left side?"

The side-to-side movement of his helmet light indicated Joe's dismissal of her idea to turn back. "This is our best hope for finding Megan in a timely manner. Martin and the others should be searching by now. Let's give it another twenty minutes. If we don't find Megan by then, we'll leave a marker to show how far we searched and then go get more help."

Joe pulled her to him, hugged her for a few long seconds, and then vigorously rubbed her shoulders and arms. In spite of the fact that she and Joe were *unofficially* going steady—Blue Horizons discouraged formal commitments of affection among its students—she found little relief in Joe's attempt to warm and reassure her. She slipped from his arms and splashed onward.

Karina felt the tightness of panic rising in her voice. A sudden heaviness settled on her chest. Worry made her careless; she nearly fell headfirst several times. Near the end of Joe's twenty-minute deadline, she stopped and shouted. "Megan!"

"Here … I'm here."

A barely perceptible voice floated to Karina, bringing a vast measure of relief. Karina and Joe shined their lights in every direction, seeking the source of Megan's voice.

"Megan! Keep shouting! We're coming!"

"Here ... here ... here," the voice echoed. "I'm up here ... here ... here. I can see your light ... light ... light."

Joe shined his headlamp and flashlight upward. The light revealed a small hole on the right side of the cave wall. The narrow opening was about two feet above the water level. Skid marks streaked the muddy wall—evidence of recent climbing.

"She has to be in there." Karina moved toward the hole. "Boost me up. I'll check it out. Megan, I'm coming."

Joe easily hoisted her ninety-eight pounds up the incline. Karina scrambled on hands and knees for nearly ten yards before her light landed on a small, muddy girl cuddled up against a rock.

Megan sat with arms wrapped around her legs. Her chin rested on top of her knees, and her teeth clicked with great intensity.

"Megan," Karina called softly, scrambling to the shivering teen. "I'm here. Joe's here. Look at me."

"Is she there?" Joe's voice penetrated the darkness.

"Yes," Karina yelled.

She removed Megan's useless helmet. Water dripped from the shivering girl's soggy hair and soaked clothing. Seconds later Karina heard a scrambling sound behind her.

"How is she?" Joe asked.

"Freezing," Karina lifted Megan's pallid face. The shivering girl tried to speak, but clicking teeth made intelligible speech impossible. "I don't think she can walk. What should we do?"

"I'll go back for help. You begin treatment for hypothermia," Joe directed.

"Okay, but hurry. Time is short. I'll try to warm Megan. Be careful. We're counting on you."

In a facetious manner, Joe saluted her stream of orders. "Yes, ma'am. Help will be here in no time." He moved close, slipped off a soggy glove, lifted Karina's mud-smudged face, and lightly kissed her cheek. Then, without saying another word, he slid down the muddy incline and disappeared.

Karina's heart fluttered from Joe's affection, but Megan's uncontrolled shivering and haggard expression did not allow time for pleasantries. In her mind, Karina reviewed all that she knew about first aid treatment for someone suffering from being cold and wet. She prayed that she had not arrived too late to reverse the onset of hypothermia—too late to save her friend.

CHAPTER 2

Hypothermia

Karina took Megan's backpack and emptied its contents onto the muddy ground. She searched for only one crucial item—the survival blanket that Martin required each student to carry.

"Here we go," she said reassuringly, trying to calm her own fears and convince Megan that she had the situation under control. "Let's get you dry and warm."

The shivering teen nodded a response. Clicking teeth made her words unintelligible.

Karina spread a thin Mylar emergency blanket on the ground. "Lean against me," she urged. "I've got to get those wet clothes off of you."

She removed her own helmet to keep from shining bright light into Megan's eyes. Then she tugged off the girl's wet sweater. Megan's blue lips and the ashen color around her eyes urged swift action. Fighting against time, Karina removed all of Megan's wet clothes, used her own spare sweater to towel the shivering girl dry, and then moved the teen onto the survival blanket.

"Hang on. I'll get you warm in no time."

In the shadowy light provided by the chemical light stick, Karina removed her own wet clothing. Shivering, she pulled a second emergency blanket from her backpack. Then she snuggled against Megan and wrapped the lightweight blanket tightly around both of them, establishing as much body contact as possible against the girl.

For a teenager, Megan was very thin and tiny, five inches shorter than Karina's five feet seven inches. Even so, the survival blanket barely wrapped around victim and rescuer. Karina slipped the lower edges of both blankets underneath them—cocoon style. Hugging Megan's cool, clammy body siphoned warmth from Karina; she shivered silently and stared into menacing darkness beyond the light stick's reach.

She prayed for Joe's speedy return. Though taller than Megan, Karina had a slim build and little body fat. She worried she might not have enough body heat to keep them both warm if unexpected events delayed Joe's return.

During the next half hour, Karina used her own body heat to warm Megan. The shivering teen drained much of Karina's body heat and left her slightly chilled, but Karina was pleased that Megan's shivering had subsided to a more manageable level.

To break the silence, Karina gently guided Megan's attention toward the dimly lit ceiling a few inches above them.

"Hey, look up there," Karina said, nodding upward in an attempt to break the uncomfortable silence and keep Megan awake. "Bats. Little browns. Ten of them are hanging on the ceiling, just a little above our heads."

"B ... big br ... owns," Megan stammered well enough to be understood. "Not ... little ... browns."

"Hey, I'm saving you," Karina teased, squeezing Megan's arm. "Don't show up your rescuer."

"Th ... th ... thanks," Megan whispered. "I'm st ... st ... still awfully c ... cold, but I'd be w ... wor ... orse if you had ... n't f ... found me."

All Megan needs now are warm clothes and something hot to drink, Karina thought.

"I'm t ... tired," Megan mumbled. She buried short, damp curls against Karina's shoulder. "How l ... long do you th ... think it will take be ... before help c ... comes? I don't w ... want anyone to s ... see me like th ... this. Do you th ... think it will be Mar ... Martin or Sa ... Sally?"

Karina thought for a moment. She knew that Sally, the lady teacher who worked with Martin at Blue Horizons, would insist on helping in the rescue.

"Knowing Martin, it will probably be both of them. He'll leave Mr. Smithson in charge of the rest of the kids. Don't worry. I'll take care of you. Unless it's Sally or one of the girls, no one is coming up here until we're dressed."

"I kn ... know," Megan yawned, no longer shivering uncontrollably, "but I feel so st ... stupid. I panicked like a little kid afraid of the dark."

Karina said, "It wasn't the dark that frightened you; it was being confined underground. You never had any trouble playing games with us outside after dark."

Megan sighed deeply and remained silent. With her friend's calm breathing and the beginning of shared warmth now that Megan had begun generating body heat, euphoria overcame Karina. She had faced an emergency and had managed to bring things under control. Amazing!

Staring into the infinite darkness, she reflected on how much her life had changed. A little more than a year ago, a juvenile court judge had sent Karina to Blue Horizons with its strict discipline and reputation of using experiential adventure education to turn troubled adolescents into responsible adults. She had been caught shoplifting, and the judge had been concerned that Karina might get into even worse trouble, so the state picked up the hefty tuition for the exclusive school, located in the New York countryside.

She had arrived angry, still trying to deal with her parents' deaths in Kyrgyzstan years earlier—the same plane crash that had also seriously injured her. Her own aunt and uncle did not know how to handle her loss, but through Blue Horizons' care, she had learned to build and fly ultralight airplanes and had experienced many adventures. In the process, Karina had found a home. Martin, the school's founder and headmaster, had become her legal guardian and surrogate father after the court dismissed her case and withdrew its financial support.

Karina reflected briefly on the petite girl leaning against her. Megan's streaked, light brown and silver hair, an indication of her rebellious behavior, dampened Karina's shoulder. Megan was at Blue Horizons by a court order, and the court paid her tuition. Megan had told Karina that her mother and father had longed to have a boy, so she didn't fit well into that plan. Worse still, her mother could not have more children. Karina knew that Megan felt she had something to prove to her parents. Karina also figured that Megan began running away at thirteen in order to get her parents' attention, much the same as Karina had shoplifted to gain attention from her own peers. Thus, they now sat together in a damp cave and waited for help.

Megan's restful slumber encouraged Karina to remain silent. The chemical light stick provided enough light to keep her from being in total darkness. It also served as a beacon for rescuers. She inched her left arm from beneath the blanket and checked the round, luminous dial on her watch. Joe had been gone over an hour. Karina sure hoped rescue wouldn't take too long. The thin survival blanket kept her warm, but it didn't protect against the cave's rock-studded clay floor. Numerous rocks pressed painfully against her legs and hips. She moved to a more comfortable position that allowed her to lie down and hold Megan close to her. In the dim light, her eyes grew heavy, and sleep eased her worries about rescue.

Karina awoke to find her left arm was asleep, because Megan lay on top of it. Karina slowly eased her arm from beneath her sleeping friend, being careful not to wake the girl. She checked her watch and a sense of fear overcame her. It had been nearly four hours since Joe had departed.

Did something happen to Joe? Why hadn't Martin arrived? Should she and Megan get dressed and try to save themselves? A multitude of thoughts raced through Karina's mind. She decided to wait another hour and then start hiking out, without waiting for help.

Minutes clicked by slowly. She was nearly ready to wake Megan and get dressed when she heard: "Karina … Karina … Karina!"

Martin's deep voice bounced off the rocky walls around her. Immediately, her heart felt more at ease.

"We're up here," she shouted, shaking her sleeping companion. "Megan's much better. She's not shivering anymore. Did you bring some dry clothes?"

"On the way. Jessica has them. She's got dry clothes and rubber waders for you and Megan. We'll wait for you down here."

She heard Megan sigh with relief at Martin's words. "Good, it's really cold in here," Karina said, placing her helmet on her head and turning on the headlamp. She and Megan sat on one of the thin Mylar blankets and wrapped the other blanket around them, keeping in warmth and protecting themselves from public view.

"Gripe, gripe, gripe." Jessica's cheerful voice interrupted her complaints. "You can't have adventure without a little discomfort."

"You've got a point there," Karina agreed, "but I've had enough adventures to last me for a *long* time."

"Hey, remember me?" Megan said in an exasperated voice. "If you guys don't mind, I'd like to get dressed. I want out of this dark dungeon."

"Tough day?" Jessica asked Megan, handing one of two large plastic bags to Karina. "Sorry it took so long to get here. We had trouble finding you a pair of jeans, and Martin insisted on getting two sets of rubber fishing waders so that you wouldn't have to wade through all that cold water on the hike out."

As Jessica sat next to Megan and handed her the other bag, Karina pulled dry clothes from her bag and wiggled into a set of rubber waders.

"By the way, where are all of your clothes?" Jessica asked Megan. "We couldn't find any in your tent. Your duffel bag is practically empty. You'll have to settle for a pair of jean shorts and a school sweatshirt."

"I dropped my clothes off at the laundry when we went into town," Megan said as she fumbled at untying the knot on the bag. In frustration, she ripped it open and pulled out its contents. "I planned on sneaking out later today and hiking into town to get them. I hate doing laundry down at the river. I'm *not* a pioneer woman."

Karina giggled at the intensity with which Megan had emphasized her last sentence. "You'd better not let Martin hear you talking like that. He might send you out on a ten-day backpacking trip without so much as a toothbrush. Seriously, you can't go sneaking out alone. It's not safe."

"It's against the rules," Jessica added. She shined her headlamp in Megan's direction.

"I know. I know," Megan mumbled in an anguished voice. She fastened the snap on her jean shorts and reached for her boots. "It's just not been my week. I'll be glad when we finish spelunking." Megan worked to slip on the waders that looked like a huge pair of plastic clothes similar to what a farmer might wear. She was barely able to get her boots into the suit and still fasten the suspenders that held the waders in place.

"You're not the only one," Jessica agreed, steadying Megan. "About half of the class feels the same way. How about you, Karina?"

"I don't know." Karina finished fastening the snaps on her waders and put on her backpack. "I kind of enjoy exploring underground."

"Well, I want out. Let's go!" Megan switched on her headlamp, which now operated with brand-new batteries that Karina had installed during the long wait.

Following behind Megan and Jessica, Karina slid down the short, muddy incline to the main passageway below, extremely satisfied that the waders kept her dry. Wisely, Martin led them out as swiftly as possible. He had simply asked Megan if she could walk. Then he headed down the same passageway where Joe and Karina had painstakingly searched for Megan. By the time she emerged from the cave and into daylight, her watch read 3:40 p.m. Karina had been underground for almost seven hours.

Karina sat on a series of logs around what had been the previous night's campfire. For the summer session, she and her classmates would not see the shiny Quonset huts and grass airstrip that made up Blue Horizons' campus. She currently sat in her summer classroom—the great outdoors. Her summer earth science session included four weeks of cave exploration in Missouri and five weeks in Hawaii where she and her classmates would study volcanoes. Her living quarters, and those of her classmates, were small two-person tents set up in a public campground. At least the campground had bathrooms with flush toilets and the luxury of hot showers.

Martin enjoyed a slightly better abode than the rest of the group. He lived in a small trailer, which doubled as his office. Listening to the small talk from her classmates, she watched Martin head toward the group. Karina couldn't help smiling. She remembered her first impression of Martin—one of an old English professor. His dark-rimmed glasses, white bushy mustache, and grayish-white hair fit that image well, but despite his slight build—though fifty pounds heavier, he stood only a couple of inches taller than Karina—Martin had excelled in a military career and worked on numerous rescue teams. He commanded respect far above his stature. Her classmates showed her impression correct by stopping their conversations and giving Martin their silent attention as he reached the group. He didn't even have to ask for silence.

"I hope everyone learned something from yesterday's episode," Martin began the morning lecture. "We were very fortunate that someone wasn't badly hurt. What did you learn, *Megan?*"

Martin's strong emphasis on Megan's name cut short any thoughts about making wisecracks. Karina looked around the class. Including Karina, seven boys and eight girls, all fourteen to seventeen years of age, sat in a semicircle on the ground.

Megan replied thoughtfully, seriously, "I spent a lot of time last night thinking about what happened—and what could have happened. I believe that I learned three things yesterday. First, I learned that panic really makes a bad situation worse. My running away from my partner not only endangered me, but it also caused Heather to sprain her ankle. Second, I don't believe that I'm a good candidate for spelunking. My claustrophobia puts everyone at risk." A broad smile filled Megan's face. "Finally, I learned that I have some really good friends. Thanks, everybody."

A number of the kids shrugged off Megan's compliment by saying that it was nothing, but Karina waited for Martin to respond to Megan's second revelation. Helping students face fears and gaining self-confidence were major goals at Blue Horizons. She didn't believe Martin would let Megan remove herself from spelunking. When Karina had freaked and almost killed both herself and Martin on her initial ultralight flight lesson, Martin had given her many extra hours of flying to help her get over her fears, and she had become a very competent pilot.

"How about the rest of you?" Martin continued without an immediate comment on Megan's statements.

None of the fifteen teenagers gathered around the campfire spoke. Each looked to someone else. Finally, Joe broke the silence. "I believe I learned that the more we practice to deal with unknown situations, the better we handle them. Except for the fact that we didn't finish our coursework, we handled a potentially dangerous situation well."

"I agree with Joe," Karina said, trying to articulate her feelings in a manner that didn't belittle Megan's feelings. "But I think we are skipping over a much larger issue. I learned that Megan must do more spelunking if she is going to come to grips with her fear of close places. She needs to get back underground as soon as possible."

Exasperated, Megan gasped and looked angrily at Karina. "I don't know what lesson book you're learning from, but we certainly aren't on the same page. I need a break. I need to work on this slowly, and spelunking is not the right approach."

"Like, I agree with Karina," Heather said. "Last year Karina helped me learn that I couldn't hide from what truly frightened me. When I did, things only got worse. Megan definitely needs to go back into the cave."

"No! I don't need—" Megan began.

"Quiet, Megan," Martin commanded. "Heather, I'm very happy that you agree with Karina." He nodded toward Karina. "I'm pleased with your assessment. It wasn't very long ago that you were in Megan's position; only, flying was your fear. You conquered that fear by learning to trust in yourself. Such a strategy doesn't always work, but I've used it often and had promising results."

"If a person is stressed out, doesn't that put the person at greater risk of an accident, especially working in a hazardous situation?" asked Paul, a tall redhead who Karina knew was fond of Jessica.

"It does increase the risk," Martin agreed. "However, under controlled conditions, that risk is manageable. Learning to face fears is crucial to developing character. Most of you came to Blue Horizons with fears of one kind or another to conquer."

"Like, wow," Heather interrupted. "Like, I thought I was the only one here to develop character."

Martin gave Heather a warning look and continued. "We'll set proper safety standards, but I agree that Megan needs to face her fears by continuing with underground exploration."

"Like, yeah!" Heather shouted. "She's got to get back underground."

"No!" Megan rose to her feet. "Stop saying *like* every time you speak. It's so annoying." She turned to Martin. "Please! I can't."

Martin held up his hand for Megan to stop. Tears formed at the corners of her eyes. "Trust us, Megan. Trust in yourself."

Tears rolled down Megan's dimpled cheeks. "I'm not sure I can. I'm so scared."

Karina moved next to Megan and hugged her. "We'll be with you all the way. Believe me; I know what fear can do. Do you remember when I panicked and almost crashed during the thunderstorm at Fulton, Missouri?"

Megan leaned against the comfort of Karina's arms and nodded. Everyone waited patiently for her response. She sighed deeply before speaking. "I remember. You swore that you would never fly again."

"I'm still flying. And I love it. You can beat this if you really want to—if you try."

Karina was surprised that Martin and the others didn't interrupt and say something encouraging. Everyone seemed to be waiting for her to take charge.

Take charge? Karina thought. *Now, that's something new.*

Megan gently pried Karina's hands from around her waist. She faced Karina. "I don't think I have your courage."

Karina took both of Megan's hands in hers before saying what was in her heart. "You're a pilot. You are every bit as brave as I am. You're as brave any of us. Right, guys?"

The other students all agreed with Karina's assessment. For the next hour, they gave many testimonies of overcoming fears in an effort to build up Megan's confidence. Martin sat aside with Sally— Blue Horizons' only female instructor—and let Megan's support group provide the fellowship that only teenagers sharing the same experiences could give. Finally, the talk calmed Megan.

"Better?" Martin asked.

"Better," Megan said, nodding in agreement.

Martin smiled. "Good. Take the day off and finish your laundry. You've got a birthday to celebrate."

The rest of that day was absolutely delightful. Martin allowed Karina, Joe, Heather, Paul, and Jessica to accompany Megan into town for lunch and a movie, which they topped off with ice cream sundaes.

Karina had even been able to call the Winfields, their daughter Penny, and Cindy—a little girl whom Karina and Joe had rescued from a helicopter crash in the Amazon rainforest. The Winfields had become Karina's unofficial second family. They lived in Fulton, Missouri, only a short drive from the campground. A year ago, on a cross-country ultralight flight across the United States, Karina had stayed with Dr. and Mrs. Winfield and Penny. They had helped her conquer her initial fear of flying, and she had been able to help eleven-year-old Penny by flying the child to St. Louis for a bone marrow transplant that helped put Penny's leukemia into remission.

During much of the year, Cindy stayed with Martin and Karina at Blue Horizons, but she stayed with the Winfields when the class was not on campus. Martin had become Cindy's legal guardian in order to help Karina fulfill the dying wish of Cindy's father that Karina take care of Cindy and find her a loving home. She looked forward to seeing Cindy and the Winfields at the end of the caving part of her summer coursework, but for this long summer day, Karina was content to enjoy an afternoon at the mall.

While she and her group enjoyed basking in the sunlight, Martin took the remaining students underground. With no immediate adult supervision, she and Joe freely held hands. They moved away from the others kids to sit on a bench outside the ice cream store. Joe put his arm around Karina; she could have sat with him for hours and hours. All too soon, the school van pulled into the mall parking lot, forcing Karina and Joe into a less affectionate relationship. It was time to return to the Meramec State Park campground, which would be home and classroom for at least another three weeks.

Mr. Smithson, a volunteer helper for the summer and a significant financial contributor to Blue Horizons, cooked for the group that evening. After a dessert of chocolate cake and ice cream, a water balloon fight left everyone soaked and content. Martin announced that Megan and part of the group would begin training for a new phase of cave exploration the next day—vertical caving.

Karina cheered Martin's announcement. Then she noticed the terror in Megan's face. She understood the girl's distress. Not only would Megan be farther underground than ever before, but she would also rappel nearly eighty feet to get there.

"Oh, my!" Megan cried, taking several deep breaths to gain composure.

"Don't worry." Heather patted Megan on the back. "You can do it. It won't be too bad."

"I'm glad you feel that way, Heather," Martin said. "You will be Megan's companion. Joe, Karina, Paul, and Jessica will round out the team. Sally will be in charge."

"Like, what about my ankle?" Heather protested. "It's still pretty sore."

"Yeah, right! You can't malinger your way out of this one," Karina said, remembering the girl's antics during the water balloon fight. She knew the thought of rappelling frightened Heather. "It didn't seem to bother you too much when I was trying to fend off that water balloon you chased me with—the one that soaked me. Remember?"

"Don't worry, Heather," Megan teased. "We'll help you through it. There isn't anything to fear about heights."

"Like, that's easy for you to say." Heather scoffed, kicked the ground, and spoke in a disgruntled voice. "You're all pilots. I'm just here for the summer. I hate heights!"

Martin ordered them to bed, ending further complaints. He told Megan to join Karina for the night and moved Jessica in with Heather. When Megan went to shower and get ready for bed, Martin called Karina to join him. He led her slowly across an open grass field and toward the series of nylon tents everyone currently called home.

"Keep building up Megan's self-esteem, but don't do the work for her. Let her deal with her own fears. Just support her."

Karina stopped long enough to slip off her squeaky, wet tennis shoes. She walked barefoot through the long, tender grass, enjoying the way it caressed her feet. "I will. Megan can do it. She just needs more time to adjust—like I did with flying."

"She should have enough time," Martin mused. "Next week you will be underground for three days on a cave mapping excursion."

"What?!" Karina exclaimed. "Underground for three days?! How will we sleep and cook?" Then, as the full realization hit her, she added, "How will we go to the bathroom?"

"I'll explain all of that tomorrow," Martin assured her. "You've got a few days of training before you begin. Do you think you can handle Megan? I'm counting on you and Joe. You are my most experienced students."

Karina felt flattered. Not too long ago, *she* had been Martin's biggest headache. Now he put her in a position of responsibility. "I think I can handle Megan, but why me?"

"I've watched how you deal with Cindy. You are a natural teacher and a very competent caregiver. Even though you are only fifteen—and sometimes still a brat—you are as good a mother-figure as Cindy could ever hope for."

Remembering the tragic set of events that placed eight-year-old Cindy into her and Martin's care brought chills to Karina. While stranded in the Amazon rainforest, Cindy's father had died in Karina's arms. His last words had been for her to give his little girl a home. She glowed in the warmth of Martin's praise.

She affectionately squeezed his hand. "Thanks, Martin." Karina admitted to herself that she owed Martin thanks for all of her accomplishments. He never gave up on her, not even when she had given up on herself. "I won't let anything happen to Megan. She can beat this. I know she can."

Martin hugged her briefly. "I know you'll take care of things." Martin released her from the hug and put a hand on her shoulder. "There is one more thing we need to discuss—Joe."

Karina nervously shifted her weight onto one foot but looked steadily into Martin's blue eyes.

"Now that I am your guardian and Blue Horizons is your home as well as your school, I can give you some freedoms that I would not accept if you were only a student. The school has a strict policy against close personal signs of affection. I know that you and Joe are developing a relationship that is cozier than school policy would normally allow."

Panic filled Karina. Sally must have seen them on the bench when she pulled into the mall parking lot to pick up the group. "Are you saying that I must find a boyfriend who is not from Blue Horizons?"

Martin held up his hand for her to stop speaking. He stared intently at her for a few seconds before a smile filled his face, curling his bushy mustache into an arch. "That is not what I am suggesting, but we need to set some guidelines. On free time, such as at the mall today, I can accept holding hands or Joe putting his arm around your shoulder. That I consider your free time, as I might if you went to some other school and had gone to the movie with a boyfriend."

Karina relaxed and shifted her weight onto both feet. Her heart felt much lighter.

Martin continued, "But I must insist that you show no signs of personal affection when you are on school-directed activities or on the school grounds when we get back to Blue Horizons. Understand?"

She wrinkled her forehead in thought. "With as little time as I have off campus and away from school-directed activities, that may be hard. What about school dances?"

Martin chuckled. "Feel free to dance with Joe or any other boy you wish to dance with." He lightly bopped the top of her head. "Just no more personal affection than the rest of the students are allowed. Now get to bed. We will discuss this more at the end of the summer when we get back on campus."

Karina hugged Martin and stepped out into the growing dusk. Thirty minutes later, she watched the rising full moon through the tent's screen door. From the comfort of her sleeping bag, she listened to Megan's troubled slumber. Karina knew Megan wanted to do something that would make her parents accept her, something that would make them praise her accomplishments, and something that would make them proud of her.

Well, Karina thought, *if flying ultralight airplanes across the United States isn't enough, maybe spending a few days underground can help. Megan's parents may have wanted a boy, but they must be proud to have a daughter who can fly an airplane at the age of fourteen. Maybe it's only Megan's view that her parents aren't proud of her. Maybe they really did appreciate Megan's courage and accomplishments?* She looked intently at the sleeping teen. *What else can I do to help boost her parent's view of Megan?*

Before Karina decided on a plan to help Megan, she drifted off to sleep. Soon she turned and tossed in anxious slumber. She desperately ran through underground passageways—running from some unseen hazard—running for a safety she could not seem to find, and she was not running alone.

CHAPTER 3

Going Vertical

Karina anxiously looked down at her friends sitting on the ground below her. From her height, they looked much smaller. She wasn't afraid of heights, but she wasn't sure about her ability to rappel. She would have rather had another day at the mall, like yesterday, than step off the side of the limestone cliff. She wiped sweat from her brow and noticed that she could see the park campground and her tent. She saw Sally and Mr. Smithson's group climbing into the van to begin another day of spelunking. At that moment, she wished she were with them. She'd rather be heading underground than standing on top of a vertical limestone wall.

Let's get this over with, she thought and tied down the loose ends of her climbing harness. Karina checked the special knot that held the one-inch tubular webbing firmly in place. The webbing ran between her legs, over her hipbones, and securely wound around her waist. This harness fit more uncomfortably than the wider commercial harnesses used by professional mountaineers, but it was easier to clean and cheaper to replace. Climbing harnesses had not been designed for crawling through cave mud.

"Ready?" Joe asked, snapping a carabineer onto the figure eight rappelling device attached to the front of her harness. "Get into a sitting position and slow or stop your descent by pushing the rope in your right hand tightly against your butt."

"Got it," Karina said. Her hand trembled as she took the rope from Joe. "Help me to the edge. How high are we?"

"We're a little higher than 135 feet," Joe answered as he positioned Karina near the cliff's edge.

She looked over her shoulder and discovered that she stood at a precipice. Besides Paul and Joe, none of the Blue Horizons students had ever rappelled before. She took a deep breath. "How should I begin?"

"Take small steps. Bend at the waist to get into a sitting position. Go one step at a time, letting out a little rope as you go. Keep your legs shoulder-width apart for balance so that you don't sway left or right." Joe attached the belay rope—her safety line—to her harness.

Karina admired Joe's thorough instructions—a repeat of the lecture and demonstration that Martin had given them an hour earlier. "I think I've got the idea," she said.

Martin had rappelled three times to demonstrate the correct procedure. His first rappel had been exactly as Joe described. Martin had taken small steps and walked cautiously down the wall. Then he had rappelled again, letting the rope out quickly. Martin had practically run down the wall. On his last descent, Martin had rappelled the wall in a series of rapid hops, which he had accomplished by pushing himself away from the wall, letting out the rope, and bouncing back to the wall some fifteen or twenty feet below the beginning of the hop. Martin had descended the entire wall in seconds. Everyone had been impressed.

"I'll go slowly," Karina assured Joe. "Let's get on with it before I lose my nerve."

"It's all yours, Rini."

Karina smiled at Joe's use of her nickname and turned to Martin, who worked the belay rope that would catch her if she made a mistake. "On belay," she said, taking a deep breath.

"Belay is on." Martin tugged the rope tightly enough that she felt secure and a little less apprehensive about her descent.

"Ready to rappel," Karina said, using the commands she had practiced earlier that morning.

"Rappel when ready," Martin said. "Have fun, Karina. Show them how it's done."

"I'll try," she said and called out the required last command. "Rappelling."

Karina felt her heart pounding as she stared down at the ground far below instead of positioning herself the way that Joe had instructed. She held her breath and inched backward over the edge. Her classmates, tiny doll-sized figures at the bottom of the sheer drop, waited with cameras raised. Unexpected fear rushed through Karina. She panicked and threw her hands into the air. The move jerked the rappel rope from her hand, and she desperately tried to regain her balance.

"Karina!" Joe shouted.

Her feet slipped. "Falling!"

Dropping vertically, her belay line abruptly stopped her downward plunge, but her left shoulder crashed into the limestone wall and her right knee scraped against coarse rock. Because she had not lowered herself into a sitting position, she had actually walked backward off of the cliff. Breathing in short breaths, Karina hung against the sheer rock wall two feet below the edge and stared at the distant ground. She realized that she would be dead at the bottom of the cliff if she had not been attached to a belay rope.

"Work yourself into a sitting position," Martin urged. "Grab the rappel rope and take control. I've got you. You're not going to fall."

Ignoring Martin, Karina yelled, "Pull me up!"

He shouted down to her, "You are over the worst part. Get into a rappel position and keep going."

Disobeying Martin's command, she grabbed the belay rope with both hands, climbed over the edge, and lay panting. Her left shoulder ached, and her right knee burned. She panted from exertion and fear.

"Let her do it," Martin commanded when Joe moved to help Karina to her feet. "Stand up and try again. This time follow your training. Don't look down until you have attained a correct sitting position for rappelling."

Karina breathed deeply and fought back an angry reply. Before coming to Blue Horizons, she would have lost control of her anger and refused. Instead, she took a deep breath to gain composure, bit her lower lip, and moved back toward the edge. With trembling hands and sweaty palms, Karina clutched the rappelling rope with her right hand.

"That's far enough," Martin said. "Now move to a sitting position."

Without looking at the ground, Karina inched over the side—squatting into a sitting position. Her right hand choked the rappel rope, which she firmly pressed against the right side of her hip. She straightened her legs until she sat horizontal to the ground. The rope attached to her webbing tugged at her waist.

"Let the rope out slowly. Then take a step and repeat the process all the way down." Joe called instructions to her in a calm, steady voice.

Karina allowed a few inches of rope to slip through her right hand. Her backside dropped an equal distance. She took a tentative step, sliding her right foot downward half a step. To her surprise, the procedure worked. By the time she reached the halfway point down the rocky cliff, Karina felt in control. Her speed depended on two things: how fast she let the rope slip through her fingers and how much slack Martin gave her from the belay rope. Feeling in control erased her fears. Because heights didn't frighten her, gaining control of the rappel made Karina feel more at ease. Except for the pain and discomfort of bruises and scrapes from her initial attempt, she enjoyed the experience.

"Like, really nice job," Heather said, unhooking Karina's belay rope and sending it back up to Martin. "I sure hope I can do as well. Like, it looks really freaky. Were you, like, scared?"

"*Like, yeah*," Karina said, imitating Heather to irritate her friend for asking such a dumb question. She hobbled over to a log and sat. "It was only scary when I fell." She sat down and removed her safety harness. "Except for the first step, it's not bad. Don't look down until you're in a sitting position and don't let go of the rappel rope. Ouch!"

Karina examined the jagged hole in the right pant leg of her jeans. Her skinned knee oozed blood. She rubbed the spot on her shoulder where it had hit the rocks and determined that she would have an unsightly bruise.

Great, she thought. *It's swimsuit time. When we finish spelunking and head to Hawaii, I'm going to look like a beat-up fish out of water.*

Megan fetched the first aid kit and placed it next to Karina. "Let me help you. It's the least I can do after you saved me from the cave. Unbutton your jeans and pull them down, so I can treat that scrape."

"Wait a minute, girl," Karina slapped Megan's hand away from the snap on her jeans. "There are boys around."

"The guys are all up top. If we hurry, we can have you fixed up before anyone reaches the ground. Boy, it's so much better being the rescuer than it is being the rescued."

All that day, Karina and her teammates took turns rappelling. After the twenty minutes it took to get Heather down on her first descent, everything went smoothly. On Karina's fifth—and final—rappel of the day, she bounced down the cliff, trying to imitate Martin's earlier performance; however, Martin didn't let the belay rope out fast enough. The rappel turned into a comic affair that jerked her around like a rag doll. Everyone laughed and cheered until she reached the ground.

A short time later, they hiked back to the campground. When they arrived, Martin ordered Karina to join him in his office, which was located in the back of a small RV camper. She fully expected a lecture and a reprimand for trying to show off. Martin was very strict about following instructions.

She left the others to store the gear, changed into more comfortable clothes, and went to see what Martin wanted. She would rather have been cleaning equipment. At least her classmates were sure of free time after they finished their chores. She feared that a different fate awaited her that evening.

"Sir, you wanted to see me?" Karina stood in the camper's narrow confines, facing Martin, whose attention focused on a map stretched across a small counter that also acted as an eating table.

"In a minute," Martin put her off, marking several places on the map before turning his attention to her. "Have a seat. How's the knee and shoulder?"

"Fine. They barely hurt at all," Karina said. She shifted from one foot to the other, curling her toes over the edge of her sandals, the preferred footwear after a day in boots.

"Good." Martin finished working, sank back into a worn leather chair, and stared across at her. "We'll do one more day of rappelling and preparation. Then I'm sending you into Ghram's Cave for a bit of extended spelunking. I believe you can handle it, and three days underground should be enough to cure Megan's fears. She isn't truly claustrophobic, or we would have had more difficulty with her than we've had. Keep an eye on her. Don't take *any* chances."

"I won't," Karina promised. This was going better than expected. She might not be in trouble. "When will you tell the others?"

"Final briefing will be tomorrow evening. You begin your descent at 0800 hours on Wednesday, and we should see you again about the same time Saturday morning. Sally will supervise the exercise. Don't give her any grief."

Karina smiled and stood to depart. "I won't. Is that all?"

"You may go now," Martin nodded. "Just remember to have a thousand-word essay about correct rappelling procedures on my desk before free time tomorrow afternoon."

Karina's heart sank. "Yes, sir."

There went her evening. While the others went to town to enjoy a movie, she'd be slaving away in her tent. She departed quickly, trying to hide her disappointment. After all, it could have been much worse. Martin could have removed her from the team.

Karina and her teammates sat around the fire ring Martin and Sally used as a gathering place for lectures and giving instructions. Karina really enjoyed the humanities classes and flight ground school course that Sally taught, and she admired Sally's flying ability. Sally was Martin's opposite in many ways. Martin was short and reserved. Sally was nearly as tall as Joe and continually cracked jokes in class. Her easygoing manner made her a hit with all of the students. Karina felt she could go into a deep sleep for a hundred years and wake to find that Martin had not changed at all. Sally was unpredictable; the students never knew what color her hair would be from week to week. The dark black hair of last month had changed to summer blonde, and Sally *always* dyed her hair red in the fall.

As her instructor approached, Karina sensed the tension build in Megan. She took her friend's hand and squeezed it. Megan sighed and gave her a weak smile in return.

"Groups are as follows," Sally said. "Jessica and Paul take the lead. They are responsible for collecting temperature and humidity data. Karina and Megan come next and concentrate on bat populations and other wildlife. Joe and Heather will bring up the rear. They will map cave formations and alternate passageways. I'll stay with Joe and Heather. Martin gave me information from a local farmer about where to find an unexplored passageway. We'll try to locate it after we spend some time working on rescue techniques. Everyone understand his or her responsibilities?"

"Yes, ma'am," Karina said aloud. The others nodded in agreement.

"Check your equipment one final time and meet over at the van. The drive will take about an hour." Sally turned briskly and went to check her own equipment.

Karina liked and respected her instructor. She was strict but always listened to what students had to say.

"Here, check your gear," Joe said, handing her a midsized nylon backpack. "It's all you've got for the next three days."

"Thanks," Karina replied, taking the heavy backpack in both hands. Inside she counted food rations, a portable stove, a fuel bottle, three one-liter water bottles, a sweater, one complete change of clothing, two pairs of wool socks, a light pair of tennis shoes, toilet tissue, and toilet bags. They had to carry out waste materials. Even though the cave was on private land, Martin *insisted* that they follow the rules of caving that the Missouri Spelunking Association established.

The slim backpack also contained five chemical light sticks, gloves, an emergency kit, extra batteries, two spare lightbulbs for her headlamp, and a small inflatable pillow. Attached to the outside were carabineers, tubular webbing, a sleeping bag, an insulated ground pad, and a heavy jacket. At least she didn't have to carry the rope or water filters. Joe and Paul carried those.

The drive to Ghram's Cave proved uneventful. Everyone enjoyed the narrow road winding through lush green forest. They sang songs and told jokes to keep Megan from dwelling on the coming event. However, everyone became silent when the school van turned off the main road and onto a narrow, rut-filled dirt path that led through a large field, across a shallow stream, and up to a small farmhouse.

Karina thought, *Wow! Such a huge farm to have fields and woods. Nearly a mile back to the main road.* The house, however, didn't indicate wealth. The two-story white wood house with brown painted window frames looked ancient, perhaps handed down from generation to generation. The large red barn located a hundred or so yards away from the house showed signs of age and weathering. Large strips of paint had peeled away from the wooden structure, and one of two wooden doors on the front was missing.

A large bald man wearing denim coveralls and leather boots emerged from the front door of the farmhouse. The small black goatee jutting from the farmer's face further highlighted the lack of hair on the man's head. As he came near, Karina noticed his calloused hands and decided this was a man who worked hard to earn a living, large farm or not.

Sally stopped the van near the man, and everyone got out and watched as she went up to the farmer and shook his hand.

"I'm Sally Truman," she said as a way of introduction, "and these are the students Martin told you about. We're extremely thankful that you are letting us use your cave."

"Tom Evans," the man said and nodded a greeting. "I should be thanking you. A local college is thinking about renting it for use as an outdoor laboratory. They put me in touch with Martin. They said that you could check the map my boy Alex made to see if it is accurate."

"We can certainly do that," Sally said.

"Once it's mapped, I can talk with my attorney to set a price. Follow me, and I'll show you the way." He turned and headed to a rather new-looking green pickup truck.

"Into the van," Sally ordered.

Driving slowly along a weed-filled dirt road, Mr. Evans guided them another mile through the woods. They came to a stop in front of a gaping hole—the dark opening through which they would descend into Ghram's Cave.

Karina climbed down from the van, and everyone went to the mouth of the gaping hole. "Wow! Looks deep!"

"I wouldn't know," Mr. Evans said. "I've never been down there. My son used to explore it before he went into the army, but I've never been inside. Can't be more than a hundred feet deep, though. That's all the rope he had."

"This is going to be great!" Paul said, punching Joe in the arm.

"Really?" Megan retorted. "For *whom?*"

Sally gave everyone a "straighten up and behave look" and turned to Mr. Evans. "We'll be out in three days. I'll stop by the house and let you know when we are finished. It will take a couple of days to turn our data into a formal map. I'll have Martin get it to you as soon as possible."

He shook Sally's hand again. "You came at just the right time. The highway department is building a road on the other side of the hill. They are going to use dynamite to blast through the limestone. Construction is set to begin in two weeks. I'm going to close the cave until they finish. Don't want to take a chance on someone getting hurt and suing me."

Karina watched Mr. Evans climb back into his truck and disappear into the woods along the same bumpy road he had led them down to get to the cave. Vaguely, she wondered whether he could make any real money just for having a cave on his property. Sally ended her speculation.

"Joe, you and Paul get the caving ladder ready," Sally ordered. "I suggest the rest of you find a spot and take a toilet break. From here on out, you carry everything with you. We don't want to pollute the cave in any way."

Accepting Sally's advice, the girls headed left into the woods. Karina found a suitable spot behind a fallen tree.

"Don't you think carrying out urine and … you know," Heather asked, grasping for a socially correct word, "is going to extremes?"

"Yeah, I sure hope I don't get diarrhea," Megan said. "That would really make this trip a nightmare."

"Ugh!" Heather said, disgustedly. "Don't even think about it."

"Grow up, you two," Jessica said. "A little discomfort won't hurt any of us."

"Besides," Karina added, "think about the opportunity we have. Hundreds of kids would love to be here in our place."

"They can have my spot." Megan's voice trembled in the warm, muggy June air.

"You'll be fine," Karina said. She fastened the snap on her jeans. "Everyone ready?"

"No, but let's get this over with," Megan mumbled. The others responded more positively.

As they hiked back to the cave entrance, Jessica whispered in Karina's ear, "Keep an eye on Megan. She's getting jumpy."

"I noticed." Karina put an arm around Jessica, her loyal companion and best friend. "I'll watch her."

A short time later, they amassed around the cave opening. Karina saw two aluminum cables, connected by round metal rungs, running down into the cave from two steel anchors that Sally had pounded into the ground a couple of feet from the entrance. She guessed that the rungs were steps, which made the contraption a ladder of some kind. Two climbing ropes also descended from anchors on the opposite side of the cave entrance. Karina knew that one would serve as the rappel rope, and Sally would use the other to belay them. Karina admired Sally's courage. Her instructor would rappel into the cave without the security of being belayed.

"We'll rappel down," Sally explained, "but climbing out on a rope is too difficult, so we'll use the caving ladder. Make sure that you don't get tangled with it while rappelling. I'll handle the belay rope, but I'll have to do it by feel. I won't be able to see you once you're out of sight, so go slow. Joe will go first."

Joe descended without any problems, as did Paul and Jessica. Then it was Karina's turn. Megan would follow her. Megan's pale face and rapid breathing worried Karina. She gave Megan a reassuring hug and a sympathetic pat on the back. Then she moved over to Sally at the cave's entrance. Karina attached herself to the belay rope. She said the proper commands and prepared for her descent.

"Hey, girl," Heather said as she switched on Karina's helmet light. "Like, you might want to see on your way down. I don't believe sunlight will penetrate very far."

"Thanks. I'll see you at the bottom." Karina smiled sheepishly, rolled her eyes at Sally, and stepped backward into the hole. After two steps, the wall curved inward. She began a free rappel, one in which she rappelled straight down. Sitting in her harness, she was a little more than an arm's length from the wall. This rappel turned out to be much easier than Karina expected. Slowly, she lowered herself to the bottom. A few uneventful minutes later, she stood on the cave floor.

"Nice rappel," Joe noted as he unhooked the belay rope and guided Karina a few steps away from the rappel landing area. "Paul and Jessica are already exploring. Stay close. Megan may need you," he whispered in her ear.

Everything went well on Megan's rappel until she descended beyond the natural sunlight seeping in through the mouth of the cave. When the sunlight ended, Megan lost control of her rappel. She started kicking, which made matters worse. The wild kicking swung her in slow circles. Finally, Megan managed to grab onto a small rock pinnacle and put her foot into a crevice. She turned upside down and lost her pack, which almost clobbered Joe. Using strength that only panic could provide, Megan righted herself and clung to the rock pinnacle with all her might.

"Come on, Megan," Joe shouted. "Just let go and move away. Sally will lower you down."

"You can't stay there," Karina yelled. "We're here for you."

"No! I can't!" Megan screamed. "I want to go home. Help me."

"Keep her talking," Joe said to Karina. "I'm going to climb the ladder and try to bring her down."

"No, I'll do it." Karina put her hands into Joe's. "This time I'm best for the job. Megan won't listen to you. She trusts me. She knows my fears. She'll believe me."

"Okay, but be careful," Joe begged. "There's no safety line on you this time. A fall from that height could be serious, maybe fatal."

"Thanks for the words of confidence," Karina said, partly teasing, partly serious. "Wish me luck."

Joe steadied the caving ladder. "Don't take any chances."

Karina carefully placed a foot onto a metal rung and grabbed a higher rung. Joe shined his helmet light and his more powerful handheld flashlight above her, giving her a better view of Megan. As she ascended the swaying metal caving ladder, determination and fear competed for her attention—determination to help Megan and fear that she might make a mistake and fall. Megan's screams, begging, and relentless crying added to Karina's contrasting emotions.

"Megan! Listen to me. Stop yelling." Karina used what she hoped was a stern tone. "You aren't in any danger of falling. Listen to me. Let go."

"I can't." Megan violently shook her head. "I'll fall. Please, help me."

Karina decided there was no way to talk Megan down. The girl was beyond rational thought—too frightened to listen. The close confines of the vertical rock walls and the darkness terrified Megan. After carefully shining her helmet light around the area near Megan, Karina spied another problem: the belay line had snagged around a rock. Even if she tried to descend, she wouldn't go anywhere until the rope was freed.

Without thinking about the repercussions of her actions, Karina reached out from the swaying ladder and grabbed the rock holding the belay rope. She found a small ledge on which to place her foot and left the limited security of the caving ladder. She hung precariously from the side of the cave wall, nearly thirty feet above the stone floor.

"Karina! No!" Joe's anxious voice reached her as she stepped from the ladder.

"Sorry," she yelled. Her arms shook with fatigue, and she couldn't reach the ladder behind her. She was committed, like it or not. Karina closed her eyes and breathed deeply to force down the panic that threatened to overwhelm her. She had little time before her arms gave way, and she plummeted to oblivion.

Karina stretched out her left leg and found a small crack for her foot. Seconds later, she found a handhold and swung to the rock pinnacle that snagged Megan's belay rope. Karina worked the rope free and tugged twice on the rope—indicating for Sally to pull up the slack.

"Help me," Megan begged. A steady stream of tears wet the distraught girl's face.

"Listen to me. I need *your* help. I can make it to you if you give me a hand."

"I can't," Megan cried. "I'll fall."

Fatigue and her shaking arms made Karina exasperated and angry. "You can't fall!" she shouted. "You still have a safety rope! I don't!"

By what strength Megan found to reach out to her, Karina didn't know. But the terrified girl extended a shaky hand and gripped Karina's wrist. One desperate leap later, Karina was perched on the same rock outcrop as Megan. Without saying a word, Karina grabbed Megan's belay rope, threw her arms around the screaming girl, and pushed away from the wall. Instantly, Sally lowered them to the relative safety below.

After unhooking Megan and ushering her toward Joe, Karina tightly hugged both friends. No one spoke; they all knew that the outcome from Karina's actions could have been tragic. As Heather neared the end of her rappel, Karina turned to greet the taller teen.

Sally descended while Heather and Joe comforted Megan. The panic-stricken teen insisted that she was not going to remain in the cave. Sally unhooked and asked what had happened. She ordered Joe and Heather to stay with Megan. Then she grabbed Karina's arm and pulled her down a passageway, away from the group.

Sally pushed Karina against the cave's limestone wall, firmly gripped both of Karina's arms, and upbraided her. "Don't ever do anything like that again. The last time I had charge of you, you went on an unauthorized flight and almost got killed. I don't need to go through that again."

"Sorry," Karina said. She hated making Sally angry. Sally had always supported her. "I won't do it again."

Sally stared at her for long moments. "You really helped Megan out of a tight spot, but it doesn't do any good to save her at your own expense, especially when she was on belay. You were in the greater danger. I need you to make decisions by using your head, not by responding to impulsive emotions."

"I know," Karina said seriously. She tried to reassure her instructor. "I'll be careful. I promise."

Sally loosened her grip and took a deep breath. "Fair enough. Get back and see if you can get Megan ready to move out. We're already behind schedule."

Karina returned to the group, which diligently worked to assure Megan that she would be okay. After retrieving her pack, Karina took a moment to gaze up at the hole from which she had descended. Because the vertical shaft was not completely straight, she saw no signs of the sun. Karina suddenly felt cut off from the rest of the world. In the cave's musky smell and darkness, she felt as though she'd entered an entirely new universe. She completely understood Megan's fears and joined her partner, allowing Joe to team up with Heather.

"Joe, lead on," Sally commanded when everyone was ready. "We need to join up with Paul and Jessica. I told them to search out a good spot to set up camp."

As Karina guided Megan through the damp cave, she viewed some beautifully colored formations. Top-growing stalactites shined like gold against the dingy gray limestone ceiling when her helmet light illuminated them. The bottom-forming stalagmites had a large amount of crystal in them, giving the formations a sparkling appearance. The passageway's floor was dry, but a small stream wound through cracks in the rock off to the side of the path. The continual sound of running water drummed in her ears.

"I see a light coming this way," Heather said. A minute later, Jessica and Paul joined the group.

"We haven't found anyplace large enough for the entire group. What do we do now?"

Sally checked her watch. "Grab a quick bite and a drink of water. Then we continue until we find a suitable site."

Everyone sat along the narrow passageway and grabbed a quick snack. Then Sally told Paul and Jessica to lead the way, and they continued exploring. Twice, Karina had to stop the group and calm Megan—each tight bend led to a new challenge. At times, it took the entire group to encourage Megan to continue. As the cave ceiling grew higher and the passageway widened, Megan finally began to move without continual urging.

Hours later, Paul called a halt to their procession. Ahead of Karina and her weary fellow explorers, the cave opened into a huge cavern filled with formations that included tall individual columns running from the floor to the roof, a huge tapestry of connected columns, stalagmites sprouting from the floor, and a multitude of stalactites hanging from the distant ceiling. Too fatigued to continue, Sally ordered a halt for the night. Karina felt that this cave was the largest and most complicated she'd explored; its length and the dozens of side passageways presented a continual challenge to not get lost. *Mapping this cave is going to be a really big job*, she thought.

After a brief meal and a less-than-pleasant bathroom experience, Karina snuggled between Jessica and Megan on the hard rock floor. It had been an exciting, emotional day. She figured that tomorrow would be even more challenging. Tomorrow they would spend most of the day learning rescue techniques. They would take turns clinging precariously to the side of sheer cave walls and learn procedures that might one day save others who were in danger.

Karina felt proud that Martin had chosen her for this experience. Without so much as a single dream, she drifted into sound slumber, lulled to sleep by Jessica's soft, rhythmic breathing.

CHAPTER 4

Cave Rescue

"Karina? Are you sleeping?" Megan's whispered voice didn't fully penetrate Karina's peaceful slumber, but the girl's elbow jabbing into her side jolted her awake.

"What's wrong?" Karina tried to sit up, but her sleeping bag temporarily restrained her efforts. "Is it time to get to work?"

"No." Megan rolled over onto her stomach, closer to Karina. "I can't sleep. It's so dark in here with only a light stick to see by. Aren't you scared about tomorrow?"

Karina looked at the illuminated dial on her watch. "You mean today? It's almost two o'clock in the morning."

"Sorry," Megan apologized. "I had to talk with someone. Everything seems to be closing in on me."

Karina unzipped her sleeping bag enough to reach out and place an arm across Megan's back. "Think about something else. Remember the cross-country flight we completed last summer? What did your parents say about your accomplishment? Were they proud?"

"Kind of," Megan said. "They couldn't believe what we did, but they lectured me more about running away and getting sent to Blue Horizons. I think I am just an embarrassment to them. They seemed relieved when it was time for me to return to school."

"Is running away why you got sent here?" Karina asked softly. "Don't answer if I'm being too personal."

Megan sighed deeply. "Yeah. After the fifth time the police brought me home, my social worker told the judge that she didn't know what else to do with me."

Karina groped for something to say. "Think how much more they will listen to you when you tell them about being trained to conduct an underground rescue."

"It won't make any difference," Megan said, inching toward Karina until their sleeping bags nearly touched. "I think I'll stay at school and not go home for summer break this year."

When Megan yawned and closed her eyes, Karina wiggled around until she found a comfortable position. The cold, rocky ground was the bad thing about sleeping in a cave. With a continuous fifty-three-degree temperature, the cave seemed warm while she was moving, but she chilled quickly when pressed against the cool rocks for any length of time. That made it essential to keep her sleeping bag on the narrow insulated pad she had lugged into the cave.

Karina thought about home. She considered herself luckier than the other kids. Figuratively speaking, she had two homes. Blue Horizons was her true home, and she was very proud to live at the boarding school. When she needed a more traditional family life, she had a home with the Winfields. After the spelunking part of the summer curriculum ended, the class was headed to Hawaii to study volcanoes for the second part of the program. The thought brought on a contented smile. The Winfields and eight-year-old Cindy were going to fly to Hawaii at the same time, so Karina could spend some time with them when she wasn't participating in classes. Karina yawned; sleep halted plans for fun-filled events on a black sand beach surrounded by luscious tropical scenery.

"Does everyone understand his or her role for this exercise?" Sally asked.

Everyone sat in a semicircle around the agile female instructor, trying not to shine helmet lights in her eyes. All morning they had practiced tying knots in the rescue rope. They had also learned how to correctly place their carabineers and other climbing equipment. Karina had trouble remembering to shine her helmet light at Sally's chest and had been reminded twice not to shine light into the other spelunkers' eyes.

"Does everyone understand what *should* and *should not* be done?" Sally asked when no one orally answered. "There's no sense in turning this exercise into a real rescue. Karina will be the injured person."

Proud that Sally chose her to be the first victim, Karina grinned and nodded her head. *I'm going to be the best victim of the day.*

This time everyone replied in an affirmative manner. Less than an hour later, Karina lay in a crumpled position halfway down the steep north wall of a large cavern. Supposedly, she had fallen from an upper ledge, injuring her left leg and right shoulder in the process. Karina's position allowed her a great view of the cave floor, some twenty feet below her. She remained still, lying on her stomach with one leg bent beneath her.

"Are you hurt?" called a male voice from high above. "Can you hear me? We'll be right down. Stay still. Help is on the way."

The voice echoed throughout the cavern, so Karina couldn't tell if Joe or Paul had called down to her. She hoped it was Joe. Because he was Heather's partner, she hadn't seen him much after helping Megan down.

"Rope," a feminine voice shouted, maybe Heather's.

A swish near her head told Karina that the first rescue rope had been deployed. Three additional ropes joined the first. Boots scraped against the rock wall, and bits of mud patted against her helmet.

"Miss, can you hear me?" Paul's voice sounded in her ear. He hung barely a foot away, using his harness as a platform. "Where does it hurt?"

Karina pretended not to hear Paul. The scenario called for her to be unconscious, which was a good thing because she would not have been able to hide the disappointment in her voice. She lay perfectly still as a second rescuer slid down next to her.

"Place an anchor above her," Heather's voice instructed. "I'll set one here. Joe and Jessica are setting the top anchors. Once we get her stabilized, they will transport her across the ravine to Sally. We'll keep her from swinging left and right."

"Belay line ready." Karina heard Jessica yell. She seemed to be far away, so she decided that Jessica must not be directly above. Karina hated not being able to talk, but her job was to play the victim, and she planned on giving a stellar performance.

"Don't move her left leg; it appears to be broken." Heather maneuvered closer to Karina. The voice seemed almost on top of her. "Her shoulder looks injured as well. Immobilize her shoulder; I'll splint her leg."

"Not so fast," Paul said, his voice next to her ear. "A-B-C's first. I'll secure her. You begin first aid."

"Like, right away," Heather said.

Karina felt Heather check her neck, then her airway and breathing, and finally her pulse and circulation. Heather used the carotid artery in her neck to determine whether or not Karina had a pulse. The speed and proficiency Heather and Paul exhibited amazed Karina. In just minutes, they splinted her leg, strapped her into a makeshift stretcher made from tubular webbing and backpacks, and began transporting her across the ravine.

"How is the stretcher doing?" Jessica asked.

"Like, great," Heather yelled. "Megan's idea to use the backpacks and their aluminum frames is better than any of our ideas."

The stretcher's comfort surprised Karina. Overhearing Heather's comment that Megan had designed the stretcher pleased her. Evidently, Martin's plan was working. Megan was becoming more comfortable being underground.

"Hang on." Joe's voice seemed near, though Karina didn't see how.

Her stretcher slid across a rope that connected the ledge that she had recently departed to the safety of the main passageway where Sally awaited her arrival. Currently, she hung twenty feet above the ground and the jagged rocks that would catch her if she slipped from the stretcher and the rope that Paul had attached to her safety harness.

"The rope is snagged on a rock. If you swing her now, it may pull the stretcher apart," Joe pointed out. His words were not reassuring; she had serious thoughts of adding her input. Before she came to a decision, Joe corrected whatever was wrong.

"Swing away," he called to someone, possibly Megan. "She's free."

Ten minutes later, everyone sat around a softly glowing light stick and discussed the rescue attempt. Karina sipped a cup of hot chocolate, relishing its sweet taste as Sally dissected each part of the rescue and each participant's performance.

"Heather," Sally said, turning toward the tall girl. "Your speed at reaching Karina was excellent, but remember to follow the rules of first aid. What is the first rule of a first aid responder?"

"Like, never do anything to hurt the victim," Heather answered without hesitation.

Karina smiled. Heather had certainly changed since Karina had first met the rich, self-centered girl last semester on a marine ecology expedition.

"What does that mean, Karina?" Sally's question jostled Karina's attention to the debriefing.

"It means that if you don't know what to do, you shouldn't guess and do something to hurt the victim," Karina answered promptly.

Sally grinned at her. "Correct. Heather, what did you not do correctly?"

"Like—"

"Stop!" Karina and Megan shouted at the same time. Karina continued, "Don't say 'like' every time you speak. It's getting on my nerves."

Sally motioned for Karina to be silent. She nodded in Heather's direction. "It is annoying, but what's important now is how Heather evaluates her performance."

"Li—" Heather caught herself. "I was in too much of a hurry to get Karina onto the stretcher. I forgot about the basics," she admitted. "I guess I wanted to be fast more than I wanted to be correct."

"Exactly," Sally said. "Speed in any rescue is important. Victims not stabilized in the first hour have much less chance for survival; however, making matters worse by doing something to harm a victim does no one any good. How about you, Paul?"

"I did well," Paul said, "until I got in a hurry while guiding Karina over the edge. The rope snagged on a rock, and Joe had to rappel down to clear the snag. I needlessly put Karina's safety at risk."

"Great. You guys don't need a teacher for debriefing," Sally praised. "What about you, Jessica?"

"I didn't have too big a part," Jessica replied. "All I did was set up the safety belay line attached to Karina in case something went wrong. I was ready to support her if the stretcher came apart. I don't know if I did anything incorrectly."

"You didn't," Sally agreed. "At least nothing that I could see. Anybody else have input for Jessica?"

"Not me," Joe said. "Everything looked fine from my position."

Everyone else agreed, so Sally turned to Megan. "And how about you?"

"I mostly watched," Megan said. She sat on her backpack and hugged her legs tightly together. Her chin rested on her knees. "All I did was figure out a way to tie the packs together to make the stretcher. I guess the only thing I did wrong was still being afraid of being in a cave."

"Are you *really* still frightened?" Sally asked, shining her helmet light on Megan's legs to illuminate the area. "You seemed more at ease than before."

"Yeah," Karina agreed. "Think about it. You sat twenty feet above the cave floor in almost total darkness and still helped supervise Joe's climb. *And* you didn't panic. That's what I call progress."

"Maybe," Megan said, but she sat up straighter and looked at them instead of at her feet. "I didn't panic outwardly, but it sure took all my willpower to stay on that ledge. I really wanted to be down and out of the cave."

Karina understood exactly how Megan felt. "But you didn't panic. Remember how frightened I was about flying? Martin wouldn't let me quit, and I learned to enjoy flying. He told me that learning to deal with fear was tough, but he also said it was a necessary skill. Martin told me that it was important to understand my limits and not let unreasonable fears keep me from becoming less than I could be. I think you've pretty well beaten this fear."

"Like, right on." Heather patted the top of Megan's helmet. "I'd explore with you anytime."

"Thanks for the support, guys," Megan said. Her face relaxed into the first smile Karina had seen since rappelling into the cave. "I couldn't do it without you."

An awkward silence followed Megan's comment. Finally, Paul said, "That's what we're here for."

Sally scrambled to her feet. "Let's eat. We change partners and do some exploring this afternoon."

"Afternoon?" Megan grumbled. "How can you tell?"

"Hey, look what I found," Karina yelled over her shoulder to Joe and Megan. She had wedged herself into a tiny hole to see if it led to a tunnel they could explore. She wanted to see if it pushed—the term spelunkers used to determine if a passageway continued or came to a dead end. "It seems to be a whole new passageway. I don't think it's on the map."

"Don't cram yourself in too tightly." Megan's voice came to her softly, full of worry. "Keep your arms forward in case we have to use the rope."

"I'm fine." Karina inched forward to show Megan that she was still able to move. She had a rope tied around her left leg. Joe would pull her out if she got wedged and couldn't move. "Don't pull on the rope."

Karina pulled herself through the tight confines one inch at a time until she entered an open space. From the scrapes on her knees and the fatigue in her arms, it seemed like she had crawled for hours and traveled a great distance, but her watch indicated only eighteen minutes had passed, and Joe informed her that only six knots were on her side of the hole—a distance of sixty feet.

Maneuvering to a sitting position, Karina looked around at her discovery. The ceiling was a good ten feet above her, and the passageway opened to a width of at least six feet. Even Megan would feel comfortable exploring here. The only negative was crawling through the tight sixty-foot passageway. Karina worried that Megan would panic. A great deal of limestone dust and small rocks had dropped on her during her exploration.

Taking one last look, she inched her way backward toward the group. Nearly an hour passed before she exited the tunnel and reported her finding to Sally.

"This is really cool," Sally said, marveling at Karina's discovery. "I'm sure it's not on the map that Mr. Evans's son made. Karina, I believe you've discovered a new section of the cave."

Everyone had crawled through the tight passageway. Megan had argued for a while, but Heather and Jessica had coaxed her into making the attempt. Karina took off her pack and set it against the cave wall next to where the other girls had stacked their packs.

Free to move more easily, she peered into the myriad of passageways with the rest of the group, except for Megan and Jessica. She noticed that Megan sat beside Jessica, who helped her practice controlled breathing to keep her from hyperventilating.

"Can we change plans and explore here?" Joe asked.

"I don't see—" Sally never finished her sentence. The ground shook violently and dislodged pieces of limestone rock that rained down upon the group. Cave dust filled the air. Karina covered her nose with her arms and crawled toward Jessica and Megan. She tried to warn them, but breathing took all of her effort.

"Cover your head," Karina finally gasped aloud. She never heard Megan's reply. The ground trembled with greater intensity, and a heavy weight seemed to sit on Karina's back.

CHAPTER 5

The Maze

In the spooky gloom that chemical light sticks provided, Karina saw a figure reach her side. Joe dabbed her forehead with a damp bandana. She recognized the salty taste in her mouth as blood. A pounding ache in her head kept pace with her heartbeat.

Joe placed a restraining hand on her shoulder as she tried to sit up. "Lie still until I've finished checking you for injuries. Part of the roof collapsed. A large rock smashed against your helmet and cracked it all the way through. Can you move your feet without any pain?"

"I think so." Karina wiggled her toes as best she could inside her boots and then slowly moved her feet. "My head hurts and my lower lip is bleeding. I think I bit it. Is anyone else hurt?"

"Lie still. I'm going to do a secondary assessment to make sure that you don't have any hidden injuries." Joe gently felt around her head and neck and began a head-to-toe assessment of her condition.

"What happened? Anyone else hurt?" Karina asked again as Joe continued his thorough examination.

Joe placed both hands on her hips and pushed. "No pelvic damage. We had a cave-in. Sally led the others a few hundred feet deeper into the cave. There is a big crack above us. I didn't want to move you before I determined if you had any head or spinal injuries." His hands moved down to check her thighs and knees.

"I'm okay," Karina said, cutting short the examination. She wanted to get away from any further danger. "Help me up."

Joe helped Karina to her feet. He picked up the light stick and handed it to her. "Lean on me. It's a tight squeeze. Be careful; the walls have some sharp edges."

Her head pounded as she walked. She felt dizzy but otherwise seemed unharmed. Karina leaned against Joe, more for pleasure than from need. She felt secure in his arms and blushed at the realization that she should be worried about getting out of the cave instead of secretly enjoying the moment.

Joe pointed toward helmet lights ahead. "Not far now. How are you doing, Rini?"

"I can walk now, but I sure could use a drink." She slipped from Joe's arms and followed closely behind him.

As they neared the group, Sally hurried to Karina and sat her down by Jessica. "Are you injured?"

Karina shook her head and immediately regretted the action. "Just a headache. A rock actually broke my helmet." She took off her helmet and presented it to Sally.

Her instructor examined the helmet and, against Karina's arguing, took off her own helmet and made Karina wear it. Then she went and rummaged through her backpack.

Jessica placed a hand on Karina's shoulder. "Bad?"

She leaned back against the rock wall. "Kind of; it's not too bad when I don't move around, and it's not as bad as when I first woke. I felt some nausea before, but that is all gone now. I don't think I have a concussion or anything."

Sally gave Karina two Tylenol tablets and a drink from one of the three salvaged water bottles. "Sip slowly. The water filters were destroyed in the rockslide."

"What do we do now?" Megan asked in a trembling voice as she cowered against the cave wall.

They sat in a tight circle around a single light stick. All helmet lights had been turned off to conserve batteries. The passageways were smaller in this unexplored section of the cave. Except for Karina's knock on the head, everyone else had come through the rockslide without harm, though only Sally and the boys had escaped with their packs. The girls' packs had been buried under heavy rocks.

"Let's look at this objectively." Sally spoke slowly, clearly. "We have plenty of air. Between us there are enough protein bars to last for about three days if we ration carefully at six hundred calories a day per person. Three water bottles should last us a couple of days if we conserve, and there is water available from the stream if we have to drink it. We still have enough batteries and light sticks for about five days. Everything else is back at base camp."

"Like, how long before someone comes searching for us?" Heather asked the question on everyone's mind.

"Another day," Sally answered. "But it will take some time for them to find us. No one knows that this part of the cave even exists. It is not on the map Mr. Evans's son made."

"We can dig our way out," Paul suggested.

"I don't think that's a good idea," Sally replied. "With that fracture in the ceiling, it's just too dangerous."

"What do you think caused it to collapse?" Jessica asked.

"Yeah," Karina said. "I thought Martin told us that there wasn't much chance of cave-ins in Missouri caves."

"Normally, that's true," Sally said. She placed a reassuring hand on Megan's shoulder. "I'm not sure what happened. The ground shook pretty hard before the ceiling came down. Maybe it was an earthquake. We aren't far from the New Madrid Fault."

"Martin said these caves were formed millions of years ago and have already experienced major earthquakes. Shouldn't that make them resistant to damage from small quakes? What we experienced couldn't have been a large quake," Paul said.

"I don't—" Sally began.

"What difference does it make? We're trapped in here and need to get out!" Megan yelled. "Who cares what caused it? The question is, *how* do we get out?!"

"Calm down, girl." Heather put her arms around Megan and hugged the trembling girl close to her. "We'll get out of this if we don't panic. Right, Karina?"

Karina smiled at her blonde-haired friend. "You bet. Does anybody here feel a breeze besides me?"

"Now that you mention it," Joe said, "I do feel a slight draft on my neck. It's so weak that I thought I was just imagining it. You know, wishful thinking."

"Let's check it out," Karina suggested.

Sally divided the group into three teams—two exploring and one remaining at their current location. After Karina said her headache was better, Sally selected a wide passageway with a high ceiling that ran off to the left for Karina and Joe to search. Paul and Jessica were assigned a search area that led to the right. That passageway was much tighter and had a low ceiling. Megan and Heather would remain where they were as a frame of reference for the searchers. Keeping Heather and Megan together freed Sally to join any group that discovered a possible means of escape or to assist any group that ran into trouble.

Two hours later, rocks poked Karina's left side as she inched her way through a tight squeeze. The walls, floor, and ceiling narrowed and just barely allowed her slender frame through. According to her crude calculations, she and Joe had followed their assigned passageway for almost a mile.

A steady breeze hit Karina and evaporated the tiny beads of sweat that rolled down her face. Cool air and the fact that her head no longer ached provided her with relief from the tormenting exertion of climbing over sharp rocks and crawling long distances on her hands and knees. The passageway became an incline; Karina crawled upward, trying to trace the origin of the life-giving airstream. She searched for a way to the surface, hoping for daylight and freedom.

"Karina," Joe called from fifteen feet below. "What do you see? Does it lead anywhere?"

"I don't see any light yet," Karina yelled, pausing to catch her breath and find a good place to put her feet. Martin's instructions— to always keep three points of contact while climbing—guided her actions. "The breeze is stronger here, and the passageway isn't getting any narrower. I need to rest a minute."

"Take your time," Joe yelled back. "Be careful."

"I will," Karina called down, trying to reassure Joe that she had the situation under control. It would be nice to help Joe out of a jam. Usually, Joe came to her rescue.

She wasn't particularly worried about being trapped in the cave. As long as they had air, their predicament annoyed her more than it presented any immediate danger. Everyone knew they were in the cave. Martin wouldn't stop searching until he found the rockslide and realized where to find them. After an uncomfortable amount of time, they would be rescued—if they didn't save themselves first.

"Enough speculating. Time to get to work," Karina told herself in a commanding tone.

Four feet above, the inclined passageway leveled out. The walls separated enough for Karina to worm her way into a sitting position and shine her light into an opening. She sat at the entrance to a large cavern, nearly fifty feet across and more than twenty feet high. A tall column stood a couple of feet from the far wall. Even more exciting, Karina spied sunlight shining on the upper end of the column.

"Joe!" Karina couldn't keep excitement from her voice. "I can see sunlight. There's a huge room here. I'm coming down."

"No!" Joe's voice stopped Karina's downward movement. "See if you can find a way out first."

"Good idea," Karina yelled down. Secretly, she kicked herself for letting her excitement and emotion get the best of her. She might have led everyone here only to be disappointed.

During further exploration, Karina discovered that most of the cave floor was muddy but level. A tiny stream of water trickled down from a small opening twenty feet above her and then disappeared down a hand-sized hole near the edge of the column. The column itself was massive, nearly ten feet in diameter.

Karina moved behind the column and held out her arm. The space between the column and the cave wall measured slightly more than two feet. The wall inched inward near the top. The opening looked tight but large enough to squeeze through. She hurried down to Joe.

"Well?" he demanded, handing Karina his water bottle. "What did you find? Is there a way out?"

Holding up a hand to buy time for a precious sip of refreshing liquid, Karina gasped. "I think so. The opening is going to be difficult to reach, but it looks large enough to crawl through. It's not going to be an easy climb."

"Do you think Paul can do it?" Joe asked.

"I think so." She wasn't surprised that Joe didn't ask if he might be able to get through. Joe always chose the most practical solution in emergencies; he knew that Paul was the best climber in the group. Every summer vacation, Paul climbed mountains in Wyoming and Canada with his father, who was an accomplished mountain climber.

"As soon as you're rested, we better get back," Joe said. He consulted his watch. "We've been gone for over three hours. Sally will be worrying."

Karina removed her helmet, used her bandana to wipe sweat away from her brow, and secured the protective headgear in a more comfortable position. "I'm ready, but go slow. My legs are just about shot."

I'm slowing Joe down, Karina thought as she ducked under a part of the passageway where the ceiling came down so low that she almost had to crawl on hands and knees. She was tired and wanted to rest, but she knew that she had to keep pace with Joe. Sally and the kids would be worried. They had been gone a long time.

"I see light," Joe called over his shoulder. "We're almost there. Hang on, Rini."

The passageway widened, and the ceiling rose, allowing Karina to walk comfortably. This was the easy part of the cave she and Joe had entered at the beginning of their search. *Thank God!* she thought.

Sally and the group stood to meet Karina and Joe as they emerged. The somber mood of the group indicated that Paul and Jessica had not found a way out. Joe shared their discovery. "I think Karina found a way out."

"Are you sure?" Megan tearfully hugged Karina.

"I'm sure that we found a small cavern with a hole that leads to the outside. I saw daylight," Karina said, returning Megan's hug and then gently pushing the girl an arm's length away. "It won't be long now, but the way out is going to be pretty scary."

"Just what are we up against?" Jessica asked as everyone gathered to listen to Karina's story.

Karina paused and looked at Joe, who nodded. She continued, "We have a long walk and a tight crawl ahead of us. Then we will have to climb up the side of a column to reach the hole."

"Before we go into any more detail," Sally interrupted, "everyone eat half of a protein bar. We'll need strength. It's almost eight o'clock. By the time we reach the opening, it will be night. We'll rest before trying to climb out."

"Why?" Megan demanded. She looked pleadingly at Sally and bartered. "If we get out now, I'll buy everyone a hamburger when we get to town."

Paul answered before Sally responded. "Everyone is tired. We'll be pretty close to exhaustion by the time we reach the cavern. It's too dangerous to climb with weak legs. Somebody could get hurt."

Karina added, "The climb is going to be tricky. I'm not sure that I can make it even with a full night's rest. It looks like we will have to climb by putting our backs to the column and pushing against the wall with our feet to inch up the column."

It appeared Megan wanted to say more, but Heather pulled the frightened girl close and whispered something in her ear. Megan sighed and settled back against Heather. Karina was impressed and wondered what Heather had said to calm Megan.

"Don't worry about the climb out," Sally said, interrupting Karina's thoughts. "Paul is the best climber here. We'll give him a share of our rations and try to help him get a good night's sleep. If it looks safe enough, he can climb out and go for help. We'll wait until he returns."

Sally's logic amazed Karina. She hadn't even thought about sending someone for help. In her mind, they would all climb out together. *Guess it's a good thing we have an adult with us*, she thought. *When will I learn to think through all of the possibilities before jumping at the first idea that comes into my head?*

Forty minutes later, the weary group had eaten protein bars, sipped water from their dwindling supply, and gathered together all that remained of their gear. Karina and Joe had also learned that Paul and Jessica's passageway ended after about a half mile.

As departure time neared, everyone seemed anxious and excited at the same time—anxious to see daylight and excited at the prospect of an early rescue. They started off without speaking, Karina in the lead, followed by Joe. The rest fell into line with Sally bringing up the rear. As tired as they were, no one looked forward to the long and demanding trip.

"I hope we don't have to do that again," Sally said, nursing a scrape above her left elbow. "How in the world did you climb up here?" She directed her last remark to Heather, Joe, and Paul—the larger ones of the group.

"Wasn't easy," Joe said, exposing his own scraped elbows. "But I'd be willing to give a pound of flesh to get out of here and get a hamburger and milkshake."

"Like, don't," Heather threatened, placing a muddy, gloved finger near Joe's lips, "unless you're looking for a mud snack. I'm starving."

Karina giggled at the hurt expression on Joe's face. "Careful, Joe. I know Heather better than you do. She means it."

"Okay. Okay," Joe said, perturbed. "I can see that I'm trapped with a bunch of humorless heathens."

The weary group settled down and made camp for the night. Then they followed Karina over to the column and looked at the ceiling. For a long time, no one spoke. The opening—their chance for salvation—was nowhere to be seen.

"It's there," Karina spoke softly, before the others could express their doubts and frustration. "I know it is."

"Are you sure?" Megan asked. "I don't see anything."

"Our lights aren't strong enough to penetrate the outside darkness," Sally said. "It's night. We won't be able to see out before the sun rises tomorrow morning. Let's get some rest. We'll get a fresh start at dawn."

Everyone agreed, and Karina joined the girls on one side of the column. There wasn't enough dry ground in one place for everyone to be together, so Paul and Joe got comfortable on the far side of the column. With only three space blankets among them, Paul and Joe shared one. Sally and Megan shared a blanket, which left Karina, Jessica, and Heather to share the third.

"What do you think?" Jessica whispered into Karina's ear. "Can we make it out?"

They lay under the survival blanket and on top of the extra clothing from Sally's backpack: Karina on the left side, Jessica in the middle, and Heather on the far side. With only a slight breeze and an otherwise constant temperature of fifty-three degrees Fahrenheit, Karina felt warm enough, though the ground could have been softer. Fatigue slowed her thinking.

"Paul should be able to handle the climb," Karina said with a confidence she didn't truly feel. "He said he's done harder climbs before in the mountains with his dad."

"I'm scared," Jessica whispered softly. "I keep thinking about what will happen if we can't get out. What if nobody finds us?"

Karina turned to face Jessica. "We'll make it out. Don't worry. Martin won't stop searching until he finds us."

Jessica changed the subject. "How does it feel having Martin for your guardian as well as headmaster?"

"I feel like I have a home now," Karina answered thoughtfully. "For the first time since my parents died, I feel that someone really cares about me, really loves me."

"I care about you," Jessica said.

She sensed the hurt in Jessica's voice. "I know you do, and I love you like a sister, but I meant an adult—a parent."

"Oh." Jessica leaned her head against Karina's shoulder. "You've been in so many tough situations since coming to Blue Horizons. I wish I had your courage."

"If you mean being lost in the Amazon and being shipwrecked," Karina said, "that was all Joe's doing. Without him, I'd have died a long time ago."

Jessica asked in a quiet voice, "Before Martin became your guardian, I know your parents died and a judge sent you to Blue Horizons because you shoplifted. Do you mind telling me exactly what happened?"

Karina gasped. Past images flashed before her eyes. *Maybe it's time to open up to Jessica.* "When I was eight, my parents died in a plane crash in Kyrgyzstan."

"Were you in the crash? Is that how you got the scars on your legs?" Jessica asked.

Instinctively, Karina ran her right hand down her trousers along the scar lines that she had received from the accident. "Yeah. I survived but got so angry that I was too hard for my grandparents to handle, so they sent me to an aunt and uncle in New York. I never really fit in there and tried to make friends at school." Karina paused a second. "I tried to join a club whose initiation was to shoplift. I got caught and ended up at Blue Horizons. Now Martin is my guardian, and I have you and Joe."

"Are you two steady again?" Jessica asked, yawning.

Heather's soft snoring and the small talk provided a calming effect. "For the moment," Karina said, "it's hard with both of us being at Blue Horizons and the strict policy about intimate relationships. Martin is giving me some freedom, but the restrictions are a drag. I can only show *close personal affection* with a boy when we are not on campus and are not on class activities."

Silence greeted Karina's last sentence; she discovered Jessica sleeping peacefully. Weariness tugged at her. Thinking about Martin and his never giving up on her became Karina's last thought before restful slumber replaced visions of her troubled past.

The sounds of Paul and Joe rising awakened Karina. She looked toward the column, and her heart brightened more than the light beam illuminating the top of the grayish-white limestone pillar. She nudged Jessica and Heather. "Get up. It's time."

Sally rose and ordered everyone to gather in a circle on a dry spot near the column. She handed out food from their meager food supply. "Chew slowly," she instructed.

Karina chewed her few bites of food and stared at Paul. *He's either not nervous, or he hides it well*, she thought. She had tried to sit with Joe and Paul, but the boys seemed to want to be alone, so she respected their privacy. Besides, Megan demanded her attention. The girl sat between Karina and Jessica and tightly held Karina's hand.

Paul drank down a few large gulps of water and moved to the column. Karina and the group followed. Sally went over instructions with Paul about how to get help. Then she moved back to stand by the girls.

"Ready?" Joe asked as Paul stared at the light shining from above.

Karina broke away from Megan and lightly tapped Paul on his jacket. "When you get out, be sure to mark a trail so you can find your way back. We'll be waiting for you." She patted his shoulder.

Paul lightly rapped her helmet. "Piece of cake. I'll bring back hamburgers and fries for all."

"Don't forget the milkshakes," Sally said in a failed effort to break the tension. Everyone else wished Paul good luck. Then he began climbing.

Karina watched enviously as Paul placed his back against the cave wall and his feet on the column. Her lungs ached from holding her breath. She watched him move up the column one step at a time. Using his hands and his back as friction brakes to keep from falling, Paul quickly inched his way toward the ceiling.

"I've made it," Paul yelled down from the opening. "I think I can grab some roots and pull myself out."

"No!" Sally yelled, but it was too late.

Karina watched in horror as Paul grabbed a thick vine and transferred his weight to it, trying to pull himself to freedom. Then, in one fateful moment, he swung back and forth as the vine dropped a full five feet below the opening. Before Karina or anyone else could act, the vine slipped farther. It stopped some ten feet above them. For a long moment, Paul held tightly to the end of the vine, but his gloved hands couldn't find enough traction to maintain his grip. Seconds later he slipped from the vine and plummeted toward the rock floor.

Karina stood frozen, but Joe acted quickly, racing to intercept Paul before he hit the ground. Joe didn't actually catch Paul, but he caught the taller boy's shoulders. Together, they landed on hard rock.

Sally commanded everyone to give her room. "Stay back."

"I'm fine," Joe said, rising to his knees. "How goes it, Paul?"

Paul grimaced. "My ankle—I think I broke it."

Karina helped Joe and Sally move Paul to a sitting position and remove his boot. She saw no deformity, but swelling indicated a sprain or fracture. Either way, Paul wouldn't do any more climbing for a long time.

"What do we do now?" Megan whined. "We have to get out of here!"

Heather and Jessica moved to comfort Megan, while Sally and Joe tended Paul. During those few moments, Karina came up with an idea—one that both energized and terrified her—an idea that she knew Joe would oppose.

"I'd like to try to climb out," Karina said. "I can climb the vine if you guys can help me reach it." She pointed to the dangling lifeline hanging some ten feet above them.

Sally looked up at the vine and shook her head. "I don't know. I don't need more injured students. We can always wait it out. Help will come eventually."

"We have to get out; we can't stay here. Please! Let her try!" Megan cried.

Heather took Megan in her arms and hugged her. "Like, not our call."

Joe shook his head. "That vine is harder to climb than it looks."

Sally looked at Karina for a long moment, then at Megan, and finally back to Karina. "Okay," she agreed. "Here's what we're going to do. We'll form a pyramid. Heather, Joe, and I will form the base. Karina will climb onto our shoulders, and Jessica will spot for her."

Joe pulled Karina aside as she prepared for her climb. "Remember to use your legs, and don't wear gloves. Watch what you grab onto to pull yourself out. A fall from the top would be much worse."

"Thanks." Karina would have hugged Joe, but Sally stood only a few feet away. "I'll be careful. I can do this." She looked at Joe and added, "This time, I get to save you. How's that for a change?"

"Don't let it go to your head," Joe said. "I'm still older and wiser."

She wanted to tease more and make a witty reply, but time and a crowd didn't allow for a longer conversation. Karina climbed carefully and stood on Joe's shoulders with Heather and Sally supporting her. Jessica and Megan shined lights on the vine.

Karina grabbed the vine with both hands, bent her knees, and pushed upward. She hoisted herself onto the vine and wrapped her feet around it to keep from slipping. The climb was easier than she expected, but she didn't see how she could climb through the hole. Keeping both hands on the vine prevented her from pushing her shoulders through the opening. Every time she reached the point where her elbows were level with her hands, her shoulders wouldn't fit. Worse still, her arm muscles trembled from exertion. If she didn't make it out soon, she'd have to climb back down and try later, an action she dreaded.

Karina decided to make a risky maneuver—one that just might work. Using the last of her strength, she pulled herself up. Only this time, she locked her feet around the vine, grabbed a bunch of smaller vines with her left hand, and clutched a big rock with her right. She grunted and pulled with all of her might, kicking her legs to find a foothold. Seconds later, Karina stood above the opening. Warm sunlight brightened her spirits. She was on the side of a large hill that overlooked a small stream. Karina saw why no one had found this entrance before. Thick bushes surrounded the opening, providing natural camouflage.

"I made it," she shouted down to her friends. "I'll be back as soon as I can."

Karina climbed the steep hill next to the cave and found herself on a wooded hilltop. She worried about forgetting the way back to the cave, so every few yards Karina stopped and marked the trail—sometimes by building a pile of dead twigs, sometimes by building a small pile of rocks, and sometimes by putting some unusual outgrowth or rock formation to memory.

Half an hour later, Karina found a dirt path that became a gravel road and led to a blacktopped country road. She hadn't walked more than half a mile when a county police car came into sight. Karina flagged down the officer, explained what had happened, and gave the officer Martin's cell phone number.

By noon Sally had taken Paul to the hospital, and everyone sat with Martin and the other students at base camp, eating a voracious amount of *real* food and telling the story over and over, exaggerating a bit more with each retelling.

"Nice going, Karina," Martin praised her and gave her a firm hug. "That was good thinking—on everyone's part."

"Can we go back and explore the new section we discovered?" Joe asked, munching on his third hamburger.

"Not me," Megan avowed. "I'm never going back into that cave."

"Why did the passage collapse?" Jessica asked between sips of iced tea. "That doesn't usually happen, does it?"

"This is only speculation," Martin began, "but the police seem to believe that it might have been caused by some blasting the county was doing to clear out rock for a new road that isn't far from where the cave-in occurred."

"I thought that wasn't supposed to happen for another couple of weeks," Karina said.

Martin nodded. "That was Mr. Evans's understanding. I don't know how or why the schedule changed, but there's no sense fretting about it now."

"We thought it might have been an earthquake," Heather said.

Martin struck down her theory. "There were no tremors anywhere else. It would have been on the news if there had been an earthquake."

"What about my idea?" Joe asked, ignoring Megan's glare. "Can we explore the new passageways?"

"Sorry," Martin apologized. "That entrance is on private land, and the owner doesn't want anyone going into the cave. After what happened, he's worried about someone getting hurt and suing him."

Joe looked crestfallen. Karina had to admit that she was disappointed too. The thought of exploring undiscovered passageways—ones that had never been explored by other human beings—appealed to her.

"If you're looking for more adventure," Martin said, looking the group over carefully, "I've got a tough one for you—one that requires working for scientists on a mapping expedition."

"Not me," Megan said. "I'm sitting this one out!"

Martin chuckled. "You are excused from this expedition, Megan. I guess you've had enough adventures for now. You can work with Mr. Smithson and the rest of the class in less adventurous caves as they count bat colonies for the Missouri Department of Conservation. You can join them this afternoon."

"What adventure? Where is it? When do we start?" Karina asked the questions for everyone.

"Devil's Icebox," Martin answered.

"Sounds intriguing," Joe mused. "Why is it so tough, and why is it named *Devil's Icebox*?"

"It's full of water in many places," Martin explained. "The cave is like a maze, and legend has it that a number of early explorers got lost and drowned. Because so many of the passages have water in them, the entrance is only accessible by either a raft or by swimming, and the water is cold. We will have to scuba dive to reach the area that we will map."

"Like, we can do that," Heather said, beaming. She turned to Jessica. "Right?"

Jessica nodded. "Let's see. Scuba diving. Wet suits. Diving along an entry line." She paused and looked straight at Martin. "No problem."

Karina knew what Jessica was thinking. She, Heather, and Jessica were accomplished PADI Master Scuba divers because of their previous semester at Ocean Quest Academy. This could be their chance to shine. They were all wreck-diver certified. This should be no more difficult that diving through a sunken ship in deep water. At least in a cave depth and decompression sickness shouldn't be a problem.

"When do we go?" Jessica repeated the unanswered questions. "And where is it?"

"We leave the day after tomorrow," Martin said. "The cave is about a three-hour drive from here. Sally thought you'd like an easy day before taking on another challenge. By then, I'll have finished helping Mr. Smithson get organized. I've hired a female intern from a local college to work with Mr. Smithson. Devon will take Paul's place. He's already certified for scuba."

"How is Paul?" Heather asked.

"His ankle is badly sprained," Martin answered. "He'll be back with us tomorrow, but he'll be on crutches for several weeks."

"I'm ready now," Karina said. She still felt giddy from all the praise she'd received for her part in the rescue.

Martin held up a hand. "Not so fast. You have some things to learn before going into Devil's Icebox. It's a living cave and very fragile. We're going in pretty far. We don't want to hurt the cave, so we have to work out exploration groups and go over special procedures."

"I'll partner with Rini," Joe offered. "We work pretty well together."

Karina blushed at Joe's comment, but she fully agreed. She was about to push the issue with Martin when his next comments stopped her short and ended the conversation until a later time.

"Sorry, Joe," Martin said. "We have a supervision problem that requires that two of the girls dive together. Because of the tight confines, we will have to go in single file and need some space between divers. A local caving club has already strung a guideline and intercom line into the cave for us, but only Heather, Jessica, and Karina have been trained to dive using a guideline. They are certified for wreck diving. They have used guidelines before. Karina and Jessica have the most experience with wreck diving, so they will dive without direct adult supervision." He paused and looked at Karina and Jessica. "Do you think you can do what I'm asking?"

Karina nodded. "No problem. We've had lots of experience."

"Should be simple," Jessica said. "In wrecks there was always the danger of falling debris or the wreck shifting. We won't have that problem in a cave. Will we lead?"

Martin shook his head. "No. Sally and Heather will lead. You and Karina will go next, and the boys and I will bring up the rear. That way, if you have a problem, you will have an adult either a few yards ahead of you or a few yards behind you. Though not directly in sight, you will still be only a short distance from help if you run into any unexpected difficulties. Understand?"

Everyone nodded, and Martin dismissed the group before further questions could be fielded. His orders were to get a nap. Then he'd drive them into town for the evening.

"This should be exciting," Joe said after Martin walked away. He turned to Karina. "How hard will it be following a guideline?"

She sensed apprehension as well as excitement in his voice. "Not hard. All you have to do is keep a hand on the guideline and try not to let your fins hit the bottom and stir up any silt."

Jessica lightly slapped Heather on the back. "If this giant of a girl can get through dark, tight shipwrecks, you won't have any trouble."

Heather tugged Jessica's ponytail. "Giant? Me? Just because you are five four, runt, doesn't make me a giant."

Joe inched up to Heather. He was only a couple of inches taller. "If she's a giant, what does that make me?"

Karina looked around to see that Martin was out of sight and then locked arms with Joe. "That makes you mine. Stay away from close proximity to all other girls without *my* okay, especially tall blonde ones."

Heather faked being insulted and batted her eyes at Joe. "Like, call me anytime," she joked. "Seriously, don't worry. Following a guideline is easy. Like, just don't get too close to the person in front of you and watch your air supply."

Joe grinned at Karina and then at Heather. "You lead. I'll follow. Perhaps not too close, though."

Jessica took Karina's free arm and pulled her away from Joe. "Nap time. We'd better do as Martin said, or we won't have free time tonight."

The group departed and headed to their own tents. Karina slipped into her sleeping bag and thought about swimming in cold water. Now that she had sufficient time to think about it, the idea of scuba diving in dark, narrow cave passageways made her nervous. She fell asleep thinking that science sure demanded a lot from a person.

CHAPTER 6

Devil's Icebox

The steady stream of bubbles flowing past Karina reassured her that Jessica was swimming directly ahead. Cold water against her bare skin reminded her of Martin's lectures about cave diving. In addition to the danger of running out of air, she knew the cold water could lead to hypothermia. She hated the darkness that surrounded her outside the penetrating beam provided by her dive light. Because they were in an extremely sensitive part of the cave, she and Jessica wore only white one-piece swimsuits; cheap, white-cotton, work gloves; and scuba gear. Because sweat, body oil, and dyes from clothes could endanger the sensitive cave formations, they had to move through the water without wearing more protective clothing. For the short dive, the cold water was more a nuisance than a danger, but Karina was eager to reach the bag of dry clothes that awaited her at the spot where they would emerge from the flooded passageway. Sally and Heather had gone first, and they had carried the dry, waterproof bag of clothes. A day earlier, Martin and Sally had transported the supplies needed to map and explore the passageways beyond the flooded area of the cave.

Karina swam into a cloud of bubbles and slowed, breathing heavily through her regulator. Jessica stopped swimming forward, backed her legs into a narrow side passageway, made a grotesque move, and suddenly appeared facing Karina. Concern was etched on her best friend's face.

Jessica motioned that she had lost the guide rope—the rope positioned to lead them safely through the underwater section of Devil's Icebox. Martin's last words before sending them through the flooded maze had been to go slow and not lose sight of the rope.

Karina searched the cave floor. Her examination proved Jessica correct, and the metallic taste of fear filled her mouth. They had lost their guideline. A quick glance at her dive computer informed her that she had less than forty-five minutes to find the guideline and navigate the flooded passageways to the caverns beyond. Failing that, she and Jessica must find an opening with air.

Frantic hands pawed at her. Jessica tried to push past Karina. The steely, unfocused look in Jessica's eyes indicated panic. Karina grabbed Jessica and pulled her close, signaling for her friend to look at her own dive computer. Because Karina had gone on a short practice dive with Joe and Devon, Karina figured that Jessica had slightly more air, perhaps fifty or fifty-five minutes. They had time.

Putting her hands on top of Jessica's shoulders, Karina forced the shorter girl to the cave floor, some fifteen inches below them. She held Jessica immobile to keep her from racing off into one of the many flooded passageways. Those few moments gave Karina time to construct a plan. Both she and Jessica were accomplished scuba divers; however, the dark and the cave's close confines added new dimensions to diving. While not claustrophobic, Karina admitted to herself that the close proximity of the cave walls and the low ceiling unnerved her. This was a tighter squeeze than she had experienced while wreck diving. She sympathized with Jessica but couldn't let fear replace reasoned thought. Panic was their greatest danger, not running out of air.

Taking the white slate and pencil attached to her left wrist, Karina scribbled a message telling her friend to calm down. She indicated that they would slowly backtrack to see where they had left the main passageway. Karina also reminded Jessica that they had been underwater for about ten minutes, so they must be close to their destination. The dive plan called for a dive lasting about twelve minutes.

Jessica took several deep breaths and signaled that she understood. Then Karina carefully inched herself back down the passageway. She didn't want to turn around. Too many turns might disorient her. Jessica faced her, so the two friends had eye contact as they used fingers to push themselves along. Clouds of silt from gloved hands pushing against the cave floor diminished visibility; Karina took one of Jessica's hands to keep Jessica close.

Less than three minutes and a distance of barely fifteen yards brought Karina to a three-way juncture. She shined her light into the first passageway but found no guideline. Karina nudged Jessica backward into the second passageway, but Jessica's fins stirred the silt, making visibility impossible.

What did Martin say to do if they lost the line in murky water? Karina thought, trying to remain calm. She grappled with rising fear, took two deep breaths, and urged her racing heart to slow down. Following Martin's predive instructions, Karina let her body settle to the cave floor. Her bare legs sank into cold, shallow silt. Lying prone, she reached out her left hand. It struck against the rough wall before she fully extended her arm. Next, she brought her hand back toward her; fingers groped through the silt, searching for the precious guideline. Nothing rewarded her effort as her hand reached her side.

She did the same with her right hand and also found nothing; however, her right hand had not touched the wall. Holding firmly onto Jessica with her left hand, Karina inched to her right and extended her arm again. This time she made contact. She breathed a deep sigh of relief that sent a burst of air bubbles into the murky water. Her right hand closed around a thin wire, only inches from her chest. It wasn't the guideline, but Karina recognized the wire. It was the intercom line that provided communication from inside the cave to the outside world. She found the correct passageway! The guideline must be near.

She pulled Jessica close enough to see the insulated, black wire running through her fingers. Jessica nodded her understanding, and Karina turned back to work. Once more she extended her arm until her hand touched the rock wall. Then she pulled her arm back to her side. Still nothing.

That isn't possible, Karina thought. She knew the two lines ran alongside each other. The rope guideline should be easy to find. They could follow the intercom line, but it was thin and black. That made it hard to see through the murky silt. She wanted the security of the thick white rope that served as their tether to safety.

For a third time, Karina reached out to the cave wall. Only this time, she walked her fingers up the wall instead of lowering her fingers back to the silt floor. Her heart beat for joy when she grasped the guideline, which she found snagged on a rock about fifteen inches above the cave floor.

"How did that happen?" Jessica wrote on her slate after Karina showed her the snagged rope.

"Don't know," Karina wrote back. "Go. Martin and the boys will be here soon."

<hr>

"Towel! Towel!" Karina gasped as she stumbled to her feet, holding onto Jessica's shoulder and walking backward because walking backward was easier while wearing diving fins. "I'm freezing!"

"Me too!" Jessica broke away from Karina to walk on her own.

Karina removed her diving equipment and gratefully took the dry cotton towel that Heather handed her. "Thanks. I've never been so cold. I don't think I could have stayed in that water much longer without a wet suit."

"Like, I know what you mean." Heather handed Karina a small bundle of clothes. "Like, my lips were totally blue by the time I got out of the water. We didn't get here much before you arrived. I kind of panicked and yanked on the rope. It slipped through my fingers, and I lost it. If Sally hadn't grabbed me, I'd probably still be swimming through that flooded passageway."

"That's why I lost the line," Jessica said, slipping off her gear. "It got jerked from my hand as I changed passageways."

"Like, really sorry." Heather moved to help Jessica and Karina store their diving equipment.

Karina patted Heather's shoulder and said, "No problem." She slipped off her swimsuit, toweled dry, and started dressing. "Please tell me that we don't have to map the underwater part of this cave," Karina begged. "It's too cold."

"No need to worry, ladies," Sally said, handing Karina a helmet and headlamp. "A spelunking club mapped that section last year.

Our job is to map all passageways that are in a radius of a half mile from this spot."

"Good." Karina slipped on wool socks and boots. "Can we work on our hair before we go? Mine's a mess."

"No time," Sally said. "Martin and the boys will be here in less than five minutes."

Disappointed, Karina finished dressing. Then she helped Jessica and Heather organize the gear. By the time they had all of the ropes, slates, and spelunking equipment unpacked and tested, Martin and the boys had arrived. The girls all moved around the bend of a passageway until the guys finished dressing. Then everyone was ready to begin.

"That was absolutely fantastic!" Karina plopped down next to Joe. For the past four hours, she and Heather had explored a tight passageway. All had been routine until they squeezed through a narrow opening and discovered a huge cavern. "Boy, am I tired. We found a cavern full of cave formations, including an entire section of crystals. You have to go and see it. It's beautiful."

"Hot chocolate?" Joe asked, holding out a cup filled with steaming liquid. "I wish I'd been there. How far is it?"

Gratefully, Karina took the refreshing chocolate. "Not far, but tough going. It's about a 175-yard crawl from here. Until you reach the cavern, it's all belly crawling, sometimes with your cheek in the dirt because the ceiling is too low to lift your head."

Heather plopped down next to them. "Yeah, there are times when it pays to be short. I'm not made for such tight places."

"Are you calling me a runt?" Karina asked, teasing the much taller, broad-shouldered girl. "I resent that. I'm only three or four inches shorter than you."

"Like, that's a lot when you're trying to crawl through a tight place," Heather said, helping herself to a cup of hot chocolate. "Where is everyone? Are we the first back? Like, I thought we were behind schedule."

"Sally and Jessica are exploring the drop-off we found yesterday," Joe said between sips of hot chocolate. "They took rope and extra equipment. Sally said not to worry about them unless they weren't back in six hours. They have almost two hours before we need to start searching. Martin got a call on the intercom. Then he and Devon put on diving gear and headed out of the cave."

"Why?" Karina and Heather asked in unison.

"I don't know," Joe said as he opened a can of tuna and handed it to Karina. "Martin didn't say anything about it, but he looked worried."

"How long ago did Martin leave?" asked Karina. She knew that Martin didn't worry easily. If he was worried, something must be very wrong. "You don't think someone got hurt, do you? Was it Mr. Smithson who called?"

Joe shrugged his shoulders. "Beats me. All I know is that it took Martin and Devon only about five minutes to get on their way. Hopefully, we'll hear from them soon. They've been gone almost three hours."

Karina finished eating in silence. At another time, she would have been delighted at having some free time with Joe, but Martin's sudden departure made her uneasy. Joe's silence indicated that he shared her feelings. Even bubbly Heather refrained from idle chatter, preferring instead to snooze on her sleeping bag. All thoughts about her and Heather's marvelous discovery were forgotten in the worry of the moment.

"Do you think we should go and let Sally know that Martin's gone?" Karina asked after twenty minutes of silent fretting.

"I think—" The muted ringing of the intercom interrupted Joe.

Karina raced to the phone, but Joe beat her, so she waited impatiently, listening to only one side of the conversation.

After a long pause, Joe said, "Yes, sir. I understand. Karina and Heather are here. Sally and Jessica aren't back yet. ... Right. ... We'll go locate them immediately. ... Yes, sir, ten minutes."

"What is it?" Karina demanded as Joe replaced the intercom phone. She practically jumped up and down with nervousness.

"I'm not sure." Joe reached for his headlamp. "Wake Heather. Martin and Devon are coming in. We're supposed to go and get Sally and Jessica and meet him back here. Martin didn't tell me anything else except that he'd explain everything when he arrived. He sounded serious."

Karina wanted more information. Patience wasn't her strong point, but she knew she'd have to wait. "I'll wake Heather. Fill the water bottles—just in case."

A short time later, Karina and Heather stood near the ledge that Sally and Jessica had rappelled down. Tension on the rope told Karina that Joe was still descending toward the distant cave floor.

"Like, Martin didn't explain what's going on?" Heather asked Karina for the tenth time.

"I told you—I don't know anything more. Joe spoke with Martin; all I know is that something is wrong. Martin and Devon should be back by the time we return."

The rope went slack, and Karina attached it to the rappel device attached to her harness. She moved into position to descend, but Joe's voice stopped her. "Wait, Karina. I see a light down the tunnel. It's coming this way."

It took only a few minutes for Joe, Sally, and Jessica to ascend. Joe explained what he knew about Martin's mysterious communication. Karina led the way back, moving more rapidly than she should, but no one urged her to slow down, including Sally.

As she neared the room they used for camping and storing supplies, Karina saw two figures in the light of the electric lantern used to illuminate the room. She called over her shoulder. "Looks like Devon and Martin are back."

She hurried into the room. Without any spoken direction, Karina and her group of explorers gathered in front of Martin. Devon eased his way behind the group.

"What's up?" Sally asked.

"Heavy rains have caused flash flooding while we were mapping Devil's Icebox," Martin announced. "High water trapped a group of teachers and students in a cave; they need help. One student and one teacher have drowned."

No one expected the tragic announcement. Karina sensed the tension building in the group. She fought back tears and noticed Jessica making a swipe at her own eyes. Karina looked at Joe and saw him biting his lower lip. She turned back to Martin.

"The local authorities have asked for our help in rescuing the trapped victims," Martin continued. He shined his helmet light on the chest of each individual before speaking. "What do you say? Can you do it?"

Cold chills made Karina shiver. She glanced slowly around at the grim faces surrounding her. Joe held his head down, and Karina saw that he was silently praying. Sally shook her head in disbelief. Heather and Jessica nodded their consent.

"I'm certainly willing to do anything I can," Karina said. "But what about professional spelunkers or the fire department? Don't they have people who can help?"

"They're on the way," Martin answered, "but it will take hours. Most of the certified rescue personnel are out of the country helping find earthquake victims in Asia, and those who remain are working on a rescue near the Arkansas border. By the time they arrive, hypothermia may kill those trapped."

"I'm in," Joe said as he stood and began taking off his shirt. "Let's get a move on before it's too late."

"Me too," Devon said.

"Like, count me in," Heather agreed.

"Let's go," Jessica said.

"Girls, follow me back into the tunnel," Sally ordered. "We'll wait for five minutes and then follow the boys. Come on; let's get into swimsuits."

Karina followed Sally. Jessica held her left hand. No one spoke. Each was lost in thought. Karina shuddered violently. Jessica put an arm around her shoulder. For Karina, the thrill and excitement of cave exploration had transformed into a living nightmare. She wondered if she would ever enjoy the marvelous underground world again.

Please God, she prayed silently. *Let us be in time.*

CHAPTER 7

A Race against Time

"Here's the situation," Martin began as he spread a map out on a table inside the park's small ranger station and pointed to one of two cave openings. "Eight students and three teachers entered the cave here. They were about halfway to the main cavern when the stream began to rise. One teacher and two students turned around and tried to get out before the cave filled. The water overcame them just before they reached the entrance. The boys couldn't swim. The teacher saved one boy, but he went back into the cave and drowned with the second boy whom he was trying to rescue."

"What about the others?" Karina asked. She dreaded the thought of pulling out bodies instead of saving desperate victims. Even inside the warmth of a full wet suit that a local dive shop had provided, shivers from pent up emotion filled her. "Can we reach them? Are you sure they're alive?"

"I can't promise anything," Martin said. "All we know for sure is that the remaining students broke into two groups. One group consisting of a female teacher and an unknown number of students went down the passageway leading to the main cavern. A second group led by a male teacher climbed onto some ledges near the cave ceiling to wait out the flooding."

Karina shifted her gaze around the table. Joe stood beside her. Devon, Heather, and Jessica stood across the small table. Sally stood at Martin's elbow, and a park ranger stood behind them. Everyone wore somber expressions. Joe took Karina's left hand in his and gave it a reassuring squeeze.

"The current inside is fairly swift," Martin continued. "We'll rope together and make our way to here." He pointed to a spot on the map that identified where the teachers and students split apart. "At this point, I'll take Devon and Heather and try to reach the group up on the ledge. Sally will take Joe and push toward the main cavern. Karina and Jessica will stay at the juncture and serve as a reserve force."

"I want to *help*!" Karina said pointedly. "I'm scared silly about the possibility of finding a dead body, but I can handle it. I can help."

"Me too," Jessica said.

"You will. By staying in this location, you will be able to assist whoever needs help. Because we don't know exactly how the students separated, we can't send too many searchers in one direction. If I sent you both with Sally and Joe and then discovered that most of the students are perched on the ledges, we wouldn't be able to help them until you got back. The reverse might be true if you came with Devon and me. Understand?"

"Yes, sir." Karina said before looking across at Jessica, who nodded agreement. "We'll be ready. What's the procedure?" Karina asked.

"Once we know where the students are and their condition, we'll use the juncture as our rally point and bring them all out together," Martin said.

"How can we bring them all out at once?" Joe asked. "There are only seven of us. We each have an extra regulator, so we can each bring one out with air, but that leaves one person behind, assuming all are still alive."

Joe's last comment brought a gasp from Heather. The tall girl seemed to go weak at the knees. Sally and Jessica helped her to a chair. Karina sympathized with her friend. The terrifying reality of the situation affected everyone. She felt light-headed herself.

Martin reached under the table and brought out a small yellow bottle. He set it on the table. "This is called a pony bottle. It has eight to ten minutes of oxygen. The dive shop sent its entire supply. We'll each have two."

Martin grabbed the pony bottle and handed it to her. Then he distributed bottles to each diver. Karina examined the pony bottle. Each bottle had its own breathing mechanism. All she had to do was put her mouth on the mouthpiece, turn the valve, and breathe— simple enough if she weren't being smashed against the rocks by a swift current in the dark, murky water—simple enough if her victim hadn't succumbed to hypothermia.

Martin looked around the room at each potential rescuer. "I know we're asking a lot from you. All of you are very competent divers, rescue-diver certified, and have faced emergency situations before except for Devon, who will be my partner. If you don't feel capable of participating in this rescue attempt, now is the time to tell me. You do not have to do this if you feel it's more than you can handle. No one will feel badly about anyone deciding against participating." Silence filled the room for several long seconds. "Grab your gear and let's hit it," Martin said. "Time is wasting; more rain is on the way."

Joe helped Karina gather her gear. Then they climbed into two park ranger vehicles for the short ride to the cave entrance. Karina sat between Joe and Jessica. A cool wind blew against her face, and a steady drizzle foretold of more problems ahead if they didn't hurry. She held hands with Joe and Jessica and rehearsed in her mind what she would do in the cave. Her companions remained silent, engrossed in their own thoughts.

"Oh my Lord!" Karina blurted out her dismay as the cave entrance came into view. "Please help us."

"Amen," Joe said.

Jessica sighed deeply. "We have to fight against that?"

The cave entrance rested about six feet above the bottom of a steep cliff. Water spewed out from the ten-foot-high opening like water from a gushing fire hydrant. A narrow, muddy path led to the entrance. Karina's determination wavered; she couldn't see how they would get into the cave, much less save anyone. A deep foreboding settled upon her. She turned to Joe for comfort and inspiration, but Joe's cold, steely expression told Karina that he had no words of encouragement.

Martin ordered them to put on their gear. A ranger helped Karina climb the path to the cave entrance. Cold water pushed her backward as she leaned into the current and struggled to keep her footing. Like the others, she wore a wet suit and scuba diving equipment. At least she wore leather boots instead of the awkward swim fins normally used when scuba diving. This would be no dive. There was no possible way to swim against the oppressive current. Inching their way against the cave wall was challenging enough. Even being tethered together for support, the going was excruciatingly slow and tiring.

When they finally reached the juncture where she and Jessica would wait, Martin shouted into her ear above the roaring sound of rushing water, "Stay here. Use this rock outcrop for protection against the current. We'll signal for you as soon as we determine where the kids are."

Karina nodded her response. Cold, gushing water pushed relentlessly at her legs, trying to knock her off her feet and purge her from the cave. The noise made communication difficult. She stood in chest-deep water behind a jagged rock that jutted out from the main passage. At least the rock protected her from the main current.

Jessica tugged at her shoulder and leaned close. "I'll keep the line for Joe and Sally. You keep the line on Martin, Devon, and Heather."

"Right," Karina agreed. She let line out for her companions. Three hard tugs on the line was the agreed upon signal to come ahead. All Karina could do now was wait for those fateful tugs or Jessica's signal that would send them after Joe and Sally.

Using her helmet light to read her submersible pressure gauge, Karina noticed that she still had at least forty minutes of oxygen. Fortunately, there had only been two sections where the water had been high enough to require breathing air from her scuba tank. Unfortunately for anyone trying to exit the cave, one of those sections was near the cave entrance. For almost fifty yards, the water had been more than seven feet deep.

A steady pressure on the rope told Karina that Martin's group was making progress. Her heart raced, and her hands were cold in spite of the thick dive gloves protecting them. She feared that any survivors would be suffering from hypothermia. According to information provided by the park ranger, their victims had been in the cave for more than seven hours—more than enough time to become hypothermic in such a cold, wet environment.

"This way," Jessica shouted in her ear. "I've got three tugs. Let Martin know. Follow me."

Karina gave three hard tugs on the rope and let it slip from her hands. She inched her way around the protective rock and shortened the rope connecting her to Jessica. The water level quickly rose enough that she had to breathe through her regulator. For several long minutes, she struggled against the current, continually bumping her scuba tank against the narrow rock walls.

Jessica stopped without warning and backed into her, knocking Karina off her feet. She went down and rolled a little in the current; however, the current wasn't as strong in the side passageway as it was in the main tunnel. Karina stopped her backward progress, only to have Jessica step on her stomach, knocking the breath from her. She bit deeply on the mouthpiece of her regulator and grabbed Jessica's leg with both of her arms, pulling the girl down on top of her.

Jessica grabbed Karina's shoulder. The move brought her face mask next to Karina's. Jessica was crying, a difficult task while wearing a scuba face mask. Tangled together, Karina looked past her friend and saw what caused Jessica's distress. She crawled out from under Jessica. Tears filled her mask as well. Tangled in the rope connecting her to Jessica was the lifeless form of a small person, probably a child.

Karina worked her way to her feet and pulled Jessica close to her. She knelt beside the figure and discovered it to be a small boy. Karina pushed her other regulator into the boy's mouth. She feared the worst. The boy's wide-open eyes and blue lips indicated that he had been under the water for some time. The child made no effort to breathe. She felt his neck for a pulse and found none.

Jessica pulled on Karina's shoulder. Karina turned to her partner and signed that it was too late to help the child. She and Jessica gripped arms together and breathed rapidly for several long moments. A huge cloud of air bubbles surrounded them. Karina couldn't force herself to look at the lifeless figure, and she might have remained embraced with Jessica indefinitely had it not been for three frantic tugs that forced her back to the mission at hand.

Drawing on courage she never knew she possessed, Karina gently pushed herself free from Jessica's arms. She took a deep breath of life-giving air through her regulator and grabbed a lifeless arm. She figured the boy couldn't be more than eleven years old. She gently closed his eyelids.

Karina shuddered, looped the rope around the boy, and unhooked it from her waist. She watched him settle to the cave floor and lodge against two sturdy stalagmites. She tied one end of the rope around a stalagmite, securing the body so that it could be retrieved later. Without looking back, Karina stepped carefully over the body and pulled Jessica with her. She headed down the passageway to where Sally and Joe desperately needed their help.

Eventually, the water level dropped enough that Karina could breathe without using her regulator. Now that she and Jessica were no longer tethered together, Karina had to continually stop and make sure that her partner followed behind her. They had not traveled a great distance, but the narrow passageway and bulky scuba tank became impediments that slowed progress.

"Look!" Jessica shouted from behind Karina. "Lights. Off to your right. Up on the ledge."

Karina looked in the direction Jessica indicated and saw small flickering specks of light. She put her head down and worked against the weak but persistent current. Her heart pounded as she forced her feet onward; she silently prayed to find only living human beings at their journey's end. The cold water made her shiver in spite of her full wet suit. She couldn't imagine how the unprotected teachers and students had lasted so long under the conditions she and Jessica currently faced.

One of the flickering lights moved to meet them. "We've got one teacher and five children on a ledge," Joe said, as he reached Karina. "They're in pretty bad shape. The teacher is in the greatest danger. She stayed in the water to help support the kids on the ledge. Sally wants to take the teacher out and for me to take one of the kids."

"What about us?" Jessica asked from behind Karina.

"You'll stay here until we return or until Martin arrives. Sally doesn't want to try to take more than one kid out at a time, so we'll come right back. Then the four of us can take out the last four kids all at the same time. It's too risky to leave one child alone."

"Sounds good if the kids can handle the wait," Karina said. "Joe, we found a boy in the water on our way in. He's tied to the rope. I—" Karina's voice faltered; she groped for words.

Joe firmly gripped her shoulder. "I know; we saw him. The kids said that one of the boys panicked and tried to go back when the water got too high for him. Try to put it behind you for now. We've got to work fast."

Karina gave Joe a weak smile. She envied his calm, measured response. He sounded so much like Martin. Without further discussion, Karina followed him to a small rock ledge crowded with five shivering children—three boys and two girls. Their teacher stood in chest-deep water, supporting one of the girls and keeping the child out of the rushing stream. Sally braced the violently shivering teacher, whose lips appeared incredibly blue in the bright light provided by Karina's headlamp.

"Karina, help me here," Sally said. "I'm going to take Mrs. Green. Joe will take Nancy." Sally shined her light on the little girl whom Mrs. Green supported.

"What about the others?" Karina asked. She noticed that the other four children cowered in a more secure position on the ledge, which stood several inches above the water. They huddled together shivering. All had blue lips but not to the degree of Mrs. Green or Nancy.

"We'll come back and take them all out together." Sally confirmed the plan Joe had mentioned. "Stay put. We'll be back as quickly as possible."

Sally pulled the teacher to her and headed down the flooded passageway. Joe lifted Nancy from the ledge, and Karina watched as he showed her how to breathe through the scuba regulator and gently led her away. Watching Sally and Joe disappear into the haunting darkness made Karina feel strangely alone.

"Karina, is the water rising?" Jessica asked.

The question returned Karina's attention to the problem of saving the four remaining children. She joined Jessica at the ledge, which held the remaining girl and three boys. All were wet and shivering. The protective enclave barely allowed the girl to sit upright, but its ceiling slanted downward so that the three boys had to lean slightly forward to keep from bumping their heads against rock. The water level was only a few inches from flowing onto the ledge.

All of the children seemed to be around eleven or twelve. Karina had no standard with which to measure whether the water had risen, so she identified a spot on the ledge that she figured was about two inches above the existing water level.

"I don't know," she answered Jessica's question. "Pick a spot above water level; we'll check it in a couple of minutes to see if there is any change." Karina turned to the children squatting on the ledge. "Hi, everybody. My name is Karina. This is Jessica. How's everyone doing?"

"Awfully cold," said the boy closest to the water. "I'm Philip." He pointed to the two boys on his right. "He's Andy, and this is Kevin." The boy patted the shivering girl on his left. "Her name is Elaine."

Karina scanned the children perched on the ledge, trying to find identifying characteristics to help her associate names with the figures that Philip pointed out. Philip was slim and had a large dimple in his right cheek. Andy, the boy sitting directly to Philip's right, was heavyset and had strands of black hair protruding from beneath his helmet. The other boy, Kevin, was slim like Philip, but Karina would remember him by the wire braces he wore on both his upper and lower teeth. Elaine's red hair and squeaky voice easily separated her from the boys.

"Can we go now?" Elaine asked in a frightened, high-pitched voice.

"Not yet," Karina said, moving to the child and putting a reassuring hand on the little girl's leg. "As soon as my teacher and Joe return, we'll all go out together. It'll be safer that way. Don't worry. It won't take long. Jessica and I will be here with you the entire time."

Elaine began crying. For the next ten minutes, Karina and Jessica worked hard to keep the children from panicking. Twice Jessica had to physically restrain Kevin from trying to climb down into the water.

"Karina, come here." Jessica grabbed Karina's arm and pulled her a few steps away from the ledge. "The water is definitely rising. How long do you think it will take for Sally and Joe to get back?"

"At least another half hour." Karina could have kicked herself. Being preoccupied with trying to reassure the children, she had forgotten all about the possibility of rising water. She quickly discovered that the water had risen at least four inches. Kevin and Andy now sat in water.

"What will we do if the water rises before they get here?" Jessica glanced back at the ledge supporting their waiting charges. "Can we make it out with all four?"

Karina quickly thought through a plan before responding. "If the water gets to the point where we can't wait any longer, you take Kevin and Andy. I'll take Philip and Elaine. We'll let each child breathe from the two air hoses on our scuba tanks. We'll use the pony bottles. It'll be tight, but it's better than waiting for our air supply to run out. If we run out of air, Joe and Sally won't have enough air to bring everyone out."

"I don't know," Jessica said. "It will be hard trying to get through that narrow passageway leading one child, much less two. What if one of the kids panics? We'd have our hands full."

"I know," Karina agreed, "but we have only twenty minutes on the pony bottles. I think that the kids would be too panicked to buddy breathe by sharing a mouthpiece. We'd have a better chance working our way out."

"I guess," Jessica said, but she didn't sound too convinced.

Well, neither am I, Karina thought. She trudged back to the ledge with a wary eye on the rising water.

Time seemed to stand still as Karina and Jessica tried to reassure the children that help would arrive before time ran out. During those long minutes, the water level climbed—first over the kid's legs and then up to Elaine's waist, which put the water level nearly to Andy's chest. All the children shivered. Karina looked at her watch. Sally had been gone for almost forty minutes. *Why aren't they back?* she wondered. *Has the current gotten worse?*

"We're going to drown!" Elaine shouted hysterically.

Even though the water only reached the child's waist, Elaine pushed her face against the rock ceiling above her. Elaine's panic settled the matter for Karina. At the rate the water was currently rising, she figured they had only another twenty or thirty minutes before the ledge would be completely underwater. She had no idea what was keeping Joe and Sally, or why Martin hadn't arrived, but it was time to exit the cave. They simply couldn't wait for help.

"Okay, guys. Listen to me," Karina spoke clearly, shouting to be heard over the rushing water. "Jessica and I are going to show you how to breathe through our scuba gear. We'll guide you out of the cave, but you've got to do exactly what we say. Understand?"

"Karina, are you sure?" Jessica asked. She spoke low enough that only Karina heard the question and doubt lingering on her voice.

She nodded and raised into plain sight the two regulator hoses that were attached to her scuba tank. "Philip and Elaine will come with me. You'll each breathe through the air hose going to my scuba tank. There is enough air for all of us, but I have only two hoses, two regulators. You will each use one, and I'll breathe through these." She dropped her air hoses back into the water and held up the two ten-minute pony bottles.

Karina heard Jessica follow her example and explain to Andy and Kevin how to use the scuba tank's regulators. Then Karina had everyone submerge for a quick practice, trying to minimize the risk of panic. They had only time for a quick practice; the water had risen to only a foot from the cave ceiling.

She had great difficulty getting Elaine to put her head beneath the water. At first, the girl panicked, pushed the regulator away, and clung to the ledge. Then after a little coaxing and help from Philip, Elaine successfully breathed underwater. During the time Elaine used the regulator, Karina held her breath, not wanting to waste any of the precious air in her pony bottles.

"Anybody want to go for a hamburger?" Karina asked, trying to break the tension. Water had reached Andy's chin and was nearly up to Elaine's neck.

"I do," Kevin said. The others remained silent.

"Are you absolutely sure?" Jessica asked the question again.

"We are *leaving*," Karina snapped. "You lead. We'll follow."

Cold water covered her head. She struggled to keep her balance with a child on each side. Karina felt awful; she hadn't meant to yell at Jessica.

In the narrow light beam from her waterproof helmet lamp, Karina saw Jessica and the boys ahead of her. The passageway narrowed, forcing Karina to adapt to the tight confines. She positioned one child in front of her and one behind her. She put Elaine in front, because the little girl seemed a greater risk for panicking than Philip. Her scuba air hoses were short, so Elaine was always in reach. Karina could only tell that Philip was still behind her when he touched her or fell far enough behind that the air hose he used tugged her backward. The pony bottle worked well, but it required Karina to use one hand to keep it to her mouth. That meant she had only one hand for balance and to help control any child who had difficulties.

Everything seemed to be working well; Karina figured she should make it out of the cave before her two pony bottles reached empty. Jessica's progress raised her hopes even more. Jessica had moved so far ahead with Andy and Kevin that Karina couldn't see her light. Even Elaine's shivering had eased as the child burned calories through the exercise required to remain upright against the current.

Though Karina expected trouble when they reached the boy's body, she was unprepared for the source. As her light illuminated the drowned figure, Karina used her free arm to hug Elaine close to her. The little girl shuddered and tried to go faster, to hurry past her stricken classmate. Karina restrained Elaine and started working her way around the drowned child.

She had almost cleared the boy when a hard jerk on the air hose going to Philip threw her off balance. Karina sat down on the drowned boy's legs. Elaine settled onto her lap. A second tug pulled Karina over completely; she lay fully on top of the drowned boy. Elaine pulled away from her, and Karina barely managed to grab the frightened girl's ankle before she broke away.

Karina locked her fingers onto the waistband of Elaine's jeans. She held the child back by her trousers and fought to gain her feet against the weight of the scuba equipment and the rushing current. Finally, Karina regained her balance and had firm control of Elaine. She forced a regulator back into Elaine's mouth. Using one arm to keep the skittish girl secure, Karina bit the mouthpiece on the pony bottle hard enough to free her left arm. Using her free hand, she pulled in the air hose Philip used. Her heart raced as it floated in front of her face mask. Part of the rubber mouthpiece had been bitten off. Philip was nowhere in sight.

Karina didn't know what to do. Heavy breathing on the pony bottle had drained it, so she awkwardly placed the damaged mouthpiece in her mouth and breathed in life-giving air. Tears filled her face mask as she firmly hauled Elaine back into the passageway in search of Philip. Her only hope was that the panicked boy held his breath long enough for her to find him. *Please God*, she prayed. *Help me. Help Philip.*

In less than a minute, Karina spied Philip's legs dangling from the ceiling. She held her breath as she grabbed a leg and pulled Philip toward her—no simple task using one hand. Karina kept her other arm securely wrapped around Elaine. She wasn't about to let the trembling child get away.

No! No! No! Karina sobbed inwardly. Tears blurred her vision even more than the murky water. Philip's face floated before her, lifeless eyes wide open. She hugged the boy to her and tried breathing through his cold lips. Over and over she attempted to pass air into Philip. She may have continued doing so until she ran out of air if it were not for Elaine.

Finally, Karina let Philip sink gently to the cave floor. She put both hands on Elaine's shoulders and gently pushed the child down the passageway. They passed the first body, turned into the main passageway, and fought to maintain balance against the much stronger current.

Struggling to hold Elaine close, Karina's strength finally gave out. Her legs buckled. She settled onto the cave floor, pulling Elaine down with her. She saw that the little girl's lips were dark blue. Breathing hard, she summoned enough strength to read her pressure gauge. It indicated a ten-minute air supply—a ten-minute air supply for one person.

By Karina's reckoning, the cave entrance and safety were at least fifteen minutes from their position. Using the last of her strength, she regained her feet and pushed Elaine ahead of her. She let the damaged mouthpiece drop from her mouth and reached for her last pony bottle. Karina was determined not lose another child without a fight.

Moving with the swift current at her back should have made the trip faster, but after bumping into sharp rock several times, once cutting her left hand, Karina had to slow down and use additional energy to maintain a safe pace.

She was about to give up when Elaine stopped abruptly. The move caused Karina to fall forward, sliding a couple of feet past the girl. She would have landed facedown on the floor, but strong arms pulled her back before her face mask made contact. Those same arms pulled Karina to her feet; she found herself supported by Martin. Relief quickly turned to panic as she discovered that Elaine no longer breathed from the scuba air hose. She hadn't fallen that far. Had the child panicked like Philip did?

To no avail, Karina frantically tried to tell Martin that she had to search for Elaine. But Martin had other ideas, and he was much stronger. While she pulled against him, Martin shoved his spare regulator into her mouth and forced her down the last hundred yards of passageway and up the steep incline that led to the cave entrance.

"There is still a little girl in the cave!" Karina shouted as a fireman and park ranger pulled her from the gushing water. "You've got to help her!"

"Karina, she's fine," Joe said in her ear. Warm arms encircled her waist, supporting and guiding her down to level ground. "Sally and I reached her on our way back to you at the same time that Martin came up behind you. We brought her out. Jessica and the boys with her are fine. Where is the other boy?"

"Gone." Karina tried to say more, but uncontrollable sobbing prevented speech.

Joe helped her from her equipment. Before she knew it, Karina found herself in an ambulance heading for the hospital. The warm blankets that covered her didn't stop her from trembling. Martin sat at her side. She used her arms to push herself into a sitting position. Dizziness from exhaustion and unrestrained grief overwhelmed her.

"Martin, it's all my fault," she sobbed. "Philip would be alive if I hadn't forced everyone to try for the exit. We should have waited."

Karina never heard Martin's response. The paramedic placed an oxygen mask on her face and stuck a needle in her arm. *Fitting punishment*, she thought. *I hate needles.*

CHAPTER 8

A Return to the Past

Falling! Karina knew that the plane was out of control. The fevered pitch of the engine blocked all possibility of speech. The plane spiraled downward, heading toward white-capped mountaintops illuminated by brilliant flashes of lightning. Fear paralyzed her. She wanted to scream. Her mother smothered her with pillows and placed her own body on top of Karina. Somehow, Karina saw the end coming, heard the rivets popping from the wings, and felt the plane disintegrating in the massive thunderstorm.

"No!" Karina screamed. She struggled to a sitting position and tried to make sense of the white walls surrounding her.

"Can I help you?" asked a tall, brown-haired lady costumed in white. A nametag told Karina the nurse's name was Virginia. "Are you in pain?" the nurse asked in a soft, reassuring voice.

Karina panted; sweat highlighted her brow as she cleared away the last dregs of nightmare. "No, I'm fine. It was just a bad dream."

Virginia took her vital signs and gently squeezed her hand. "Call if you need anything. I'm only three doors away, and I'll be on duty all night. Press the call button if you want something, even if you just need to talk with someone." The nurse gave her a friendly smile and departed, softly closing the door.

Karina lay back on the hospital bed, trying to gain her composure and fighting back the anger and panic that she hadn't had to contend with for months. For years after the plane crash that killed her parents, nightmares and domineering anger had plagued Karina. But until tonight, she had not had a nightmare in more than six months.

Sitting up and swinging her legs over the bed, Karina saw that the clock by her bed read 12:23 a.m. It was after midnight! The ambulance ride and the realization of the events that brought her to the hospital rushed to the front of her memory. Tears flooded her eyes. She pulled the large hospital pillow to her chest and hugged it like a small child would hug a teddy bear.

A small, terrified face floated before her eyes. Karina strangled the pillow, wallowing in her agony. Philip was dead—and it was all her fault. She had made many mistakes since coming to Blue Horizons. Her impulsive and stubborn actions had gotten her into some pretty tough situations, but the ending had always turned out positive, even when Cindy's father died in the Amazon rainforest. Now, however, things weren't going to be fine. She'd made a horrible mistake, and a little boy had died because of her decision. Why hadn't she listened to Jessica? What gave her the infinite wisdom to be bossy and tell others what to do?

Karina rolled onto her back and pushed her toes against the metal end of the bed. Gasping, she pushed against it with all of her might. Her nerves taut, she wanted to run, to scream, to close her eyes and never open them again. All the while, tears streamed into the soft pillow she clutched to her chest. There was no recourse for her actions. No matter what anyone said or did, Philip would still be dead.

"Hey, you're awake," Martin said, quietly entering the room. "You okay?"

Karina cried out in anguish, "No! I'm never going to be okay again. He's dead. I killed him!"

Martin walked across the room, sat beside Karina, and held her tightly. She put her head against his shoulder and cried for a long time. When her pent-up emotions finally drained, she looked teary-eyed at Martin. He brushed back her bangs and placed a tender kiss on her forehead, an unusual gesture for Martin.

"Karina, I know you blame yourself for what happened to Philip." Martin gently held both of her hands as he spoke. "And I know what I'm going to say will give you little comfort, but I want you to listen closely.

"I talked to Sally and Joe about the plan of action that Sally instructed you to follow. I also spoke with Jessica about what led to your breaking with Sally's plan. Jessica even told me about disagreeing with your decision not to wait for Sally and Joe to return. I wish I could tell you for certain that you acted correctly, but I can't.

"When you made that decision, you demonstrated leadership. As a leader, you must live with the decisions that you make. However, before blaming yourself for Philip's death, take all of the factors into consideration."

"What do you mean all of the factors?" Karina asked, voice trembling. *What was he trying to say?*

Martin continued, "The cave completely filled with water, something that Sally had not considered when she told you to wait for her return. The children already showed early stages of hypothermia. Nancy, the little girl whom Joe had rescued, almost died in the emergency room. Her body temperature was so low that she went into shock. For a while, it seemed as if the doctors would lose her as well.

"If you had stayed, Elaine would have been subjected to at least another thirty minutes in cold water, enough time to lower her body temperature still further. The passageway *completely* filled with water. Even if you had remained, breathing from your air tanks would have pushed your air supply to the limit. And even if Sally and Joe arrived in time, taking Philip out without having to manage Elaine wouldn't have guaranteed his survival. The only way out was to walk past the boy's body."

"Martin, every time I close my eyes, I see Philip's face," Karina said, tears wetting her cheeks. She leaned her head against Martin's shoulder. "I wish it had been me instead."

Martin firmly moved her an arm's length away. His face held a stoical expression. "You want the easy way out? Well, there is no easy way out. Philip is dead; there is nothing that you can do about it. You'll remember what happened the rest of your life—every detail. And you will either learn to accept it, live with it, and get on with your life, or you will never have a moment's peace. No one is blaming you except you. I am very proud of how you helped those who needed you. If the situation had not been so extreme, I would have never let teenagers—no matter how qualified—attempt such a rescue. The ranger in charge of the rescue feels absolutely certain that none of those trapped in the cave would have survived if we had not been able to assist. The professional rescue crew didn't arrive on the scene until two hours after we reached the hospital."

Martin's firmness and the force of his speech calmed Karina. Her tears stopped, but the turmoil and anger inside her remained strong. "What can I do?" she asked him. "I don't think I'm strong enough to live with this. The nightmare has already returned."

"You've dealt with tragedy before," Martin said sympathetically. "You've handled plane crashes, losing your parents, being stranded in the Amazon, and surviving a shipwreck. You can handle this. However, I think you need some time to sort things out, so I'm sending you to the Winfields for the next couple of weeks while we finish this unit on earth science."

"What about my grades?" Karina asked, but her heart felt lighter. "What about helping Megan?"

"Joe and Heather can help Megan," Martin said. "You've done enough spelunking for the practical exam. Study your notes and textbooks. I'll mail you the final exam. Dr. Winfield can proctor it for you. Now lie down and get some rest. I promised Elaine that she could see you first thing in the morning."

Martin kissed Karina's cheek and tucked her into bed. His words and her spent tears relaxed her. She thought back through the day's events and her decisions. Karina wished that she could say that she'd have done something differently, something to keep Philip alive, but she was resolute that she would have made the same decisions all over again. She rolled over, clutched her pillow, and prayed that she had made the right choice. Karina also prayed for forgiveness and peace of mind—something that so often eluded her. Her thoughts centered on the harsh words she'd had for Jessica—words that seemed destined to haunt her for eternity.

Early the next morning, the nurse informed Karina that she was being discharged. She got dressed, packed, and decided that she'd use the time before Martin arrived to honor his promise that she'd visit Elaine. Karina placed a note on the bed informing Martin where she had gone. She also notified the nurses at the nurses' station and then chose to walk up the two flights of stairs to the pediatric ward instead of using the elevator. All too soon, she found herself opening the child's door.

Elaine sat up in bed and brushed red hair from in front of her eyes. "I was hoping you'd visit me before you left the hospital. The doctors said I have to stay for another day."

Karina walked over to the redheaded little girl and took her hand. "I certainly couldn't leave without saying good-bye." She bent over and hugged the youngster.

"Thanks for saving my life," Elaine whispered in Karina's ear.

"I didn't do anything, really," Karina said, turning her head to wipe tears from her eyes. "I'm sorry about your friends."

Tears moistened Elaine's eyes. "Me too. Sometimes I can't believe they're gone. This morning I learned that Mr. Quinlin, Pablo, Timmy, and Philip drowned in the cave." Elaine squeezed Karina's hand tightly. "I'd be with them if it wasn't for you. I was so cold that I didn't even care if I got out. If you hadn't forced me to keep moving, I wouldn't have made it. I'll never forget you."

Emotions surged through Karina. She hugged Elaine several times, said that she had to get ready for Martin to pick her up, and promised to call her as soon as possible. Elaine wrote her home phone number on Karina's hand. Karina did the same to Elaine, writing the Winfields' phone number on the girl's right palm. After a few more hugs, Karina quickly departed the room for the relative solitude of the hospital waiting room, where she immediately broke down. Sitting in a soft lounge chair, Karina placed her head against her knees and cried out her agony.

After Martin fetched her from the hospital, he took her to an IHOP pancake house for breakfast and then headed down the highway toward Fulton, Missouri, and the Winfields' home. Karina looked forward to seeing Cindy and the Winfields, but memories of yesterday's rescue attempt dampened her enthusiasm. She sighed deeply when Martin exited the highway and the Winfields' large white farmhouse-style home came into view. She bit her lips to hold back tears as Martin turned on the Winfields' driveway.

"Karina!" A sturdy, fair-haired girl raced across the lawn as Karina slipped down from the passenger seat of the fifteen-passenger van. "I've been looking for you all morning. You're hours late."

She almost didn't recognize Penny as the girl hopped over the short picket fence that separated the lawn from the gravel driveway. Just a year ago, before Penny's bone marrow transplant, she had been a small, frail child—a child who looked and acted much younger than her years. Now she looked like any normal, healthy twelve-year-old girl.

Karina hugged Penny. "You must have grown four inches and gained twenty pounds since last summer."

Martin interrupted the reunion. "Karina, it's nearly noon. I have to get back and help Sally and Mr. Smithson. I'll see you Friday. Penny, thank your parents and tell them hello for me."

Karina hugged Martin and then held Penny's hand as she watched the van speed down the long gravel driveway. All too soon it turned onto the paved road and disappeared. A lump filled her throat. She shuddered in spite of the warm summer afternoon. Penny squeezed her hand, breaking Karina's semihypnotic trance on the empty roadway.

"Sorry," Karina said weakly. "Where is everyone?"

"Around," Penny said, guiding Karina through a gate and toward a large, white house. "You can have the guest room all to yourself. Cindy and I are sharing my room. Mom thought it would be better if you had a place to be alone when you needed it." Penny stopped with a hand on the front door handle and turned to face Karina. "I'm really sorry."

Karina faked a smile. "I know. I'd rather not talk about it."

Penny nodded and led Karina through the front door. Karina suddenly found herself to be the center of a surprise party. Eight-year-old Cindy locked her arms around Karina's waist. Joe hugged her from behind, and the rest of the crowd took turns patting her on the back. It took Karina almost a minute to find her voice.

"What is all this?" Karina asked. She read a banner that hung along the upstairs banister. It welcomed her and informed her that she was loved.

Dr. Winfield came to her rescue. "Just a little support from those who care about you. Be a good girl and accept it."

Karina rode an emotional roller coaster during the next two hours. Reminiscing about the events of the tragic cave rescue, she cried alternately, first in Jessica's arms and then in Joe's arms. She laughed at Cindy's antics and felt comforted by all the sincere sympathy her classmates heaped upon her—that is, those classmates who were present. Martin had only excused Jessica, Joe, Heather, and Devon from the day's activities to participate in the surprise party. Karina guessed that Martin was giving them the day as a means of closure to the previous day's calamitous events.

When the conversation turned into awkward periods of silent reflections, Dr. and Mrs. Winfield ended the reunion and drove Karina's Blue Horizons classmates back for more spelunking activities. Penny went to a friend's house for the night, which left Karina to get Cindy ready for bed. She sat Cindy on her lap and brushed the little girl's hair.

"You did the best you could," Cindy said, patting Karina's thigh. "Martin told us all about what happened. You did everything possible. I know you did, just like you handled everything in the Amazon."

Karina wanted to disagree—to argue the point—but she decided against arguing. Arguing with an eight-year-old child—even a child with an IQ of 182—wouldn't change the facts; it would only increase the anger she felt burning inside her. Besides, Karina didn't want to hurt Cindy's feelings. The little girl had been through so much already that Karina didn't see any need to add to Cindy's emotional trials. After all, only a little more than six months had passed since Karina had helped Cindy bury her father.

"I know. But I still feel bad," Karina said, brushing the last tangles from Cindy's hair. "Now, young lady, off to bed."

"Can't I sleep with you?" Cindy asked, sliding from Karina's lap. "I've missed you so much. Since you got back from your semester at Ocean Quest Academy, you've been gone more than you've been with me."

A pang of guilt added to Karina's burden. She had promised Cindy's father before he died that she would take care of Cindy and help her find a good home. That home had turned out to be with

Martin and Karina at Blue Horizons, except when they traveled. During those times, Cindy stayed with the Winfields. Still, Karina wanted to be alone. She didn't have the patience or energy to deal with the mischievous child.

"Sorry," Karina said, tweaking Cindy's nose. "Not tonight. You can sleep with me tomorrow night."

"Promise?" Cindy asked.

"I promise," she said. "Come on. I'll read you a story."

"Great," Cindy called over her shoulder as she ran from the room. "I'll get the book."

A deep sadness fell upon Karina as she walked to the room that Cindy shared with Penny. She wasn't sure why, but she felt useless. She usually loved reading to Cindy. Now Karina simply wanted to crawl into bed and cry.

For the next forty minutes, Karina read Cindy a story titled *Pennies for the Piper*. The book told about how a little girl had lost her mother and, through a series of mistakes, began a journey that helped her work through the grief of her loss. While reading, Karina remembered Philip's face and wondered what type of journey would be necessary for her to get past the grief that weighed so heavily upon her heart. All night, Karina tossed and turned. Philip's face haunted her each time she closed her eyes. She rolled restlessly in bed, kicking off the covers and then pulling them back over her. Finally, around three o'clock in the morning, an idea came to her. *It just might work,* she thought. *I'll call Martin tomorrow and see what he thinks.*

As Martin pulled into the Winfields' driveway, Karina ran out to meet him. Two days had passed since she'd called Martin. He had agreed, but he wasn't sure it was a good idea.

"Karina, are you sure about this?" Martin asked, raising his bushy, brown eyebrows.

She climbed into Martin's little station wagon and adjusted her seat belt. Karina felt uncomfortable in the tight dress shoes that accented her black skirt and ash-colored blouse. "I'm sure. This is something I must do. Please hurry. I don't want to be late; we have to get Jessica."

Martin nodded, started the station wagon, and drove down the driveway in silence. As he turned onto the main road, the lump in Karina's throat caused her to gasp for air. The last couple of days had been pure misery. She had put on a good face for Penny and Cindy during the daytime: laughing, swimming, and playing games. But in sleep, nightmares defeated her defenses. Each night she woke in a sweat; her screams brought Penny and Cindy to her rescue.

Karina decided that her journey for peace lay in attending Philip's funeral. The idea had come to her from Cindy's book. Perhaps knowing he was at peace might free her heart from the continual torment and anger raging within her—an anger that grew stronger each day.

That morning she had even snapped at Cindy for coming to breakfast in her nightshirt, something that was forbidden at Blue Horizons but was common at the Winfields' home. Karina remembered her own embarrassment after yelling at Cindy and looking around the table to see Penny wearing pajamas and Mrs. Winfield in a robe. After a moment of silence, Karina had turned and escaped upstairs to her room without eating breakfast. She remained in her room until it was time for Martin to arrive, refusing to come out or let anyone inside to speak with her—even Mrs. Winfield.

Karina clenched and unclenched her hands as she groped for control. Martin turned from the main road onto the gravel road that led to the campsite Karina had called home before the tragic rescue attempt. Jessica wanted to be with Karina for Philip's funeral.

"Hey," Jessica said, greeting Karina and Martin as she opened the front door. She wore a navy blue skirt, white blouse, and tennis shoes. "Sorry, I didn't have anything black to wear." She spoke to Martin, "Heather, Joe, and Devon want to come with us. Can they?"

"Sure," Martin said. "I gave everyone the day off. We'll finish mapping tomorrow. Tell them to hurry. It's an hour's drive from here."

"Be right back." Jessica turned and ran back to the series of tents that served as home.

Karina put her head back against the seat's headrest. She felt as if she might vomit. Her stomach churned, and tears crept from the corners of her eyes. Martin handed her a tissue, and she struggled to make herself a bit more presentable before Jessica, Heather, and the boys returned.

During the drive, Karina spoke few words. She chewed her lip and listened as everyone except Martin recounted the events that led to Philip's death. By the time Martin pulled into the church parking lot, the kids had decided that they had done their best. Jessica even went so far as to agree that she and Karina had acted correctly by leading the children out when they did. Even if they had not been able to save Philip, they had certainly saved three kids.

Karina walked slowly up the concrete steps and entered the little white church. Rows of wooden benches lined the chapel. Each bench looked as if it could hold about ten adults. A huge stained glass window that showed Jesus rising to heaven on a cloud filled the wall behind the altar. Light streamed in through the window and made Jesus look alive.

Philip's casket lay in front of the pastor's pulpit. Martin led the group down the carpet-covered aisle to view Philip's body. Karina trembled as she peered at the boy who had once seemed so alive and who had been so helpful during the rescue attempt. His face seemed peaceful now. Philip's eyes were closed; his hands were folded across his chest. He wore a gray suit, and makeup gave color to his pale cheeks.

Philip's mother sat in the front row, crying into a handkerchief. His father greeted them. Martin explained who they were, and Philip's father solemnly shook each would-be-rescuer's hand. He thanked Karina for trying to save his son.

Karina tried to speak, but tears prevented intelligent conversation. Joe led her away to a seat several rows behind Philip's mother. Wiping her eyes with a second tissue provided by Martin, Karina noticed that the little church was nearly filled to capacity.

Karina listened to the preacher and tried to make sense out of his remarks. She believed in God, but she was still uncertain about her faith. Until coming to Blue Horizons, Karina had seldom attended church services. In fact, she had attended few church services during her time at Blue Horizons. A visiting pastor held church services in the school's chapel every Sunday, but students weren't required to attend. Until Martin had become her guardian and she had begun attending church with him, Karina had skipped most services in favor of sleeping late. Now she wished that she had paid more attention to the sermons.

The funeral service began with the hymn "What a Friend We Have in Jesus." Then the pastor walked to the podium. "In the Book of John, we read: 'I am the resurrection and the life. He who believes in me will live, even though he dies; and whoever lives and believes in me will never die.'"

After the Bible reading, he spoke about how about Philip would live again and one day be reunited with his family. The pastor then spoke about Philip's life for about ten minutes. Karina cried throughout the service, but that didn't seem out of the ordinary. Jessica, Heather, and almost all of the girls and women cried.

Philip's mother and little sister laughed when the pastor reminisced about one Halloween night when Philip was eight years old and dressed up as a black cat. He went out trick-or-treating and came upon a dog loping down the street. Philip went up to the dog, hissed at it, and extended his hands as though they were claws. The dog promptly bit one of boy's hands, and he had to go to the doctor, ending his night of fun and hopes of accumulating a large stash of candy. Their laughter turned to tears when events brought back the reality of his death.

The service concluded with a couple more hymns. Everyone was invited to the cemetery for the interment and then to a small reception in Philip's honor. Thankfully, Martin declined the invitation.

As Karina followed Martin down the church steps, Philip's mother ran over and hugged each of them. "Thank you so much," she said, hugging Karina. "It helps me to know that he was not alone when he died—to know that he was with friends."

Karina wanted to confess that it was all her fault and that Philip might still be alive if she hadn't ordered Jessica and the children out before help arrived. She wanted to say that she was sorry. But she only managed to hug Philip's mother and share tears of grief.

Martin finally took her arm and led her to the station wagon. They sat silently and watched as the funeral procession turned left from the parking lot, crossed the street, turned onto a gravel driveway, and passed a sign that read "Cemetery." Then Martin turned onto the blacktop road and headed away from the direction the funeral procession had taken.

Karina sniffed quietly. Joe placed a protective arm around her shoulders, and Jessica held her hand. The drive seemed to take forever. Martin stopped at McDonald's and bought everyone lunch, but the treat of fast food—usually devoured instantly—went mostly uneaten.

Martin dropped Joe, Heather, and Devon off at camp. He drove Karina and Jessica back to the Winfields. Martin told Karina that Jessica could stay with her for a couple of days. He said that might help her put the incident behind her so she could get on with life. A few minutes later, Karina and Jessica slept, arms entwined, on the large four-poster bed in the guest room Karina currently called hers.

Brushing her light brown hair and putting it into a ponytail, Karina looked at herself in the mirror of the dresser in the guest room she shared with Jessica at the Winfields' home. She examined her red-rimmed eyes from a recent sob session with Jessica that had been therapeutic but tiring. She had fallen asleep and awakened to an empty room. She looked at her wristwatch. She'd been asleep for only twenty or so minutes.

"Karina, come quickly," Jessica called from downstairs. "Martin's on the phone."

Karina raced down the steps, taking two at a time, praying that nothing was wrong. She took the phone from Jessica. "Martin?"

Martin's voice sounded in her ears. "There has been a major volcanic eruption in Hawaii, much larger than usual, so we are packing for the trip to Hawaii. Where are Dr. and Mrs. Winfield?"

"They're shopping with Penny and Cindy," Karina answered. "We aren't scheduled to depart for another week. Will I travel with you or wait?"

"I'll let you know later this evening after I've had a chance to speak with the Winfields," Martin said. "My inclination is for you to stay with the Winfields. We'll fly over and get situated. I'm shipping two ultralight trainers over; we can use them to get some aerial photographs."

The thought of flying excited Karina. She had not piloted a plane in such a long time. She also wanted to see an erupting volcano. "What about Jessica? Can she stay with me?"

"That will be for the Winfields and Jessica to decide," Martin said. "Put Jessica back on. I'll call you later tonight."

Karina handed the phone to Jessica and impatiently waited for Martin to stop speaking. Until Jessica spoke, Karina had little insight into the conversation.

"Yes, sir. I understand," Jessica finally said. "If I have the choice, I'd like to stay and travel with Karina and the Winfields." Jessica smiled at Karina. "I think we both need some more time together."

Karina nodded agreement. The long conversations, often tearfully painful, had helped Karina. But she still had frequent nightmares, and her anger often got the better of her. That morning she had yelled at Cindy for talking back, which led to a long talk with Dr. Winfield.

Dr. Winfield had reminded her that discipline came from love and should be directed at the child's disobedience and not at the child; anything less broke the trust that Cindy's father had bestowed upon her. Karina had apologized to Cindy. They had talked the situation over, and Cindy had melted into her arms. Afterward, they both felt better about the incident, but Karina still felt on edge, as if she might explode without warning.

"If Dr. and Mrs. Winfield agree, we're traveling partners," Jessica said after hanging up the phone. "It's almost time for the news. Let's see if there is anything on about the eruption. Do you know how lucky we'd be to see a major volcanic eruption?"

"Very," Karina agreed. "But with my ability for finding disasters, we'll probably crash into the volcano for one final *hot* time."

"Don't even think about it," Jessica said, turning on the evening news in time to see fantastic pictures of lava spewing from the Kilauea volcano on the big island of Hawaii. Large red streaks of lava flew hundreds of feet into the air.

Sitting on the floor in front of the television, Karina never took her eyes from the screen, not even when Jessica sat beside her and grabbed her arm during a particularly magnificent scene in which the rushing lava spilled into the ocean, sending huge plumes of steam high into the sky.

Aghast at the sight of such awesome power, Karina shuddered. She realized that she would soon be watching it in person, thought about being caught in the lava's path, and worried about the possibility of something going awry.

CHAPTER 9

Hawaiian Holiday

Warm sand squished between Karina's toes as she walked slowly along the shoreline at Ehukai Beach Park in Pupukea on Oahu's North Shore. She and Jessica had arrived in Hawaii the night before with Cindy and the Winfields. Martin had given her a few days to relax and have vacation with the Winfields. He had even said that Heather could join them the next day for a bike ride down from the top of a volcano.

Karina had been delighted the previous night when Martin informed her that the ultralight airplanes had arrived. He told her that everything was moving ahead of schedule, so he'd given everyone three days to enjoy Hawaii before beginning the science unit on volcanoes. Cindy and Penny had demanded they spend the first day at the beach learning to surf. The only disappointing news was that the volcanic eruptions seemed to have ended. There had been no new lava flows for the past four days.

"Wow! Look at those waves!" Cindy tugged Karina's arm and pointed to eight-foot-high waves. "Can I learn to surf?"

Karina took Cindy's hand and turned the child toward an area farther down the beach. "Learning to surf is why we came to the beach, but you don't begin here. See that area with the *small* waves down the beach. That's where *we* begin. The big waves here are a part of the beach called the Pipe; only expert surfers dare to challenge those waves. Even then, some have died."

"I could do it," Cindy said confidently.

"Yeah, right," Penny retorted. "Well, I'd like to live to be thirteen, so let's go to the beginner's beach." Penny started down the trail without waiting for a reply.

"Right on," Jessica said. She trudged barefoot down the beach toward a white shack lined with surfboards. A large sign above the surfboards announced surfing lessons.

Karina gently pushed Cindy in the direction that Penny and Jessica had chosen. She marveled at the beautiful, cloudless sky and exquisite patches of emerald and blue ocean water that stretched all the way to the horizon. Karina felt a little fatigued from their long flight and the five-hour time difference. She was happy to have a few days to relax and have fun before joining Martin and her classmates.

As Karina and her group reached the hut, a young, muscular man came out to greet them. "Can I help you, ladies?" He wore only a bathing suit, and his skin sported a light tan that accented his sun-bleached blond hair.

I sure hope so, Karina thought. "We have only one day at the beach. Can we learn to surf in a day?"

"You can certainly get a good start," the boy answered. "It's your lucky day, because I've been dying for a challenge. I'm Tommy, but everyone calls me Wings 'cause I've got this dream of being a jet pilot. Follow me; we'll get some surfboards." Wings led them through the shop to a rack of stacked surfboards lining the back wall.

"Forget surfing," Jessica whispered in her ear. "Find out if he's free after work. I think I'm in love."

Using a bare foot, Karina lightly kicked her jaunty friend's butt. "I thought you and Paul had a thing going."

"We do." Jessica picked out a red-and-yellow surfboard that stood several inches taller than her five-foot, four-inch frame. "But there isn't any harm in considering all of my options."

"I want this one," Cindy yelled, distracting Karina from making a teasing remark.

Two hours of slips, falls, and several mouthfuls of seawater later, Karina finally managed to stay on the surfboard as she rode a foot-high wave all the way to the warm, sandy beach. She turned and saw Cindy heading back out with Penny toward larger waves down the beach.

Karina picked up her surfboard, walked over to the large section of carefully placed beach towels, dropped the surfboard, and settled onto a towel. She grabbed sunscreen and began liberally applying it to bare skin, which was substantial considering the bikini she wore.

She watched Cindy and Penny begin their run to the beach. Karina marveled at their progress. She barely kept her balance on a one-foot wave, while the little girls rode on top of three-foot waves. It had taken Karina a whole hour of body surfing before she learned to stand on her board.

"Cold soda?" Jessica asked as she plopped down beside Karina and offered an ice-filled cup of soda she had obviously purchased from a snack-shop vendor.

"Thanks." Karina took two large gulps. "Just what I needed. I swallowed so much salt water my stomach is doing flip-flops."

"You should have stayed with me and Wings," Jessica said. "He's a great teacher."

"Teacher?" Karina teased. "But what was the lesson? Every time I saw the two of you together, you seemed to be practicing hugging techniques."

"He was just helping me ride the waves. He showed me how to place my feet for the best balance," Jessica said. "Hand me the sunscreen."

Karina tossed the bottle to Jessica. "Twelve times in a row?" she asked. "Did it really take that many times?"

"I'll never tell." Jessica kicked sand in Karina's face. "Don't be a prude. Live a little."

"I'm committed to Joe at the moment," Karina said. "I don't need any more complications in my life. It's all I can do to face each day."

A long silence greeted her comment. She felt awful for breaking the magic of the day. Jessica had always been such a faithful friend. Jessica was the one who slept with her each night and awakened her when the nightmares started, and it was Jessica who held her until she could drift back to sleep.

Karina gulped down the last swallows of soda. "Race you," she called out, not waiting for a reply. She grabbed her surfboard and ran into the waves. Looking over her shoulder as she paddled out to catch a wave, she saw Jessica paddling behind her. Lying flat on the surfboard and using arms and legs, Karina quickly reached the open ocean. She worked herself into a sitting position.

Jessica already straddled her own surfboard. She pointed to a wave building behind them. "That one."

"It's larger than I'm used to," Karina said, "but let's do it." She dropped prone on her board and paddled for speed, hoping nothing bad would befall her.

She got a good jump on Jessica, but her friend's skill at surfing surpassed Karina's ability. By the time Karina managed to stand atop the surfboard and find her balance, Jessica led by at least ten yards. Karina leaned into her board, trying to increase her speed, but it was a bad move. She became top-heavy and started sliding down the wave rather than riding its crest. Karina lost balance and dove into the water; her surfboard continued its journey without her.

She plunged to the sandy ocean bottom. Her experience at Ocean Quest Academy had taught Karina how to handle the ocean, so she wasn't worried about being in the water. She simply kicked and skimmed along the bottom until she had to rise for air. Breaking the surface, Karina saw Jessica dismount and turn to search for her.

She waved and swam the last fifty yards to the beach. By the time the sun neared the western horizon, she had mastered three-foot waves. Pride in her accomplishment dovetailed with Penny's success when she came surfing in on a three-footer.

All in all, this has been a good day, Karina thought. She hoped that there would be many more such days as she signaled the others that it was time to meet Dr. Winfield for the drive back to the motel.

Looking out at the deep blue ocean from the base of the Haleakala observatory, Karina marveled at the beauty below her. She had seen the ocean numerous times and had even spent a semester at sea with Ocean Quest Academy, but she had never seen the ocean from the top of a volcano. A famous artist could have set the view to canvas. *What a place to begin a bicycle ride,* she thought.

Cindy tugged at her arm. "I can't get this helmet to fit."

Karina adjusted the helmet and checked that Cindy's elbow and kneepads fit securely. "How's that? Look at that view."

"Pretty. When can we start? I want to ride."

"Pretty?!" Karina thumped Cindy's helmet. "I'm riding with an insensitive brat. You're standing on top of an inactive volcano surrounded by a beautiful ocean panorama on all sides, and all you can say is *pretty?*"

"I said it was pretty," said Cindy, smirking at Karina. "And we are standing on top of a dormant volcano," she said, flaunting her high IQ. "It has been inactive long enough to be considered dormant. Didn't you read the material Martin assigned you to read?"

Karina paused, trying to decide whether to accept Cindy's challenge. Though only eight, the little girl had been endowed with the IQ of a genius, possessed a high school vocabulary, and remembered almost everything she read. Karina capitulated and let the remark slide. Besides, she had not read all of Martin's assignments.

She changed the subject. "Go get the others. It looks like it's about time to begin."

Karina watched Cindy run to the tourist observatory to summon Penny, Jessica, and Heather. She marveled at the child's athletic ability, being able to run without panting at an altitude of almost ten thousand feet. Fatigue drained Karina's energy; she had not slept well. The late flight from Oahu to Maui, a vivid nightmare, and a heated argument with Cindy over the morning's downhill ride from the top of Haleakala—instead of snorkeling at Molokini Atoll—had left Karina tired and moody.

The scenic ride to the observatory parking lot had been exciting enough for Karina, but it had tried Cindy's patience. The tourist van had slowly climbed the curve-filled road, partly to let the tourists see the sights and partly because of the heavy trailer full of bicycles that would be used for the bicycle ride down the side of the massive volcano. Twice Karina had warned Cindy to watch her manners and have patience. She had warned the child that she would spend the afternoon in her motel room instead of learning to windsurf.

After waiting a few minutes for Cindy to return with the others, she checked the bicycles. Karina wondered what kept everyone. She had been the first to go to the enclosed observation platform to view the expansive summit depression that dropped 3,028 feet, but she couldn't see how such a breathtaking sight would slow Cindy down enough to take this long. Even Penny wouldn't be able to keep Cindy's curiosity going long enough to prevent a quick start to the adventure and excitement of the bicycle ride.

Karina finished checking the bicycles. Most of the other tourists had returned. They were ready to begin. Embarrassment made Karina impatient. One father complained to the guide that his family had plans for the afternoon, and Karina didn't want to be responsible for other tourists being inconvenienced. Karina kicked the dust at her feet and began the steep trek to the observatory. A shout from above halted her progress.

"Hey, Karina," Penny called. "Wait there; we're on our way."

Shading her eyes from the sun, Karina saw five figures trotting down to meet her. *Five*, she thought. *Who could the fifth person be?* She continued watching until the fifth figure became a little black girl about Penny's age, eleven or twelve.

"This is Kiwi," Penny said. "She's in another group but wants to ride with us. Can she?"

Karina said, "I'm not sure. Have you asked her parents? You'd better check with our guide."

"I'll ask the guide." Cindy darted away.

"Kiwi's father said she could," Penny said as she took hold of Kiwi's hand. "He's riding in one of the vans. He doesn't know how to ride a bicycle. Can you imagine that?"

Karina looked into Kiwi's dark brown eyes and couldn't help admiring the child's beauty. *Someday boys are going to stand in line for this girl*, she thought. She smiled and extended a hand. "My name is Karina. I'm pleased to meet you."

Kiwi smiled back with exquisite, pearl-white teeth. "I'm Kiwi, spelled the same as the fruit." The little girl formally shook Karina's hand. "My mother always liked kiwi, so I inherited the name. I'm eleven, and I want to be a scientist when I grow up. I live in San Francisco, and my dad is a very successful accountant, but he doesn't have much time for me. I've been dying to come to Hawaii. I met Penny at the top. She's fun to be with, and I'd really like to join her for the ride down. There aren't any kids my age in our group. My group leader and my dad said I could if you don't mind."

The child's disarming smile convinced Karina. She grinned at the bubbly girl and interrupted. "You can ride with Penny and Cindy. We're stopping to eat at some little roadside inn on the way down. What about your group?"

Sliding to a halt next to Kiwi, Cindy breathlessly answered Karina's question. "The tourist company that we are with also owns Kiwi's tourist company. We're all doing the same thing; we'll all come together at the same parking lot when we're down."

"I guess it's settled then," Karina said. A few minutes later she found herself with Jessica at the end of a long line of bicyclists heading down the winding road.

Karina counted more than fifty riders from various groups in front of her. Heather had joined them for the ride and rode in front of the three kids; Karina rode in the rear with Jessica. Penny, Cindy, and Kiwi rode three abreast directly in front of her except when congested traffic or narrow turns dictated otherwise.

Dropping her bicycle down one gear, Karina remembered earlier instructions on how to safely ride a bicycle down the thirty-four miles necessary to reach the bottom. She hoped Cindy used lower gears and wasn't depending on her bicycle's brakes. Worn brakes could lead to a serious accident.

She watched Cindy effortlessly guide her bicycle around the curves and decided to stop worrying about the girl and instead concentrate on her own progress. It took all her efforts to keep the bicycle under control and still take in the magnificent view surrounding her. After half an hour and five miles of practice, Karina relaxed and enjoyed the ride. The scenery became less dramatic when she descended into the fields and forests on the lower part of Haleakala and lost sight of the ocean.

"That was great," Karina said, skidding to a stop beside Jessica. "But I sure could use some time away from this bicycle seat." She awkwardly dismounted her bicycle.

"Me too," Jessica agreed, pushing her bicycle into one of the many bicycle stands in front of a quaint little inn. "Much longer on that thing and I won't be able to sit for dinner. How long before we're down?"

Karina secured her own bicycle, noting its location for later retrieval. "Two hours riding time if I remember correctly. Let's get inside before Heather and Cindy eat everything. I swear that kid eats her own weight at least three times a day."

Breakfast consisted of fresh fruit, a choice between pancakes or waffles, fried eggs, and buttered toast, washed down with an inexhaustible supply of milk, coffee, or fruit juices. Karina sat with Jessica and Heather at a small table near the front door. She kept a close watch on Penny, Cindy, and Kiwi. The girls sat at a long bar near the back of the inn. She noticed that Kiwi fit right in with Penny and Cindy. They giggled and laughed and seemed to be enjoying each other's company. Kiwi's dark skin and short, curly black hair sharply contrasted with Penny's blonde hair and the light complexion with which Penny and Cindy had been born.

"Hey, we better get a move on," Heather said, downing the last of her orange juice. "I think almost everyone else has departed for parts unknown."

Shifting her attention to the tables that filled the dining room, Karina saw that only about a third of the tables held bicyclists, and only one table held bicyclists who were in her group. Sounds drifting in from the open door indicated that the majority of riders were getting set for the final leg of the adventure.

"Good idea," Karina said. "After delaying everyone at the beginning of the ride, we'd better not loiter." Even though she had been told it was not necessary, she pulled a dollar bill from her pocket and left it for the waitress. An earlier lecture from Martin about manners and appreciating the good works that others had done encouraged Karina to leave the cheerful waitress a tip—assurance that her work and friendship were appreciated. As she pushed her chair up to the table, Karina inwardly admitted that Martin's guidance continued to influence her behavior even when he was miles away.

Once underway, the trip continued through rolling downhill forests that left little additional sightseeing. Karina felt that she could have been riding anywhere, perhaps even back in the hills of New York. Except for the palm trees, the hills behind Blue Horizons looked very similar. Ninety minutes of riding led her and the rest of the group to the parking lot from which they had begun their journey. Dr. and Mrs. Winfield waited for them, freshly returned from their tour of a macadamia nut plantation.

Karina held Cindy at bay as Penny introduced Kiwi and Kiwi's father to her mom and dad. After putting up the bikes and using the restrooms, Dr. and Mrs. Winfield invited Kiwi and her dad to join them for lunch at an interesting village across the island. Kiwi's dad agreed. He got directions from Dr. Winfield and headed off with Kiwi in a small economy car. Then Dr. Winfield herded everyone into his rented van for the hour-long drive.

"I'm not hungry. Let's stop now," pleaded Cindy, her head hanging out the side window as the highway wound its way along Maui's coastline.

Karina looked out the window and saw a beautiful black sand beach and dozens of windsurfers effortlessly cutting across the waves on brightly colored surfboards that had even more brightly colored sails. She understood Cindy's excitement.

"Lunch first," Karina said. "We're going to what used to be a whaling village. There will be time for windsurfing this afternoon. A lesson on history will be good for you."

"But—" Cindy's whining tone hinted of rebellion.

"Remember, we're meeting Kiwi at the restaurant," Penny said.

Relief flooded through Karina at Penny's intercession. It had been a good day; she didn't want anything to ruin it. Unless things got out of hand, she was in charge of Cindy—Martin's way of teaching Karina to be responsible.

A sharp curve in the road turned them away from the windsurfers, so Cindy and Penny delved into making plans for windsurfing with Kiwi. Karina wasn't much of a history student herself, but Dr. and Mrs. Winfield wanted to explore the former whaling village of Lahaina, its giant banyan tree, and the whaling museum. Karina wanted to please them. After all, Dr. and Mrs. Winfield gave them ample opportunity to explore and enjoy Hawaii on their own. It certainly wasn't too much to expect a short outing together.

Lunch at the ocean-side restaurant in Lahaina was delicious and interesting. Two navy ships—a destroyer and a frigate according to Dr. Winfield—ran some type of maneuver about a mile offshore. The huge navy vessels held everyone's attention, even Cindy's. The addition of Kiwi and her father provided intrigue.

Karina suspected that something strange was going on between the little girl and her father. He readily agreed to join them for a tour of Lahaina and bought a round of ice cream cones, which they ate under the massive banyan tree in the center of the town. Kiwi's father seemed devoted to filling Kiwi's every request, but when Kiwi begged to join them for windsurfing, Kiwi's father seemed angry. A short argument ensued; Kiwi won and joined Penny and Cindy for the afternoon. To appease Kiwi's father, Dr. and Mrs. Winfield invited him to join them on a snorkeling trip.

Karina didn't know what conflict existed between father and daughter, but she sensed something was wrong—something that caused him to back off. The way Kiwi's father always kept an eye on her, even when speaking with Dr. Winfield, made Karina nervous. If the child had been covered with bruises, Karina would have suspected abuse.

Heather paddled a sleek windsurfing surfboard up to Karina. "Follow me out. Like, I want to try one without the little kids tagging along."

Karina glanced down the beach and saw Jessica supervising the girls. Watching Jessica help Kiwi onto a surfboard, she smiled at Jessica's patience—a quality Karina had only in short doses.

"Hey, Karina," Heather called. "You coming with me or not?"

"Coming." She settled into a prone position with the sail snugly pressed between her body and the surfboard.

Heather headed to where the more experienced windsurfers caught larger waves, and Karina worried that Heather wouldn't stop before entering the strong, outgoing current that could take them far away from shore. She hurried to catch Heather and warn her not to go farther, but the long-legged girl stopped paddling and began erecting her sail.

"What were you trying to do, paddle back to the mainland?" Karina asked, placing her own sail into the slot that secured it to her surfboard.

"I know what I'm doing," Heather said. "I wanted to speak to you without the kids. Like, I figured this was far enough out that we'd be alone."

Karina squinted against the glare of the setting sun, trying to read the expression on Heather's face. Heather wasn't a permanent member of Blue Horizons, and they had not always been friends during Karina's semester at Ocean Quest Academy.

"I've really enjoyed sharing this time with you," Heather said. She paused.

Karina sensed that Heather had more to say. She finally broke the awkward silence. "I'm glad you're here."

Heather smiled. "Thanks, but what I'm really trying to do is— like—ask you to come back to Ocean Quest Academy. In February, we're going on an expedition across the ocean to the Mediterranean Sea to do some research on global warming."

The offer astonished Karina. She had been sent to Ocean Quest Academy for a semester aboard a ship at sea—to learn some discipline. Her penchant for impulsively breaking rules had almost gotten her expelled from Blue Horizons. Now that she was back in *good graces* at Blue Horizons and Martin had become her permanent guardian, Karina had never thought about ever leaving.

Heather seemed to take her silence as a rejection. She continued, "I know it's too much to expect that you come for the fall semester, but I really want you to join me for the winter semester. Like, you were the only true friend I had at Ocean Quest."

Karina gave Heather a perplexed look.

"If you don't want to come," Heather said, a hint of disappointment lingering on her words, "I understand."

"It's not that," Karina said quickly. "I need some time to think about it. I'd love to see some of the kids again, but I need to think about it for a while. I've got to consider Cindy. I promised her dad before he died that I'd look after her. Martin may not want me to be gone that long."

Heather's disappointed expression broke Karina's heart. "Tell you what. I'll think about it, and when we're through with our volcano unit, I'll discuss it with Martin and Cindy. Let's take one thing at a time."

"Good," Heather said, a smile creeping across her face. "You're coming. Like, I knew you would."

"What?!" Karina exclaimed in response to Heather's audacious conclusion. "I didn't agree to anything, Heather!"

The much taller girl didn't answer. She released the restraining strap from her sail, stood awkwardly, and let the wind fill the sail. In a moment, Heather raced across the waves.

Karina followed Heather's example, though more slowly. She was not as comfortable or balanced on the surfboard as Heather. She placed her feet against one side of her surfboard. Then she held onto the pole that supported the fully extended sail and leaned outward toward the ocean. Almost immediately, the surfboard surged forward. The wind blew her shoulder-length hair behind her. Skimming across the waves thrilled Karina and took her breath away. She would have been content to surf forever, but the beach rushed to meet her. She was running out of ocean.

By the time Heather reached shore, Karina trailed by only a few yards. She moved the sail so that it lost the wind and hung limply. With a thump, the surfboard landed on the soft beach. Warm sand clung to her wet feet as she carried her surfboard to join Heather and the rest of her group. Penny and Kiwi ran to Karina.

"That looked great," Kiwi said. "You looked like an expert."

"Thanks," Karina said. "It was fun."

"Will you take us out?" Penny asked.

Not prepared for such a request, Karina paused before answering. Penny seldom asked her for anything. Karina wanted to fill the request, but she wasn't sure of her own competency. What if she got out there with the kids and had trouble? Could she help them? And the sun was setting. Time might become another critical factor.

"Gee, guys." She searched for a plausible excuse to deny the request. "It's getting pretty late. Do you think you can do it?"

"I can." Kiwi awkwardly used one bare foot to cover the other with sand as she spoke.

"Me too," Penny said.

"I don't know," Karina said, pausing again. "I'm not sure I can handle both of you out there."

"I'll help." Heather joined the conversation. "You take Penny; I'll take Kiwi."

Heather's offer of help and the idea of each taking a child settled the issue. "Well, if you agree to ride with us on our surfboards, it's a deal."

"I want to ride my own board," Kiwi said, pouting.

"It's with Heather on her board or not at all." Karina gave Kiwi a mother-said-no look, hoping to end the argument.

"We agree." Penny looked at Kiwi. "It's better to ride with Karina and Heather than not to ride at all. Karina won't change her mind."

A short time later Karina and Penny positioned themselves for a run to the beach. To Karina's right, Heather stood on her surfboard with Kiwi between her and the pole. To her left, Jessica worked to get her sail adjusted. Cindy rode with Jessica because the child had threatened mutiny at being left out of the opportunity.

"Thank you, Karina," Penny said as Karina slipped her sail into place. "This means a lot to Kiwi. I know you didn't want to do it."

"It's not that," Karina said as wind filled the sail. "I was nervous about my own ability. Get up; we're being left behind. Let's show those *mainlanders* how to windsurf."

Karina and Penny held onto the sail and gingerly leaned away from the surfboard. Balanced perfectly, they quickly overtook Jessica and Heather. Reaching the beach seconds before the others, Karina and Penny ran onto the beach and waved, showing off their first-place finish.

"Like, I want a rematch," Heather said as she and Kiwi ran to meet them.

"Me too. Can we?" Kiwi jumped up and down. "We'll beat you next time."

As Cindy reached them and joined in the challenge, Karina gave Heather a warning look. She would have vocalized her displeasure and ended any talk about more windsurfing, but Kiwi caught her attention.

The little girl stopped jumping. She held her head with both hands and cried as if she were in great pain. Before Karina could ask the cause of her distress, Kiwi crumpled to the ground—not in the dramatic manner seen in movies. Kiwi's knees buckled, and she collapsed straight downward onto the warm sand.

CHAPTER 10

Make-A-Wish Foundation

Karina raced to the fallen child and knelt. Jessica helped roll Kiwi over. The little girl's eyes were closed; her face was taut, as if she were in pain. Karina glanced over her shoulder. Heather comforted Cindy, who cried hysterically. Penny stood motionless, dumbfounded. A crowd gathered around them.

Karina gently placed a hand on Kiwi's shoulder and shook the little girl. "Kiwi, can you hear me? Are you in pain?" She got no response. Taking a deep breath, she turned to Penny. "Your dad should be in the parking lot waiting for us. Go and see if he's there."

At first, Penny didn't respond. Then she shuddered and sprinted across the sand toward the concrete steps leading to the parking lot.

The next few minutes seemed longer than a lifetime. Karina followed her first aid training and checked the little girl's airway, breathing, and pulse. Kiwi breathed in shallow, rapid breaths; her heart beat rapidly but so softly that it was barely perceptible. There was no lifeguard at this beach, so the crowd was her only hope for help if Dr. Winfield wasn't waiting for them.

A kind Hawaiian man used his cell phone to call for an ambulance, and Karina fanned Kiwi with a paper plate someone from the crowd provided. Tears slipped from her eyes as she faced the prospect of another child dying in her presence. *Please, God*, she prayed silently. *Don't let her die. I couldn't stand to look into the face of another dead child.*

Fortunately, she didn't have to wait long for an answer to her prayer. Dr. Winfield reached her at almost the exact moment that

Kiwi opened her eyes. The little girl gently squeezed Karina's hand and smiled weakly.

Dr. Winfield quickly took charge. He thanked the crowd, informed them that he was a doctor, and encouraged them to go on their way. Kiwi's father arrived with Mrs. Winfield. Mrs. Winfield ordered all of the kids to follow her to the van.

Karina's emotions bounced out of control. Tears streamed from her eyes. She wanted to be with Kiwi. At the same time, she never wanted to see the child again—as if removing Kiwi from her mind would erase the fear that clutched her heart.

Mrs. Winfield herded everyone into the van. As Karina entered, Mrs. Winfield gave her an awkward hug. Then she told them about an earlier conversation with Kiwi's father that took place on the snorkel boat—a conversation that broke Karina's heart.

"Kiwi is very ill," Mrs. Winfield explained. "She has been for a long time. She is here through a grant given by the Make-A-Wish Foundation."

Penny said, "Isn't that an organization that helps dying children fulfill their biggest wishes?"

Mrs. Winfield nodded. "Correct, honey. Kiwi has an inoperable brain tumor. She came here because her final wish was to visit Hawaii and see an erupting volcano."

The van seemed to close in on Karina. She couldn't breathe. She needed fresh air. "Let me out! I've got to get out of here!"

Karina opened the sliding van door on her left and ran blindly; she didn't stop at the end of the parking lot. At the curb, she stubbed the bare toes of her left foot, staggered onto the dry grass beyond, and then ran down the road. Tears and the gathering dusk blurred the headlights of oncoming cars. Slowing to a walk, Karina cried out her misery.

She wasn't sure how long she walked, but darkness overtook her before she stopped crying. She stepped away from the road, sat on the grass, pulled her knees to her chin, and examined her painfully scraped toes. An ambulance and a police car passed, sirens blaring and red lights flashing a warning.

Karina felt ashamed. She should have stayed and consoled Penny. Kiwi was Penny's friend. Penny would certainly understand how Kiwi felt. Just over a year ago, Penny had faced a lifesaving operation—a fight against leukemia. Penny had won, at least for the present. Her bone marrow transplant had been a complete success.

"How could I be so selfish and run away like a frightened brat?" Karina bitterly lashed out at herself. After long, painful minutes, she decided to walk back and apologize for her cowardly behavior, but Dr. Winfield's van stopped at the side of the road before she had enough courage to stand.

She watched as the door opened and Cindy ran out to meet her. Karina stood in time for the little ball of fury to lunge into her stomach, hugging her so tightly that she could barely breathe. She pried Cindy away and caught her breath. Dr. Winfield left the van and joined them. Then Mrs. Winfield drove the van down the road.

"Ready?" Dr. Winfield asked. His one word brought more tears.

Karina brushed them away with her arm and immediately wished she hadn't. Salt from the dried saltwater on her arm burned her eyes. "I'm sorry. I don't know what came over me."

"There's nothing to be sorry about. Let's walk. I'll try to explain Kiwi's situation as best I can. She's on her way to the hospital; we won't know anything for certain until the doctors run some tests." Dr. Winfield answered Karina's unspoken question. "We'll catch the van at the service station near the bottom of the hill. It's only about a mile walk. Sorry. I didn't think about shoes."

She gave Dr. Winfield a weak smile, took Cindy's hand, and began walking down the gentle incline. Dr. Winfield took her free hand, and Karina felt comforted by the extraordinary gesture. She squeezed his hand, and he patted hers.

"I think you know that Kiwi regained consciousness," Dr. Winfield said. "She asked me to tell you that she had a great time. She also asked if she could do it again, sometime."

"Do it again?" Karina asked, hesitantly. "I thought Kiwi was dying."

"She has a brain tumor that is located in a place where an operation would either kill her or leave her a vegetable for the rest of her life," Dr. Winfield explained. "Chemotherapy on her type of brain tumor has never proven to significantly prolong life and usually makes the patient very ill. Kiwi and her parents decided on quality of life instead of length of life."

"How long will she live?" Cindy asked, butting into the conversation.

"No one can say for sure," Dr. Winfield said. "According to the information her father gave me, Kiwi's tumor has become large enough that it's beginning to interfere with her brain's ability to run her body. Kiwi may have hours, days, or even weeks to live, but probably not much longer than a few weeks."

The sob escaped Karina before she realized she was crying again. She felt like such a baby. Cindy took the reality of the situation calmly. Karina wondered why she couldn't get control of her emotions.

Dr. Winfield put his arm around her and led the way down the hill in silence. No one spoke. As the hill leveled out, Karina saw the lights of the service station half a mile ahead. Finally, she controlled her emotions and stopped crying.

"I'd like to see Kiwi again … if it's possible," Karina said, breaking the deep silence.

"Me too," Cindy said. "Can we go to the hospital?"

"Not tonight," Dr. Winfield answered. "Kiwi's fatigue from all of the exercise and excitement today may have contributed to her collapse. The doctor's will make sure that she has a good night's rest. Let's talk about visiting in the morning when everyone is rested."

Karina pulled Dr. Winfield's arm tighter around her shoulder. Then she reached up and gave him a quick kiss on the cheek. "Thanks. I feel better now."

Few words were spoken during the ride back to the hotel. Penny had cried herself to sleep by the time Karina reached the van, and Jessica and Heather also slept. Karina held Cindy on her lap, and the little girl fell asleep almost before Dr. Winfield pulled out of the service station parking lot.

The silence gave Karina time to think back over the day. Until Kiwi's collapse and the discovery that the energetic little girl was dying, it had been a great day. Now she felt sad and happy at the same time. When she thought about Kiwi dying, her heart broke all over again. It took all her restraint to hold back tears. But when she remembered Dr. Winfield's care, Karina felt loved and special.

In only a year, she had found the love of Martin and the Winfields. Now two men loved and cared for her, either of whom she would gladly call father.

When they reached the motel, Dr. Winfield woke Penny and left Karina the job of getting the girls into bed. She carried Cindy into the hotel room that Cindy shared with Penny. While Karina undressed Cindy and slipped her into a thin summer nightgown, Penny got ready for bed without speaking. Karina gently kissed both girls on the forehead before turning off the light and quietly departing.

Back in her own room, she escaped into the bathroom and hoped Jessica would be asleep by the time she finished getting ready for bed. She had no desire for conversation. Karina stood in the shower and let its warm spray massage her body as she tried to mold her emotions into something controllable.

In her mind, she rehearsed what she would say to Kiwi in the morning, provided the little girl lived through the night and was and able to receive visitors. In each scenario, Karina lost control and burst into a fresh round of tears when she tried to rehearse words to comfort Kiwi. She turned her thoughts to the times in her life when she had witnessed death: her own parents in Kyrgyzstan, Cindy's father in the Amazon rainforest, the boys in the cave, and finally Kiwi's imminent death.

After much reflection and many emotional highs and lows, she turned off the water, toweled dry, and slipped into her own nightshirt. Karina climbed quietly into bed; her last thoughts were about life and death—serious subjects to which she was no stranger. As clouds of sleep replaced despair, unconscious tears wet her pillow.

Standing at the boat's rail, a fresh breeze fluffed Karina's light brown hair. The gentle waves lapping under the boat brought back memories of Ocean Quest Academy and the times she'd had during her semester away from Blue Horizons. Karina had learned to love and respect the ocean and its inhabitants. She hoped to instill in Cindy the same appreciation and respect. Karina despised people who defaced nature.

The motorized tourist boat headed for Molokini Atoll, a submerged, dormant volcano now maintained as a protected game preserve loaded with colorful fish. Along with Jessica and Heather, Karina planned to snorkel and enjoy the tropical, marine environment with Penny, Cindy, and Kiwi.

She turned her attention away from the sea and saw Kiwi standing across the deck. The little black girl seemed overjoyed at the prospect of the day's adventure. Kiwi's broad smile radiated her joy. She pointed out objects for Penny and Cindy to observe. Worrying that the day might be a drain on the child, Karina's thoughts drifted back two days—to the day she and Penny had retrieved Kiwi from the hospital.

The sterile hospital smell had attacked Karina and made her slightly dizzy the instant she stepped from the crowded hospital elevator onto the floor of the cancer ward. A sign labeled "oncology" had informed Karina that she and Penny were on the right floor. Room 472, Kiwi's room, had been located at the far end of the sparkling white corridor. Karina had stopped to rest at the small waiting room next to the nurses' station in order to regain her composure, but she had not been able to proceed, which forced Penny to go on alone.

In the warm ocean breeze, Karina shuddered and turned her gaze back out to the open sea and their destination. She had spent more time in hospitals than she cared to remember. Karina detested them and hoped that she wouldn't grace their presence again for many years to come. Her heart went out to Kiwi, and she prayed that the little girl would never see another hospital room.

Kiwi had been enthralled with joy when Karina had informed her that Martin had given permission for Kiwi and Penny to join Karina and her classmates at Hawaii's Volcanoes National Park for the start of the volcano unit. This snorkeling trip would end Karina's vacation and recovery period. Tomorrow she would be a student, and school would be in session.

Since gaining permission from Kiwi's father and rescuing the child from the hospital, Dr. Winfield had taken them on a harrowing drive along the Hana Highway—miles of narrow roadway, one-lane bridges, and hairpin curves—to the little town of Hana. The ride had been beautiful; magnificent waterfalls and luscious rainforest adorned one side of each winding curve, while dazzling ocean panoramas filled the window of the other side.

An afternoon excursion from Hana had taken them to the gravesite of Charles Lindberg. While paying homage to the famous aviator, Penny had explained her desire to be a pilot. She had told the story about how Karina had fulfilled her greatest dream by flying her to the hospital for a bone marrow transplant.

Karina had turned away at that point, not able to look Kiwi in the eyes, but she had heard the excitement in the conversation as Penny revealed Karina's status as an accomplished ultralight pilot. Hearing about her exploits—some highly exaggerated—had made Karina proud that she had been able to help Penny in her time of need.

"Cat got your tongue?" Heather handed Karina an ice-cold can of lemonade. "Like, it brings back memories; doesn't it?"

Karina took the can and looked out at the volcanic island coming into view. "Sure does. I hope the girls learn to appreciate it as much as I have. I hope Kiwi loves it."

"That kid has spunk. I called my father last night, and everything is set." Heather sipped lemonade. "The Make-A-Wish people readily agreed to let Kiwi join us as long as the bill is paid. Dad offered to pay all of the expenses. Like, about time he did something worthwhile with his money."

Karina ignored Heather's last remark. She knew that Heather's father was very wealthy, but Karina also knew that he spent far too little time with Heather. They were practically strangers. She decided to change the subject. "Where's Jessica?"

"She's with Dr. and Mrs. Winfield. Mrs. Winfield seems a bit nervous. She's concerned about sharks after reading about the thirteen-year-old surfer who got her arm bitten off. Jessica is trying to convince her it's safe to go into the water."

Karina passed the last twenty minutes of the trip talking with Heather and enjoying the boat ride. She watched as Molokini Atoll rose from the sea and formed a shield, protecting the area from strong currents and providing an excellent snorkeling area more than a mile across.

Shortly after arriving at the atoll, she gathered the little girls and paired each of them with an older girl. Cindy wanted to snorkel with Jessica because the two had become great friends. Heather took Penny for a partner, leaving Kiwi and Karina to snorkel together.

Karina stepped from the boat into comfortably warm, crystal-clear water. Thirty feet below, the sandy bottom stood out as a perfect backdrop for hundreds of colorful fish darting about. Karina instantly recognized the long-nosed trumpet fish, various parrot fish, and sleek barracuda. She surfaced and signaled for Kiwi to join her. The little girl jumped into the water and surfaced next to Karina.

"This is great," Kiwi said, spitting out water. "Look at all the fish."

"Hold on, tiger," Karina said as she pulled Kiwi close to her and adjusted the snorkel attached to the girl's face mask. "You'll be able to breathe easier if the snorkel is *out* of the water."

"Thanks." Kiwi gave her a sheepish grin. "This water sure is salty."

"It'll make you sick if you swallow too much of it," Karina said, slowly moving her fins back and forth to keep her head above water. "We've got over an hour, so let's just swim facedown on the surface for now. We'll note some places that might be fun to examine more closely and then go down to take a look."

"Anything you say," Kiwi agreed. "You're the boss."

"Can I trade Cindy for you?" Karina asked jokingly. "Cindy challenges me every time I tell her to do something."

"If you'll take me for a plane ride like you did Penny," Kiwi said.

Karina choked up at the request and didn't immediately answer. She didn't want to tell Kiwi that even if Martin granted such a request, it wouldn't be the same. No lifesaving procedure loomed in Kiwi's future. "I had special permission to take Penny for that flight. I'm not allowed to fly with passengers under normal circumstances."

"Oh," Kiwi said disappointedly.

"But I can see to it that you get a plane ride," Karina added quickly, noting Kiwi's crestfallen expression. "My guardian is a great pilot. We'll get you a good view of an active volcano one way or another."

"Thanks." Kiwi gave Karina an awkward hug and then placed her face mask in the water and began looking at fish.

For thirty minutes, she guided Kiwi around the cove. After locating some good places to explore, Karina stopped and made Kiwi practice snorkeling a few feet under the water. Finally, she decided to take the girl to the bottom. Karina was pleasantly surprised at how long Kiwi could hold her breath. Then she reminded herself that Kiwi suffered from a brain tumor, not asthma.

Karina called Heather and Penny to join them for the bottom dives. Snorkeling required one partner to stay on the surface while the other dived. For Karina to dive down with Kiwi, she needed someone to stay on the surface. The same would be true for the others. Karina had wanted Jessica and Cindy to join them, but they were with Dr. and Mrs. Winfield.

Kiwi turned out to be very competent at snorkeling. Karina followed her to the bottom, which lay nearly twenty feet below the surface. The agile child headed for a series of small volcanic boulders surrounded by fish. Karina followed closely behind and watched intently as the girl took a picture with the disposable underwater camera she had purchased onboard the boat.

Next she led Kiwi under an arch of rocks that formed a shallow cave. Inside Karina stopped and pointed out some eels hiding among the rocks. She had to pull Kiwi back to keep her from grabbing onto an eel—an act that could be extremely painful.

Karina surfaced and allowed Heather and Penny the chance to dive. She turned to Kiwi. "Look but don't touch. Respect nature."

"Sorry. I wasn't thinking," Kiwi said. "Should we be wearing dive skins?"

Karina smiled. She remembered the mate on the boat trying to convince everyone to wear a dive skin—a thin suit a diver wore for protection against contact with stinging marine life. The mate had exaggerated the danger of brushing against jellyfish and ruining the trip.

"In clear water, jellyfish are easy to see and avoid," Karina reassured her. "He just wanted to make some money off of the unreasonable fears of inexperienced tourists."

The answer satisfied Kiwi. For the remainder of that morning, Karina enjoyed pointing out mysteries of the sea. The trip's highlight came after they had piled back onto the boat for a short ride to Turtle City, an area frequented by green sea turtles. Kiwi, Penny, and Cindy tried valiantly to touch one of the large turtles, but the nimble creatures easily avoided all contact.

"Great day," Jessica said, sitting down between Karina and Cindy for the ride back to shore. Kiwi sat on Karina's lap, soundly sleeping. Cindy rested her head against Jessica's shoulder.

"I wish we had more time before returning to work," Karina said. "I want to see the volcanoes, but I've enjoyed spending time with Cindy. Do you think we have a chance to see an eruption?"

"When I talked to Martin yesterday, he said that Kilauea was erupting into the ocean from a lateral lava tube," Jessica said. "We're going to fly over and take some photographs."

"Really?" Karina said excitedly. It had been far too long since she had flown. She wanted to get back into the air. "That would be great. What time do we leave tomorrow?"

"Early," Jessica said, running her fingers through Cindy's tangled hair.

Pleasant conversation, the exertion, and a warm afternoon breeze made Karina sleepy. She lowered her cheek and rested it against Kiwi's head. She didn't know whether she drifted into sleep, but her mind focused on the image of a small ultralight flying above a sea of molten lava. Without warning, a huge stream of lava shot skyward and slammed into the ultralight's right wing. The small plane tumbled toward the bubbling, red death below. Then the plane ignited into flames and exploded.

She jerked to a sitting position with such a start that she almost rolled Kiwi off her lap and onto the deck. Glancing around, she verified that everyone was safe. Jessica and Cindy slept next to her. The others either slept or enjoyed Maui's beauty as the boat neared the harbor. Karina felt ill. The dream seemed so real. She had not seen who was flying the ultralight, but she had the uneasy feeling that trouble lay ahead.

Karina hugged Kiwi close to her. She wondered if her dream held any meaning and feared that more death was close at hand.

CHAPTER 11

Volcanoes National Park

"Watch your head." Karina helped Cindy step from the lighted surface of the Thurston Lava Tube into the dark, wild section. She allowed Cindy and Kiwi to lead, but she was determined to keep the energetic duo under control. Penny walked at her side, and several classmates followed a few yards behind her. Martin trailed behind everyone.

Kiwi shined her headlamp around the curved roof of the lava tube. "Look how round this cave is. It's almost like a tunnel."

"Hot lava flowed through here," Karina explained. "It cooled from the outside and let the hotter, runny lava flow through. That made the tunnel. Sometimes lava comes in different densities, even within the same lava flow. That allows for different types of lava formations."

Kiwi listened intently to her explanation. The child seemed genuinely interested in anything to do with volcanoes. She had expressed her desire to become a volcanologist, a scientist who studied volcanoes. Karina prayed the child would have the chance, but she knew that the next few days that she spent with Blue Horizons during their volcano science unit was probably as close as Kiwi would get to reaching her dream.

"Race you to the end," Cindy said, bolting into the darkness. Kiwi darted after her.

"Don't run!" Karina yelled, somewhat miffed. She had warned Cindy twice already not to run, not only because running was risky but also because she didn't want Kiwi to overexert herself.

"I'll get them," Penny offered, racing after the miscreants.

"Great," Karina grumbled. "Now I've got three to worry about."

"You're not alone." Joe stepped from behind her and shined his much brighter handheld light down the shadowy tunnel. "Loosen up."

Karina increased her pace. "Guess I'm becoming an old mother hen. It's just that Cindy doesn't seem to think of anybody but herself. She keeps forgetting how ill Kiwi is."

Joe's brighter light illuminated the adventurous trio hunched over something about twenty yards down the tunnel. Karina shortened her stride and slowed to a comfortable walk. She made a mental note to have a serious discussion with Cindy after they returned to camp later in the day.

"Karina, look," Cindy called, kneeling. She reached down into a hole. "I moved a rock and found a hole. I think I can squeeze into it. Can I try?"

"Let me see." Karina nudged Cindy away from the hole and knelt beside Kiwi, who also seemed ready for some unauthorized exploration. Martin and her classmates walked past. She called to Joe. "Keep an eye on Cindy."

"Right," he said. "I've got her; she's not going anywhere."

Lying on her stomach, Karina shined her light into the hole. She didn't remember reading in the brochure Martin had given her about any side passageways. Karina figured she might be able to squeeze through the narrow hole, but it made a sharp turn downward only a couple of feet into the passageway.

"Can we explore it?" Kiwi asked.

"No," she said, rising to her feet and brushing dark volcanic dust from her knees. "Too dangerous. It drops down a little way in. We don't have the proper equipment for such exploration. It probably narrows too much to explore." Karina felt the disappointment from her young charges and changed the topic of conversation. "Besides, we don't have the time. We have two other places to visit before lunch and an aerial photography flight this afternoon."

Her reminder about the afternoon flight quickly refocused her little group. She led the way down to the end of the lava tube. The rest of her classmates huddled around Martin, listening to his lecture.

"Most lava is classified by the type of silicate rock it forms." She overheard as she joined her classmates. "Karina, can you tell me what silicate rock is?"

"Yes, sir. Silicate rock is rock that consists of silicon and oxygen. There are three different types of silicate lava rocks: basalt, rhyolite, and andesite."

"Excellent," Martin praised her. "Joe, can you tell me a trait that identifies basalt rock?"

Karina realized that Martin's grilling was a mild reminder to stay with the class. She also knew Joe spent each evening studying for his upcoming test to become a fully licensed private pilot and was behind on his reading. Joe probably couldn't answer Martin's questions. She was about to come to his aid when another voice answered the question.

"Basalt rock is very dark in color because it doesn't have much silica, less than 50 percent by weight. Basalt rock is made up mostly of magnesium and iron," Kiwi said clearly, confidently, and without hesitation. "Rhyolite, on the other hand, is light in color because it has a lot of silica—at least 65 percent by weight—and not much magnesium and iron. Andesite contains between 50 and 65 percent silica, and its color is darker than rhyolite but lighter than basalt."

"Outstanding!" Martin lifted Kiwi and gave her a hug. "Can I hire you as a tutor?"

The rest of the Blue Horizons students also added their praise to Kiwi, who proceeded to show off her knowledge of volcanoes.

"I'd love to help tutor," Kiwi said as Martin set her down. "The type of lava and its viscosity determines what type of eruption a volcano has. You do know what viscosity is, don't you, Joe?"

Karina saw that Kiwi's pointed question caught Joe off guard, but he made a quick recovery. She was also relieved that the question had not been directed at her.

"Viscosity refers to a liquid's resistance to flow," Joe answered. "It determines how fast a liquid will flow. The greater the viscosity, the slower a liquid flows."

"That's correct," Kiwi said, but her voice indicated unhappiness that Joe knew the answer. "Jessica, what is the viscosity of basalt lava?"

Jessica shrugged her shoulders. "Uh … high, I think."

"Nope!" Kiwi said, beaming that she had another chance to flaunt her knowledge about volcanoes. "Basalt lava has very low viscosity. It is runny and flows quickly. Basalt rock also erupts at a very high temperature, somewhere between 1,000 and 1,200 degrees Celsius. Mauna Loa and Kilauea, as well as other shield volcanoes, are made from basalt lava."

Karina chuckled softly at Jessica's expression. She seemed vexed at being embarrassed by a child.

Kiwi continued, "Karina, what about rhyolite? Does it have high or low viscosity?"

Karina turned to Martin for help, but Martin seemed happy to let Kiwi take over the morning lecture. "Rhyolite lava has very high viscosity," Karina finally answered. "I can't remember at what temperature it erupts."

"Good on the viscosity part," Kiwi said. "Rhyolite lava erupts at temperatures between 650 and 800 degrees Celsius. You should know that, Karina."

Penny giggled; the muffled laughter embarrassed Karina. She prepared a retort to tell Kiwi that little girls shouldn't be arrogant, but the ground shook violently and negated her response. She lost her balance and sat sharply down onto the hard rock floor. Panicked shrieks sounded from several directions, and Karina recognized Cindy's high-pitched scream.

"Don't panic," Martin said. His calm voice halted the screams. "It's only a tremor. It will pass."

Almost before Martin finished speaking, as if he controlled the forces of nature, the shaking stopped. Karina shined her light around. Martin's right hand gripped Cindy's shoulder. His left hand firmly held Kiwi. Joe leaned against the wall next to her. Penny and the rest of the kids huddled together on her right.

"Let's finish this discussion outside," Martin suggested. "With the recent eruptions that have taken place this year, we might be able to see something if that tremor was an indicator of another eruption."

Karina rose to her feet, took Cindy's hand, and worked her way through the dark passageway. At the incline that separated the wild section from the lighted tourist section, she boosted Cindy and Kiwi onto the smooth, concrete walkway. Less than a minute later, she stood in bright sunshine, searching for signs of an eruption in progress.

Karina shaded her eyes with her hand. "I don't see anything."

"Me neither," Jessica said.

"Nothing unusual." Penny's voice hinted the disappointment everyone felt.

"Don't be too discouraged," Martin said. "Few people are lucky enough to see a major volcanic eruption. We'd be fortunate, indeed, if we were to have front row seats at an eruption. Let's pile into the vans. We'll stop at the museum and then take a look at Kilauea's main crater."

Karina sat between Joe and Heather as Mr. Smithson drove them to the volcano museum in Volcanoes National Park. She was edgy but didn't know why. Even though the little kids rode with Martin, she didn't like them traveling in a different van.

Inside the museum, Karina quickly regained control of Cindy, Kiwi, and Penny. She guided them from one fascinating display to another. She relaxed and enjoyed the informative displays until she came to a display that set her teeth on edge. Inside a glass case stood the thermal protection suit a volcanologist had used while examining a lava flow. The suit was badly burned from the waist down. An informational sign told Karina that, while collecting data, the scientist wearing the suit had fallen through the crust of cooling lava into the hotter lava beneath the surface. He had died from severe burns.

This particular revelation worried Karina. Martin's schedule included an evening walk on recently cooled lava. Kilauea currently erupted into the ocean from a lateral lava tube, and he wanted them to observe how the lava added new land to the big island of Hawaii. She knew such mild eruptions drew hundreds of people to watch cold ocean water rapidly cool the hot lava and spew magnificent steam clouds speckled with small globs of glowing lava high into the air.

But the burned suit hanging in the display added a sober reminder to be very careful when walking on recently cooled lava.

Leaving the museum, Karina wrapped her arms around Cindy and hugged her. The child smiled and hugged her back. Yet, the uneasy feeling persisted, and Karina struggled to breathe normally as she climbed into the van for the short ride to Kilauea's crater. A few minutes later, she experienced her first sight of an active volcanic crater. She climbed down from the van, collected the girls, and worked her way to the volcano's rim.

Joe stood beside her. "Look how far it is across the crater. It must be a mile and a half. Can you imagine the force it took to lift the millions of tons of rock to form this rim?"

Karina stared down at the solid rock floor lying hundreds of feet below. "I'm not sure that I'd like to be standing here to find out."

"I sure would," Kiwi said. "But it's highly unlikely. I think we're in the wrong spot. The eruption earlier this month came from Mauna Loa. I wish we could go there."

"Not a chance," Jessica said. "Martin told us that the road leading to Mauna Loa is only open to scientists at this time. There's still a chance for another eruption."

"That's why I want to go," Kiwi said, earnestly. "That's my biggest wish: to see an erupting volcano."

"Karina, can't you fly Kiwi over by Mauna Loa this afternoon?" Penny asked.

Karina gave Penny a stern look. "Not possible. Too many tourist planes are flying that way to show tourists the signs of the last eruption. Besides, I'm following Martin. Remember?"

Penny said, "I just thought that maybe you would be able to fulfill Kiwi's wish like you did mine last year."

Karina knew that Penny wanted Kiwi's dream fulfilled, and she wondered if Penny thought fulfilling Kiwi's dream might spare the child's life—something that would take more than a simple flight could provide.

"I—" The ground shook violently, forcing Karina to grab the crater's protective fence rail for balance. On the crater floor below her, a patch of the dark rock split apart. A glowing ribbon of lava burst into the air. The thin red stream rose only a hundred or so feet into the air, but it held everyone's attention, including Martin's.

Karina stood mesmerized. Lava spurted into the air and then dropped into a scarlet pool forming on the crater floor. For almost a minute, she focused her eyes on the amazing scene.

"Look at that!" Kiwi yelled and pulled out a disposable camera. She put the camera to her face and began snapping pictures. Joe and several other students produced cameras. Karina reached into her pocket, removed a small digital camera, and documented what she hadn't thought possible: a volcanic eruption—a sight not witnessed by many who yearned for such an experience.

Karina snapped three pictures in rapid succession. Then she positioned herself to get a shot with Heather, Jessica, and Megan in the background. She wanted some perspective. She focused the camera and started to push the button, but the lava suddenly dropped to the crater floor, ruining her shot and ending the limited eruption.

"What happened?" she asked no one in particular.

"Looks like it's over for now," Martin said. They all stood at the rail hoping to see more.

"That was something," Kiwi said, not taking her eyes from the pool of red lava that had already begun forming a black crust.

"Does this fulfill your dream?" Penny asked.

"That was certainly an eruption," Karina said, putting an arm around the little girl's shoulder.

Kiwi shook her head. "Too small. I want to see rivers of lava flowing, and lava sailing high into the sky. You know—a major eruption."

Secretly, Karina agreed with the child. The red lava bursting from the caldera floor had been exciting, but it left Karina wanting more.

"Let's head back to camp and get some lunch." Martin said. He moved along the line of students and urged them to return to the vans.

As they turned to leave, several park rangers arrived, followed by other cars full of scientists and reporters. The reporters asked the students what they had seen while the rangers and scientists spoke with Martin, Sally, and Mr. Smithson. It took almost an hour before

Martin was able to get all of the students into the vans for the trip back to their camp.

Their base camp was more modern in Hawaii than it had been during the spelunking expedition in Missouri. Martin had rented a number of cabins, an action that thoroughly pleased Karina. She didn't particularly enjoy living in a tent for extended periods of time. Living in a tent forced her to be more organized than her nature usually allowed.

After a brief lunch—tuna salad sandwiches, chips, fruit, and iced tea—Martin ushered everyone into the motel's large conference room, which they used as a classroom. Karina sat beside Joe and Jessica. Heather, Megan, and the kids sat in the row of chairs directly in front of her. She fretted about what all the excitement might do to Kiwi's condition. The child had been full of energy ever since the eruption.

"Here's the routine for this afternoon." Martin stood in front of an easel that supported a large aerial map of the park. "Jessica and Joe will fly the first pass—right here." Martin used a pointer to indicate an area near the ocean. "Joe and Jessica will fly in *Bluebird*. Joe will pilot. Jessica will sit in the front seat and handle the camera. Cindy will fly with me in *Jet Stream*. After refueling, Megan will pilot *Bluebird* with a member of the ground team. Heather will join me. On our third and final run for the day, Penny will fly with me in *Jet Stream* while Karina flies *Bluebird* with Kiwi in the front seat. Mr. Smithson will be in charge of those staying behind. Those students not selected to fly will work as ground crew and will have the opportunity to fly tomorrow. It would also be a good time for everyone to write their reflections on the day's events."

Kiwi squealed at Martin's announcement. Karina smiled; she was pleased that Martin trusted her enough to fly the kid out to see Kilauea's steam plume, which Martin had informed her was higher than usual, perhaps the result of the day's earlier eruption at the main crater. She hoped that other aircraft wouldn't be too much of a problem.

Over the next couple of hours, Karina patiently tried to keep Kiwi entertained. Because Martin kept the airplanes at a small roadside airfield outside of the park, there was not much to see or do. Karina used the time to explain the principles of flying an ultralight airplane to Kiwi. Cindy told Kiwi about the time Karina and Joe had flown into the Amazon to save her. Karina fought back tears when Cindy talked about her father dying. She walked away with the pretense of checking on the afternoon weather report.

Her turn eventually came for the afternoon flight. Karina helped Kiwi climb into the front seat of the two-seat airplane and showed her how to use the radio. She started the engine and waited for Martin to taxi down the narrow runway. Then she took off immediately behind Martin. Effortlessly, she pulled back on the control stick and climbed to the required altitude: one thousand feet above sea level. The thirty-two-foot wingspan on the ultralight gave her plenty of lift. Karina worked her rudder pedals and shifted her control stick to the left. The plane responded by lowering its left wing and banking left. She leveled out and flew directly over the park, following a few hundred yards behind Martin. In the distance she saw a thick steam plume rising from the sea.

"Isn't it beautiful?" Kiwi asked from *Bluebird*'s front seat. "Can we go closer?"

The child, encumbered by the bright red lifejacket she wore and the plane's restraining shoulder harness, had her head glued to the left side of the cockpit window as Karina slowly circled the huge plume of steam rising high into the sky. She flew at one thousand feet, and the plume rose well above her. Karina kept her distance from the column of steam and followed Martin's plane. She had no desire to get closer. The ultralight trainer she flew had a skin made from treated cloth and wings covered with Mylar. The plane wasn't very heavy, making it highly susceptible to sudden changes in the wind. The rising steam promised turbulence for anyone venturing too close.

"Not possible," she said. "It's too dangerous; see the lava being thrown into the air with the steam?" Karina pointed out red specks visible inside the white steam plume. "If one of those hit us, we'd be in real trouble."

"I guess you're right," Kiwi agreed. "But I'd sure like to get a closer look."

"Kiwi, can you hear me? Over." Penny's voice came through their headsets.

Karina told Kiwi how to respond, and the little girl maintained a steady chatter as Karina slowly circled the area. She kept a close eye on the steam plume, which seemed to be growing taller. Without warning, a large glob of molten rock intersected her flight path. Karina moved her control stick to the right. The little plane rolled out of its slow left turn and veered away from the steam plume. She guided the plane out to sea—away from any danger.

"Nice move," Martin radioed to Karina. His usually calm voice seemed strained. "Head back to the landing strip. We've seen enough for today. This area is too unsettled for the moment. Over."

Karina keyed her microphone. "Copy that; heading back to the landing field. Over."

"Do we have to leave?" Kiwi asked in a pouting tone, ignoring correct radio procedure.

"As quickly as possible, Kiwi," Martin said. "Stay off of the radio. Out."

Karina flew her ultralight airplane back to the little grass strip they used as a runway and made a perfect landing. Then she shooed Kiwi off to play with Penny and Cindy. Martin ordered her and the other Blue Horizons students to report for debriefing.

Upon entering the room, Karina saw Sally and Paul talking with her classmates. Paul walked without a cast on his ankle; he informed her that he was back to normal, but he wasn't interested in spelunking anytime soon. Martin cut short the greetings and conversation.

"I'm suspending the aerial photography for now," he informed the class. "The volcanic activity in this area is just too unsettled to fly with the light planes we have. It would be putting everyone flying at unnecessary risk."

Sounds of grumbled disappointment ran through the students, especially among the students who had not flown. "Why can't we just fly above the danger?" Megan asked.

Martin held up his hand for quiet. "Karina had a very close call today when a red-hot piece of lava unexpectedly sprang from the top of the steam plume. She was well outside the half-mile safety zone, and the rock still descended through her flight path. It is just too difficult to determine what is and what isn't a safe flight profile." Martin looked at Karina. "You did a great job. Your instinct and flying ability did you proud. You demonstrated great finesse in making such a smooth turn out to sea."

Martin's praise thrilled her; she was pleased that she had handled the plane so effortlessly. If there were no more volcanic surprises, she'd be even happier.

"What do we do now?" Heather asked.

"We are going to plan B. Instead of going down to the ocean to see the steam cloud at night, we are going to hike to here." Martin pointed to a spot on the map. "We'll camp out there for a few days. The park ranger informed me that Kilauea is erupting inland, and we might be lucky enough to see significant lava flows."

"From a safe distance, I hope," said Karina, grumbling loud enough for Martin to overhear.

"We'll be camped away from any eruption," Martin assured her, "and we'll observe the lava stream from a ridge. We should be safe. As you know, shield volcanoes don't usually have violent eruptions. The park rangers have approved the plan and given us a camping permit."

Karina wasn't fully reassured by Martin's remarks. She wasn't happy about leaving the comfort of her cabin for the cramped confines of a tent. She packed in silence, took a shower, and made the little kids shower and pack. Dr. and Mrs. Winfield and Kiwi's father would not join them for the first couple of days of camping. Kiwi's father had some important work to do, and Mr. and Mrs. Winfield were going on a two-day cruise. If not for Dr. Winfield vouching for Martin's expertise, Kiwi would have been left behind.

When all of the kids finished packing, Martin and Sally piled them into the vans for the drive to the drop-off point. Mr. Smithson remained at base camp. He would be their direct contact to the park rangers. Karina looked out the window at the results of years of earlier eruptions—dark black rock that stretched for miles. If she hadn't known better, she might have been on another planet.

After dismounting from the van and putting on heavy packs, Karina followed Martin into lush rainforest. The hike took more than five hours, and darkness settled on them before they finally reached the site for their camp. During the last three hours of the hike, the kids took turns carrying Kiwi. Karina had mentioned to the group that she was worried about the child exerting too much energy, and the kids took over. Kiwi arrived rested but still ready for bed. Using flashlights, Karina and Jessica set up their tent. They ate a cold dinner consisting of sandwiches and lemonade. Then Karina got the three little kids into their tent before she crawled into hers. Jessica already slept, curled into a tight ball in her sleeping bag.

Though tired, Karina still couldn't find sleep. Lying on hard ground, she felt slight tremors every few minutes. She held her breath during each tremor, fearing that the ground was about to be torn apart. Her instinct told her that she shouldn't be there, and she got angry with herself for not trusting Martin's judgment. Still, somehow she *knew* she should be a long way off.

She decided to tell Martin her hunch and fears the first thing in the morning but doubted it would change anything. At least she would speak her mind. Karina turned on her side, pulled her pillow around her head, and snuggled deeper into her sleeping bag. Long hours passed before sleep calmed her and replaced the uneasy feeling in her stomach.

CHAPTER 12

Earthquake

"Watch your step." Karina led the way up a steep, vine-covered path to get a better view of a volcanic eruption they had been seeking since early morning. A quick glance at her watch informed her she had about forty minutes before turning back. "Heather, don't let Cindy stray from the path."

"She's fine," Heather reassured her. "I've got the kids. Slow down. You're going too fast."

Karina glanced over her shoulder and saw Heather and Jessica struggling on the steep hillside. Heather led the way. Jessica brought up the rear, safely confining the three little girls between them. Brushing sweat from her brow, Karina surveyed the path ahead. She figured that one more push would put them on the top, maybe giving them a good look at the erupting volcano—or maybe not.

Testing the strength of a think vine, Karina made a dexterous move and scrambled the last few feet. She stood on a bluff overlooking the most fantastic sight she had ever seen. "Hurry up! You have got to see this!"

Karina removed her backpack and pulled out a digital camera; she snapped incredible pictures, one after another, without ever taking her eye from the camera's viewfinder. Across the valley, less than a quarter of a mile from her current position, two streams of lava flowed slowly down the adjoining hill. The streams met at the valley floor and formed a mighty river of red, traveling down the lush green valley and setting everything it touched on fire.

"Let me take a picture," Cindy begged from beside Karina. "Look at that lava."

Karina handed Cindy the camera and helped Kiwi into a position that gave the child a better view. "Does this qualify as a major eruption?"

"Close," Kiwi said, pulling out her own camera. "There is a lot of lava, but it's not really a major eruption." She put the camera to her face and snapped three quick pictures. "It is exciting though. The other kids will be jealous that they didn't come with us."

"Like, you got that right," Heather said.

Karina smiled at Heather's enthusiasm. Heather had not been interested in the long climb. She had only come to help Karina keep an eye on the little kids. Martin had given everyone free time to study or just relax. No one else had wanted to explore. Everyone was still tired from yesterday's long hike. If it hadn't been for Kiwi, she might not have come either. "Better move back a step. You don't want to fall off."

Heather stepped back from the steep bluff. "Good idea. A fall from here could be really serious. Like, if you didn't die from the fall, the lava might get you."

Penny moved next to Karina, stepped on tiptoes, and whispered in Karina's ear. "Thanks. Kiwi would never have gotten this chance if you hadn't brought us here. I think she's really happy."

Tears welled in Karina's eyes, forcing her to shrug off Penny's thanks and turn away before the others saw her cry. She wasn't exactly sure why she cried. At the moment, Kiwi seemed as happy and healthy as any child Karina had ever seen. If it hadn't been for that day at the beach and the tyke's stay in the hospital, Karina would have thought the girl was totally healthy.

For almost an hour—longer than Karina had planned—they sat watching the lava flow down the steep valley. After a while, Karina noticed different aspects of the lava flows. The left stream ran slightly faster; she figured it was hotter, because it had specks of white lava dotting the bright red of the main flow. She knew that white lava was really hot. However, she couldn't remember exactly how hot and didn't want to ask Heather or Jessica for fear that Kiwi would show off with another lecture on volcanoes. Grudgingly, Karina had to admit that Kiwi knew considerably more about volcanoes than she did.

"Time to go, gang," Karina said, mentally noting that Martin would be worried if they didn't return soon. He had not been excited about letting them explore on their own. "Martin is going to have our hides if we don't hurry back."

With great effort and much grumbling, Karina pried her group from the exciting scene and headed them carefully down the steep hillside. Climbing down proved much easier than the ascent; it took only half an hour to regroup with the rest of her classmates. Her revelation of a great view of the flowing lava settled the tasks for the day. Martin decided the entire class would eat an early lunch; then Karina would lead everyone up the trail to take pictures of the lava flows.

The afternoon passed swiftly. Because the viewing area from which she and the little girls had watched only had enough room for Martin, Sally, the little kids, and few students at a time, she led small groups of students to and from camp to take pictures of the flowing lava. Penny, Kiwi, and Cindy stayed with Martin and Sally to watch the flowing lava. By the time she guided the last group to the observation ridge, she and her classmates were not the only observers of nature's grand show. Dozens of tourists, news crews, and scientists had worked their way into the area. A couple of park rangers set out warning markers to keep unwary tourists from venturing too near the action.

The last group of students begged Martin and Sally for more time to take pictures, so Karina volunteered to return to camp and fix dinner, giving her classmates more time to view the eruption. After a heated argument, Karina forced Cindy to return also, leaving Penny and Kiwi under Martin's care.

Hiking back to camp took time. Karina passed dozens of sightseers on the narrow trail, and she had to stop numerous times to look at the digital pictures that Cindy had taken of the eruption. When they reached camp, Karina tossed her gear into her tent and began the process of cooking dinner. Most of the students who were not with Sally and Martin were sleeping, but Jessica and Heather were awake and offered to help make dinner—an offer she gladly accepted.

"Wasn't that fantastic?" Jessica asked. She handed Karina another opened soup can.

"Fantastic and frightening." Karina poured the family-sized can of vegetable soup into a large pot she heated on a camp stove.

"Frightening? Why?" Jessica asked, kneeling beside Heather, who made ham sandwiches and placed them in a large plastic container.

Karina finished stirring the soup, lowered the lid, and sighed. "I keep thinking how horrible it would be to be trapped with lava flowing closer and closer, nowhere to run, just waiting for a painful death." She shuddered. "I can't get the image of that burned suit we saw in the museum from my head."

"I'm with you," Heather agreed, placing the last sandwich into the container. "I don't like camping this close to the eruption. Like, if it weren't for the rangers saying that it's safe to camp here, I'd feel in real danger. What if that lava begins flowing faster, fills up the valley, and flows our way? What if Kilauea explodes like Mount St. Helens did back in 1980?"

"No way," Jessica said. "That is a deep valley. The lava is almost a mile away. We'd have plenty of time to get out, and shield volcanoes don't explode like Mount St. Helens did. Mount St. Helens is a composite volcano, consisting of andesitic lava. Kilauea's lava is mostly low viscosity basaltic lava."

"You sound like Kiwi," Karina giggled. "That kid is a walking encyclopedia on volcanoes."

"Yeah, too bad the kid is so sick. Like, she'd make a great scientist." Heather's comment silenced further speech for long, awkward seconds.

"Where's Cindy?" Jessica changed the subject.

Karina absently plucked strands of grass with her left hand. "She's resting in her tent. I told her she couldn't come with us tonight if she didn't take a nap. It was the only way I could get her to come back with us, short of dragging her by her hair."

"She's a stubborn little thing," Heather said.

"I guess we would be too, if we had been through all she's been through," Jessica said, lying on her back with her hands behind her head.

"That's no excuse." Karina stretched out beside Jessica. "According to what her father told me before he died, Cindy has been stubborn since she was a baby. I think it might be because she's so intelligent. It's just her nature, but she's got to learn to obey without every command becoming a battle."

"I guess you're right," Jessica agreed. "But I'm glad she's with us. I like watching the way you deal with her. I think you're going to be a great mother some day."

"I hope not too soon," Karina laughed. "I'm still learning to be fifteen. Sometimes when I fight with Cindy, I see myself in her and don't feel like I have the right to correct her."

"From what you've told me, you're obligated—*mother dear*." Heather threw a clod of grass at Karina, which transformed serious conversation into a free-for-all as the three teens frolicked in the grass, wrestling and tickling each other, all thoughts about obligations and unseen dangers momentarily forgotten.

"Look, there goes another one." Cindy pointed to a glob of glowing lava sailing into the darkness of the night sky.

Karina held Cindy tightly to her, partly for affection and partly to keep her under control. "I see it, honey. It's beautiful. Did you get any good pictures?"

"Bunches. I'd take more, but I'm out of batteries." Cindy placed her arms around Karina's waist and squeezed tightly.

She returned the hug and tousled Cindy's dirty, tangled hair. At that moment, Karina felt happy and contented. Martin had taken Kiwi and Penny on a trek to a higher ridge to get a different perspective for pictures. Joe stood at her side, clicking pictures with his digital camera. She wished that time would stand still and freeze the contentment within her. Happy moments had been few and far between since her parents died. Now she felt that maybe things would be better—if she could get over the nightmares that still haunted her. Last night she had screamed in her sleep, waking Heather and Jessica. While sleeping, she had returned to the flooded cave and stared into Philip's accusing eyes.

Karina heard Martin calling everyone to head back to the campsite. Reluctantly, she took Cindy's hand and turned to go. Joe took her other hand. Her heart fluttered, and she blushed, hoping the dark night hid her pleasure. Cindy noticed her holding Joe's hand and giggled, but Karina didn't let go until camp came into sight.

After a short debriefing on the day's activities, Martin ordered everyone to bed. Midnight passed before she crawled into the sleeping bag next to Jessica. She felt like talking, but Jessica was already asleep, snoring softly. A myriad of emotions filled Karina. The happy feelings and love she felt for Joe and Cindy provided comfort, but a persistent fear that something bad was about to happen still nagged at her.

Karina rolled over onto her stomach and squirmed to get comfortable. She tried to logically relieve the uneasy feeling by reasoning that she was not totally past the tragic cave rescue. She also rationalized that Kiwi's terminal condition weighed heavily upon her emotions. After much thought, she decided to take her concerns to a higher authority.

She folded her hands to pray. "Lord, please give Kiwi a chance to grow up. Give her a chance for a long and happy life." Karina ended her prayer with a petition for everyone to be safe. Then she sighed deeply and closed her eyes.

Karina beamed with happiness as Joe slipped the necklace around her neck and fastened it into place. She felt his strong hands on her shoulder. Then his grip tightened; he began shaking her violently. She gasped and tried to tell him to stop, to tell him he was hurting her, to tell him that was not the way to treat a girlfriend. But the shaking intensified.

"Wake up!" Jessica's voice penetrated the darkness around her. "Something's wrong."

Karina opened her eyes and saw the tent walls shaking in the dim beam from Jessica's flashlight. The ground beneath her shuddered and worked against her every move. She managed to crawl from her sleeping bag, but the ground shook violently. Jessica tried to kneel, lost her balance, and fell back against Karina, forcing both of them to the ground and against Karina's side of the tent. The tent suddenly shifted downhill.

"Hang on." Devon's voice reached into the collapsed tent. "I'll get you out."

Karina and Jessica struggled to free themselves as the welcome sound of a zipper in action vented cool air. Bright moonlight revealed the most devilish scene Karina had ever witnessed. Fewer than a hundred yards away, trees burned brightly and the landscape glowed red, as if a huge electric stove had been set on high and left unattended. It took only seconds to realize that the *stove* was, in reality, a stream of lava.

With Devon's help, Karina gained her feet and extended a hand to Jessica. Dressed in only panties and an oversized T-shirt, Karina rummaged through the collapsed tent for her jeans and boots. Jessica also searched frantically. Karina found her boots and stepped into them without even searching for socks. Finding her jeans, she threw them over her shoulder. She wanted to get to the little kids. She could put her jeans on when they were in a safer position.

"I've got to get Cindy and the kids!" she shouted and moved toward the tent the three little girls shared.

Devon pulled her back and pointed to a spot thirty yards away. "Joe's already got them. They're with Martin. Didn't you hear us yelling? Martin sent me to get you."

"I heard but couldn't wake Karina," Jessica said, holding onto Karina's free hand. Like Karina, Jessica slipped on boots and carried her jeans.

"I thought I was dreaming," Karina said. "Let's get dressed."

A sudden blob of red lava hit the little girls' tent and the entire area burst into flames, cutting off any possibility of reaching the spot where Martin collected the other kids.

"This way. Come on!" Devon yelled. By flashlight, he led them across the unsteady ground. They headed downhill on an overgrown path. The trembling stopped. It happened so quickly that Karina's legs seemed unsteady on the solid ground beneath her. Devon explained the situation as they hurried behind him. "We can't reach Martin. There is a ravine at the end of the field too steep for us to cross. He'll lead everyone out using the path we hiked in on; we've got to work our way downhill and then try to cut over in his direction. It's our only chance."

Holding onto Jessica's shoulder, as much for security as for balance, Karina followed Devon. Soon they overtook Heather, Megan, and

Sally, who told Karina that they had also been cut off from the rest of the group. Stopping to catch her breath on a little hill, Karina saw the incredible devastation below and behind her. The valley that had once been their campground now pooled with hot lava; it was black and crusted near the edges as the outlying lava cooled, and glowing red where lava continued to flow down the valley, setting fire to the trees and brush in its path.

Karina made some mental calculations. "The lava is flowing at about sixty feet a minute. That's less than a mile an hour. We should be okay. Let's catch up with Martin."

Sally pointed ahead of Karina. "It may not be that easy. We're being cut off."

To Karina's horror, she saw that a lava stream several hundred feet wide already flowed down the opposite bank across from their current position and ravaged everything in its way. In the distant glow that the lava provided, Karina saw a crowd of tiny figures cross in front of the second lava flow and climb the hillside above, thus escaping the entrapment she and her group faced. She prayed that the figures included Martin and the rest of the kids.

"What should we do?" Heather asked. "Like, we can't stay here, we can't go that way, and we certainly can't go back."

The danger of their situation hit Karina like a boxer taking a jab to the chin. She staggered and would have fallen if Jessica and Sally hadn't steadied her. "What are we going to do?" Karina asked.

"We've got to work our way down the valley and try to get far enough ahead of the lava that we can safely cross its path." Sally pointed down the dense shrub- and brush-covered hillside.

"Wait a minute," Jessica said, slipping off a boot. "If we're going to be running through that, I'm getting dressed."

Blushing, Karina joined Jessica's frantic quest to get dressed. "We have to hurry. If we make a wrong turn or can't get through the thick shrubs, we'll be trapped between the streams of lava."

For the better part of an hour, Sally led them down the rugged hillside as fast as they could scramble. Karina worried that someone would slip and sprain or break an ankle—a situation that presented dire consequences. Speed was everything; speed was life.

Sally came to a halt near a tall tree. "I can't tell where the lava is. Does anyone see anything?"

"The hillside is burning above us," Devon said, "but I can't tell how far ahead of the lava we are."

"I'm light," Jessica said. "Lift me up against the tree. I might be able to see something."

"I'll help." Karina moved to Jessica's left side, while Devon positioned himself on Jessica's right. Sally helped lift Jessica until she stood on Devon's shoulders. Karina saw Jessica grab a scrawny tree branch to keep from falling.

"We're ahead of the lava," Jessica reported. "But not far enough. We've got to keep moving down and farther to the right."

Jessica's unwelcomed announcement sent them off again, sometimes running, sometimes sliding, and sometimes crawling down the steep, rocky slope—racing against time to gain an advantage against their lethal adversary. Branches lashed at Karina as she pushed her way through the thick shrubbery. She was thankful that she wore jeans. Her arms already bore several painful cuts where thorns had scratched her.

Time stood still. Nothing seemed to matter except her headlong rush downward. Putting one foot in front of the other, Karina forgot everything as she struggled through weeds and brush that seemed intent on denying her access to safety. She wasn't sure how long she scrambled, maybe fifteen minutes, maybe twenty. Fatigued muscles screamed at her every move, and her heels blistered in her boots, making each step a new misery. Breathing heavily through her mouth parched her throat, and her side ached from a terrible cramp that refused to go away.

Finally, when she thought she could go no farther, Sally called a halt. Everyone sank to the ground while her instructor shimmied up a small tree for a better view of the situation.

"I can't run anymore," Heather moaned beside her.

Karina gulped air before agreeing. "I can't go much farther either. I need to take physical education classes more seriously." She hoped she'd have the chance to attend another physical education class.

Sally rejoined the tired, dirty group. "I think we've gained a safe margin. We'll need to hurry, but we should be able to make it. Once on the other side of the lava, we can find a high spot and rest."

"Do you think the others got out?" Karina asked. She worried that Martin and the rest of the kids, especially Penny and the little girls, might not have made it to safety.

Sally shook her head. "I don't know, Karina. All I can tell you is that they had an easier trail and a more direct path." Sally ended further discussion in favor of moving to safety. The sun rose and bathed them in bright daylight as they fought exhaustion to reach the top of a ridge. Once there, Karina saw that they had safely crossed in front of the river of lava that flowed steadily, neither increasing nor decreasing speed.

Lack of water and terrific thirst kept Karina and the rest of the group silent as they rested on the luscious, green ridge and watched the ever-creeping lava flow past. Sally allowed them almost an hour to rest before urging them to follow her westward, away from the lava.

Around ten o'clock in the morning, they reached a road. Less than an hour later, a park ranger found them. He transported Karina and her group to a staging area where all of the displaced tourists and campers anxiously sought news of lost friends and relatives.

On the way, Karina asked the park ranger about Martin and the kids, but he informed her that he had not been to the staging area and didn't know who was there. Seeing her dismay, he informed her that, as far as he knew, no one had been injured by the eruption. He also told her that only a handful of campers and hikers had not been found.

In spite of the park ranger's reassurance, Karina's heart raced. Butterflies filled her stomach and left her queasy until the car pulled into the relief staging area. Even before Martin reached her, Karina knew things were okay. Martin's smile eased her torment and told her no harm had come to any of those she held dear.

"Penny, Cindy, and Kiwi are with Dr. and Mrs. Winfield," Martin said as a way of greeting her. Then he did something so unlike him that Karina didn't know what to say. Martin lifted her off her feet and hugged her to him. "I'm so happy you're all safe. I hated leaving you behind."

Warm tears filled her eyes. She didn't know what to say, so she simply returned Martin's hug. He set her down and greeted Sally and the rest of the new arrivals. By the time Martin finished congratulating them on their successful escape, Joe and the rest of the troop crowded around. Happy tears flowed as story after anxious story circled among the teens and adults. Karina discovered that Martin's group had easily made it to safety before the advancing lava. He had paced nervously all night and morning, waiting for news about them.

Martin commanded everyone to get something to eat and drink. Then he ordered them to get some rest, which brought an end to the reunion. Karina made her way to a Red Cross food tent and drank five glasses of water before eating a bowl of soup and a toasted cheese sandwich. She wanted to talk with Martin more about the little kids, but the long night and exhausting day had drained her energy, leaving her barely able to finish her meal.

Joe helped her to a large tent that served as the women's dormitory. He quickly pulled her around to the side of the tent—away from sight—and kissed her. Then he hugged her tightly. She wanted to return his kiss but hesitated too long and missed her chance. Joe hugged her tightly and left without speaking.

Karina entered the large tent, which held twenty cots. She found a cot next to Heather, slipped off her boots and jeans, and slid under a crisp white sheet. She wanted a shower and something for her blisters, but fatigue pushed all other priorities from her mind. Even the slight aftershocks that frequently rattled the tent couldn't command her attention.

Two days had passed since Karina's frantic escape. She sat in the last row of seats inside Martin's new command center: a large tent he had rented. Martin stood before a white marker board. "Lava is flowing in two streams from Kilauea: here and here." He made two wide red marks indicating the flowing lava. "We've already had one close call, so we're changing gears a little. The FAA has forbidden any flights over the lava except for scientific flights, so we are going to break into two groups. One group will head overland to observe and make a video of the continuing eruption. The other group will join me at sea to do some underwater photography of the lava flowing into the ocean. As we have a number of highly qualified divers with us, I think this would be a fantastic opportunity to see how lava becomes new land."

Karina glanced at her watch, noting that it was twenty-three minutes after ten o'clock in the morning. Less than an hour earlier, she had phoned Penny and Cindy. Both girls were doing well, and Kiwi was back with her father, who was preparing to take her back home. He evidently felt Kiwi had seen enough volcanic eruptions, even for a last wish. Penny had told Karina how Kiwi had cried at the news, but her father had been firm.

"Karina, are you paying attention?" Martin's question broke through her thoughts.

She shook her head. "Sorry, sir. I didn't mean to daydream."

Martin gave her a warning look before continuing. "I was saying that you, Heather, and Jessica would join Joe and me at sea. We will leave within the hour. I've arranged with the American Geological Institute to use their boat. A team of Institute divers will be in charge of the overall dive; however, I'm placing you as the team leader for our students. Get your gear, and let's hit it."

Karina felt privileged that Martin trusted her. She was a better diver than Joe and Heather. Still, she didn't really want the responsibility. She just wanted to be told what to do. Karina decided that responsibility weighed heavily on one's conscience. For once, she wanted only to follow orders.

She gathered her gear and climbed into the van. A short time later, she sat next to Heather aboard a small cabin cruiser as it sped to their destination. "You should be in charge. You have more diving hours than I do."

"No chance," Heather said, smirking at her. "I learned long ago how to stay out of positions of authority. I don't do them well. Like, you're a natural. Live with it."

Heather's remarks made Karina feel proud. Not long ago, she doubted that anyone would have thought her responsible. "Thanks, but I don't feel up to responsibility at the moment."

The boat came into sight of a huge steam cloud ascending into the sky and ended all conversation. Karina saw red specks high in the steam cloud and marveled at the sight. The awesome power that they would soon witness from beneath the sea silenced everyone.

Karina took a deep breath and wondered what the next few hours might bring. She climbed into her scuba gear and checked her equipment. Jessica and Heather were her partners for the dive. She slipped on her fins, stepped from the platform, and plunged into the cool ocean water. After Jessica and Heather entered the water and joined her, she began her descent.

Karina trembled and felt slightly nauseated as water covered her head. She checked to make sure that Heather and Jessica followed her. Descending through the churning water, she saw the reason for her apprehension—a bright red glow that instantly turned cool ocean water to steam.

CHAPTER 13

A Hot Time at Sea

Karina grabbed Heather's buoyancy control device, usually called a BCD. The BCD was a jacket that held the scuba air tank. It had an air pocket that helped her stay at a certain level without sinking or rising. Heather had been so intent on taking video of the lava below them that Karina wasn't sure she had seen the signal to ascend.

Heather made eye contact with Karina and shook her head. She took the white slate and pencil attached to her left wrist and scribbled a note to Karina saying that she was in a good position for filming and wanted to stay.

Pointing upward toward the bubbles trailing Jessica's ascent, Karina again indicated for Heather to surface. The tall, lanky teen obeyed and began slowly ascending. Karina kept pace. She wasn't sure why Jessica suddenly started an ascent without first notifying her, but Jessica always followed safety procedures, so Karina knew something was wrong.

Upon breeching the surface, Karina spit out her regulator. "What happened?" Automatically, she inflated her BCD, turning it into a life preserver that kept her afloat and in rhythm with the two-foot waves sweeping the area. She floated close to her friend.

Bobbing on the waves, Jessica turned to face Karina. "I had a free-flowing regulator that I couldn't stop. I was low on air, so I made straight for the surface while I still had enough air to do a controlled ascent. Sorry, I guess I kind of panicked."

Karina relaxed. "Don't worry about it. You did the right thing."

Heather approached from behind Jessica. "Like, what's up?"

Jessica raised her malfunctioning regulator. "Equipment problem."

Karina motioned for the girls to swim to the boat. "Let's go ahead and change tanks while Jessica changes her regulator. We've got a great view of the eruption. If we change tanks and replace camera batteries, we should be able to get another thirty minutes of video before lunch."

Heather and Jessica agreed. All three exchanged excited tales of what they had seen below as Karina led them to the boat. After climbing onboard, she explained the situation to Steve, the Geological Institute diver in charge of her team. Then Karina slipped out of her scuba gear for a quick trip to the ship's bathroom, or *head* as sailors called it. Twenty minutes and two glasses of water later, Karina herded Jessica and Heather over to the entry platform.

"I'm getting great video, but it needs scale," Heather said, slipping into her scuba gear. "Karina, why don't you and Jessica swim down a little closer to the lava? That way I can get some video with perspective?"

"Closer?" Karina asked. "What do you mean by closer?" She looked at the steam cloud rising high into the sky.

"Yeah," Jessica added, "that's a lot of heat and power you're talking about."

"Not real close," Heather said, adjusting her scuba gear. "Like, just close enough to give me some scale. You don't have to go too far. Descend another fifteen feet or so from where I am. That should give the video perspective and a frame of reference everyone can understand."

Karina performed some mental calculations. "We should be able to do twenty feet without any problem, but we stop as soon as the water temperature becomes uncomfortable. I don't want anyone taking any chances."

Jessica pointed seaward. "Martin and Joe are coming. Maybe we should run this by Martin first. Fifteen feet closer to the lava would put us right at the safety limit that he set."

"Probably a good idea," Karina agreed, sliding her face mask into place. "Let's do it."

She didn't wait for a reply. Instead, she took a long stride off of the platform and hit the water, scissor kicking to keep from sinking too far. Karina surfaced and gave the okay signal to Steve. After checking that Jessica and Heather had entered safely, she intercepted Martin and Joe.

"How was your dive?" Martin asked, stopping to speak with Karina. Joe swam to her side.

"Great," Karina said, gently kicking her legs to fight against a slight current. "Jessica had a regulator problem, so we came back to get her a new one and change tanks. Heather is getting some great video, but she wants Jessica and me to go down another fifteen feet; she wants to get some scale for her video. That depth takes us close to the safety limit you set for us."

Martin paused for a moment before speaking. "No deeper than sixty feet, I don't want any accidents."

"Be careful," Joe said. "I've got two pictures where the lava had gas bubbles burst and throw hot globs of lava out from the main flow."

Karina smiled at Joe's concern. Knowing that he worried about her thrilled her. "We'll be careful," she promised. "See you after our dive."

The descent was uneventful, but Karina kept a wary eye on the slowly flowing lava. Only three minutes into the filming session, a small section of lava bubbled and flung hot red globs high into the water. Even though the molten rock came nowhere near her or Jessica, Karina heeded Joe's warning and forced her group—against Heather's objections—to move another twenty feet from the glowing lava that oozed its way across the ocean floor. Heather quickly returned to filming the scene. Karina and Jessica swam around and pointed toward the lava so that Heather had perspective for the video.

When Heather moved away to film a section with Jessica, Karina hovered motionlessly and watched, totally amazed at the raw power creeping toward her. The steaming, red glob gently rolled forward relentlessly. Water continually turned to steam and headed for the surface, but the current pushed the steam cloud behind the lava, leaving a perfectly clear view. Only the leading edge was red. Cold ocean water quickly cooled the glowing liquid. The cooled basalt lava quickly turned black, making it look like a huge black snake with a bright red head.

Fish swam much closer to the lava than Karina dared. She was comfortable at her distance—some seventy feet away—but she figured the water temperature would rise sharply if she moved closer.

Jessica signaled Karina and pointed to her right. Karina couldn't believe her eyes. Six divers on three underwater propulsion devices shaped like miniature torpedoes with handles—two divers to a device—neared the lava flow. Using the propulsion system's greater speed, each pair of divers seemed to be playing chicken with the lava, trying to see who could come closest to the head of the flow, which was the hottest part of the volcanic stream.

Karina indicated to Jessica that the divers were crazy. Without warning, a large spurt of lava burst from the main flow and sprayed one group of divers as they raced near the front of the oozing danger. One diver—the one in control of the propulsion device—let go and drifted toward the ocean floor. The other diver grabbed the device and desperately tried to gain control of the erratically zooming machine but couldn't and slammed into the ocean floor.

Karina pointed to the diver drifting to the ocean floor and indicated with hand signals for Heather and Jessica to help that diver. She descended to help the scooter driver, who now lay motionless on the rocky ocean floor—only yards from the red death inching steadily closer. If she didn't hurry, the diver had no chance.

The water warmed dramatically as she neared the motionless figure. Her depth gauge read seventy-two feet. Rocks shot past her; one barely missed her head. The seawater became a sauna. Steam bubbles and small rocks hurtled upward not more than a few yards from the injured diver. As she reached her victim, Karina immediately noticed that the diver was a young female who was still breathing through her regulator.

Steam bubbles burst forward; a small rock hit Karina above her left forearm. She bit down hard on her regulator's mouthpiece to keep from screaming. Her left arm felt as if someone had taped a hot coal to it. Fighting against pain, she reached down and released the diver's weight belt. The injured girl floated toward the surface. Using her good right arm, Karina grabbed her victim's tank and held on tightly.

At the same time, she frantically kicked—angling her ascent away from the advancing lava. Burning pain spread throughout her left arm, but she grimly fought back the pain and continued a controlled ascent, releasing all of the air from her BCD.

Ten feet from the surface, she tried to reach the injured girl's BCD to release air, but searing pain in her arm made her dizzy and forced her to abort the effort. Unable to hold on any longer, she released the girl's leg and watched her shoot upward. Karina's ascent brought her close to her victim.

"Help!" Karina yelled. She pushed the power inflate button on the girl's BCD. She vaguely noted that the injured diver floated with her head out of the water. The intense pain in Karina's left arm forced her to reach across with her right hand to reach her own inflator button. She hit the hose that held the button and knocked it from the snap that held it in place. The hose moved out of her reach, and she couldn't force her left arm to work. The heavy weight of her scuba gear pushed down on her, and her legs quickly fatigued. As she sank below the surface, she dimly thought Joe was going to be really angry with her for drowning.

In shadowy darkness, pain seared through her arm. A malicious tormenter peeled her flesh away. *Funny*, Karina thought. *I didn't think anyone felt pain in heaven. Perhaps I'm not in heaven! With my record, I probably got turned away.* More pain discouraged further rebuke of past behavior; she screamed aloud. Then she panicked and held her breath. She didn't seem to have trouble breathing, but she couldn't find her regulator. A horrible smell brushed away the darkness; she yelled again.

"Stop kicking, Karina," Martin said firmly, wafting an ammonia inhalant under her nose. "I've got to cut away the rest of your wet suit. I can't see how bad that burn is until I get your suit off."

Karina stopped yelling and kicking. A weight suddenly pressed upon her legs, and a second weight restrained her arms. Martin's figure came into better focus; she noticed that Heather held her legs still, and Joe pinned her arms to the bunk. The low white ceiling and the steady rocking informed Karina that she was back on the boat. Evidently, she hadn't drowned, but she had no idea how she had survived.

"How did I get here?" she asked. A sudden fear made her gasp. "What about the others?"

Joe answered as Martin began the devilishly painful act of cutting off the part of her wet suit that had melted onto her arm. "Heather and Jessica brought up one diver; he's going to be okay, but he's got a nasty burn. The girl you saved has a broken collarbone and some cracked ribs, but she's going to recover."

"Ouch!" Karina screamed as Martin finished cutting off the wet suit's sleeve, exposing the burn on her left arm. She looked at it, expecting to see charred flesh all the way to the bone. "Is it bad?"

"More painful than serious," Martin said, applying a cold, wet compress to the area. "You were lucky. It was a glancing blow. Had the lava hit you directly, it would have given you a very severe burn."

"Hey, hero." Heather pinched Karina's right thigh. "Next time I go with you. We're a team. Remember?"

Karina smiled weakly at Heather's teasing. "No, we aren't. Next time I stay back and supervise. You and Jessica can do all the work. I'll applaud your efforts."

"Next time," Joe butted into the conversation, "Karina dives with me. Every time you two get together, someone gets hurt."

"There won't be any more diving in this area for us," Martin said. He placed an ice pack on Karina's head and patted her good arm. "We have all the video we need. We're going back to shore and doing some editing. This young lady is on her way to the hospital to have that arm examined by a doctor."

Karina noticed Jessica's absence. "Where's Jessica? She isn't hurt is she?"

"Jessica's fine," Joe said. "She volunteered to go with Steve on the other boat. They are transporting the injured divers back to the marina in their own boat. Steve wants to make sure the kids' parents are aware of the stupid stunt they pulled."

Joe and Heather finished filling in the blanks on the trip back to shore. The divers were a bunch of girls and boys from a private school for rich kids. One of the boys had *borrowed* the boat and equipment without his father's knowledge. The oldest kid was only thirteen. Joe felt they were lucky to be alive.

Karina spent a miserable afternoon at the hospital. A nurse started her on an IV, which really upset her. Though her injury turned out to be only a second-degree burn, that didn't make the treatment pleasant. Karina squirmed and bit her lip as the doctor treated and dressed her wound. The burn covered a circular area nearly two inches in diameter. Being shuttled from one room to another—in a less-than-fashionable hospital gown—caused Karina's mood to take a turn for the worse.

When her treatment finally ended, she dressed in clothes that Martin had dropped off for her. Currently, she sat outside the discharge window, waiting for Martin to finish getting her released. The hospital policy required her to remain in a wheelchair until she was discharged.

"What took so long?" Karina stood and started to push the wheelchair away. "I'm ready to blow this place. My arm is killing me; I want to go and rest."

Martin shook his head. "Sit down. You have one more obstacle to face before we go, so get back in the wheelchair and let's get to it."

Martin's tone left no room for argument, so she seated herself into the uncomfortable confines of her *chariot*. "What obstacle? Will it hurt?"

"Maybe, maybe not." Martin pushed the wheelchair to the elevator, hit the button, and waited for the door to open before saying more. "Your presence has been requested by one of the patients of this establishment. I think it would be good for you to pay a short visit to the requester."

Karina tried to pry more information from Martin as he punched the button that took them to the fourth floor, wheeled her down three long hallways, and deposited her outside a private room. Fear that another seriously ill child might be inside clutched at her heart. Martin knocked on the door.

A tall, dark-haired Asian man dressed in a black business suit opened the door and shook Karina's hand. "Thank you, for coming. I'm Bob Lee, Victoria's father. She has something to tell you."

"Do I know you?" she asked the man, looking to Martin for an explanation. "Who's Victoria?"

In place of an explanation Martin said, "I'll be back in an hour." He nodded to Mr. Lee and departed, leaving Karina totally frustrated.

"Victoria is my daughter. You saved her from drowning—or worse—this morning," Mr. Lee said. "She wants to see you. I've not had much success in speaking with her since her mother and I divorced. I'd really appreciate it if you could take some time and find out why she did such a stupid stunt. I threatened to send her to live with her mother, and she began throwing things. Being a teenager yourself, I thought maybe she'd speak to you, especially since she begged me to bring you here. I'm grateful your father agreed."

She didn't tell Mr. Lee that Martin wasn't her father. She felt warm inside that he mistook Martin for her father. "I'll speak with her, but don't expect too much."

Mr. Lee thanked her and pushed her into a luxurious private room. A pretty Asian girl wearing a flowered nightgown sat on a hospital bed. The bed was raised so high that the child was almost in a sitting position. Her bare feet stuck out from beneath the short sheet covering her lap. Her right arm lay in a sling perched across her chest.

"You wanted to speak to me?" Karina said, awkwardly.

"Yes," Victoria said loudly. She looked at her father. "Alone."

Karina watched Mr. Lee leave; his shoulders sagged as if they held the weight of the world. She felt like reaching out and slapping the girl.

"I ..." Victoria paused, "I wanted to thank you for saving my life. Today's my thirteenth birthday. The gang thought a diving excursion would be a great way to celebrate. I guess we were wrong. Are you hurt?"

"I've had better days," Karina said sarcastically, surprised that Victoria was thirteen. The petite child looked no older than ten or eleven. Her anger rose but ebbed somewhat as Victoria grimaced. "How about you?"

The girl shook her head bouncing her black ponytail from side to side and took several shallow breaths before answering. "It hurts when I breathe, but it would hurt a lot more if that lava had reached me before you did. Forgive me?"

Karina looked into the child's green eyes. "No. My arm is killing me. You aren't sorry; I can tell. I've been a spoiled brat long enough to know one when I see one. If you don't get your act together, you might not be so lucky next time."

During the awkward silence that followed, Karina reflected on the truth she had spoken. Victoria didn't really want her forgiveness. The kid wanted to escape responsibility for her actions. She wanted Karina to let her off the hook. Yet, Karina reasoned that there had to be *some* good in the kid. She did ask to see her, and—to some extent—she did apologize. Karina decided that Victoria was searching for something to help her make sense out of her world. A sudden inspiration gave Karina the necessary compassion to break the awkward silence.

She rose from her wheelchair and sat on the bed next to Victoria. "You can't find what you're looking for by getting yourself hurt. As I said before, I've been a brat myself. When I was your age, I was about the worst person on Earth. I was angry beyond belief—mad at the entire world."

"How … how did you change?" Victoria asked in a soft, trembling voice. "My father doesn't want me, and I can't stand my mother. She ran out on us—on me. I hate the things I do, but I can't seem to stop. Every time I promise myself that I will change, I break the promise as soon as I speak with Dad."

Remembering back to the terrible fights she had with her aunt and uncle before coming to Blue Horizons, Karina felt some sympathy. "You've got to find someone to trust, someone who won't put up with your nonsense."

Victoria stared out the window, and Karina saw a tear roll down the girl's cheek. "I don't think such a person exists."

Karina figured now was a good time to pass her inspiration on to Victoria. If her idea worked, the child was certainly in for an attitude adjustment—maybe a lifesaving attitude adjustment. "That school you go to must cost a lot of money. How do you afford it?"

"Dad pays for it. He makes a lot of money." Victoria's tone expressed disgust. "Why?"

Karina gently placed her hand on the girl's good shoulder. "I think it's time you changed schools."

For the rest of that hour, she explained about Blue Horizons and how the school had changed her and many other kids. By the time Martin returned, she had Victoria convinced. Another hour convinced Mr. Lee. Blue Horizons would have a new student for the fall semester.

"Nice going." Martin helped Karina out of the wheelchair as they reached the hospital entrance. "I thought you might be able to relate to Victoria's situation and offer some advice. Blue Horizons might be able to help her—once we come to an understanding."

Karina smiled at Martin's poorly disguised suggestion that Victoria had some really tough times ahead. "I had a good teacher," she said.

Martin patted her head and led the way to the parking lot. Karina felt important. She turned to Martin with the intent of bragging, but a shout stopped her. Dr. Winfield ran across the parking lot.

"Penny and Kiwi have run away," Dr. Winfield said between deep breaths. "Penny left me a letter saying that she was going with Kiwi to see another volcanic eruption. The child had a very bad seizure last night. Penny is trying to fulfill the child's last wish, just as Karina filled Penny's."

CHAPTER 14

Eruption

Karina staggered at Dr. Winfield's announcement. Martin steadied her and guided her over to the van he had rented. Leaning against Martin, she mumbled, "We've got to find Penny. I know something bad is going to happen if we don't find them soon."

Martin opened the door and sat her in the front passenger seat. "We'll find them."

Dr. Winfield put a hand on her shoulder. "The police are already searching, and park rangers are covering areas where Kilauea is erupting inland. They will find Penny and Kiwi if they go anywhere near an eruption. Joe and Sally are already flying search patterns around the lava flows, and the sheriff's department has a helicopter standing by."

"I want to help," Karina said in as steady a voice as she could muster. "I can't sit by and do nothing."

She expected Martin to go fatherly on her and tell her that she needed rest and that there were enough searchers out. To her amazement, he drove her to the ultralight field and radioed Joe. A short time later, she spotted for Joe as he flew.

All afternoon, Joe flew her over rivers of lava that flowed slowly down to the ocean. Flying in the front seat of *Jet Stream*, Karina watched for any sign of the two girls. She had wanted to fly, but logic dictated that Joe pilot the ultralight while she spotted. Joe had twice the experience, and he wasn't injured. Karina's emotions fluctuated from extreme anger—she was going to thrash Penny within an inch of her life—to wanting to hug both kids.

"Sorry," Joe said. "We're running low on fuel and sunlight. Time to head for the airfield."

"Right," Karina agreed. She didn't try to hide the disappointment in her voice. She knew Joe was just as concerned and just as frustrated. "Let's return using a different course; swing left over by that ridgeline to the east."

He did as she directed. Flying low, only five hundred feet above the trees, Karina used a hand to shield her eyes from the setting sun. Joe banked left toward the area where their landing field was located, and Karina slumped back against her seat.

"They have to be—" A flash of bright red set against the black boulders of a streambed drew Karina's attention. "Wait. Swing right up that streambed. I thought I saw two figures, one wearing a red T-shirt."

Joe did as commanded. "Are you sure? Martin said Penny was wearing a red St. Louis Cardinals T-shirt."

"I'm not positive," Karina said, truthfully. Instinct told her she had spotted the girls. "But I definitely saw something."

As the sun set lower and lower in the west, Karina searched to no avail for another sight of human presence. Joe helped by staying until the very last second, and he expertly landed the ultralight as the sun set. Heather and Jessica met them as Joe lifted the airplane's canopy and helped Karina out.

"Martin said to wait here until he gets back," Heather said, handing Karina a cup of ice water. "He and Sally have gone with a ranger to search the position you radioed in. Like, they're on horseback."

Heather handed Joe a cold drink. "He said for you guys to get something to eat and then to get to bed. He wants you in the air at first light if they don't find the kids tonight."

Karina gulped down the refreshing liquid. "Where's Dr. Winfield?"

"He's on foot with some park rangers." Jessica put an arm around Karina and ushered her toward one of the dormitory tents that Martin had rented so everyone could be close to the ultralights until someone found the little girls. "Dr. Winfield is amazing. He's really worried, but he doesn't let his emotions run wild. I bet it comes from being a doctor. I wish I could be as cool in an emergency."

Jessica left Karina and Joe outside the girls' dormitory tent and headed back to help fix dinner. Joe gave Karina a hug and kiss before departing for the evening. While she showered and climbed into clean underwear and an oversized T-shirt, Heather fetched her some soup and sandwiches.

"Get to bed," Megan ordered after Karina finished her meal and began discussing the situation with the rest of the girls. "Martin left me in charge."

"Right away, ma'am," Karina teased, saluting. But she obeyed Megan's command. Her bed, a cot, didn't exactly invite sleep. She rolled onto her good side. Her left arm ached in spite of the fact that Dr. Winfield had given her some medication to help control the pain.

Fatigue weighed heavily upon her. The day had been long, physically and emotionally demanding, and extremely frustrating. As hard as she tried, she couldn't sleep. Being tired but not sleepy led to hours of tossing and turning. A little past midnight, Karina slipped on a robe and went out to the bathroom.

Upon returning, she pulled a chair outside the tent and admired a beautiful star-filled sky. As far as she could tell, everyone else was asleep. A cool breeze fluttered, lifting the hem of her robe. Karina put her knees to her chin, tugged the robe around her legs, and enjoyed the solitude. Only worrying about Penny and Kiwi ruined the moment.

A shooting star flashed across the sky, and she made a wish for the little girls' safety. Penny had always been such an obedient and thoughtful child that Karina had trouble believing this situation was real and not one of her insidious nightmares.

A brilliant moon illuminated Mauna Loa's summit. She marveled at the massive volcano, but she knew it wasn't Hawaii's tallest mountain. Karina remembered Martin telling her that, with a total height of 32,000 feet, Mauna Kea—north of their location—was the highest mountain on Earth, even higher than Mount Everest, although the first 18,000 feet rose from the ocean floor to sea level. With a sigh, she decided to try to get some rest. She didn't want to be exhausted if Martin needed her. Karina doubted he would find the girls before morning. After a long look skyward, she retreated to bed.

The vibrating cot awakened Karina even before Megan's shouts. She sat up, firmly grasped the cot, and swung her legs over the side, searching with bare feet for her boots. Flashlights wobbled erratically inside the dark tent. Frightened yells from her classmates added to the confusion. Karina decided to forget her boots and ride out the earthquake. Except for the large tent poles in the center, nothing could collapse on her and cause any real damage. She figured she was safer staying put than running blindly into one of her friends. The tent was in an open area, so she wasn't in any danger from falling trees or other objects.

As the shaking lessened, Karina felt that she had made the correct decision, but then the ground buckled and tossed her off her cot, as a wild stallion might throw off an inexperienced rider. She landed squarely on her rear and yelped in pain as the shock radiated to her tailbone. Rolling onto her stomach, she clasped her hands behind her head only seconds before the tent's heavy canvas collapsed around her, cocooning her in total darkness.

While the ground shook, Karina lay trapped beneath the canvas. The earth gave her chest and abdomen a violent massage. A hard rock pressing against her left hip bone sent sharp pain through her pelvis. She tried to move from the spot by curling her toes and pushing forward. The heavy canvas resisted the attempt, so she tried to move her left arm to get some leverage. Moving her arm happened to be a mistake; the canvas caught the bandage covering her burn and sent waves of pain cascading through her arm. Resigned to waiting out the quake, rock or no rock, she concentrated on controlling her breathing.

The violent trembling ended, but Karina lay still and silently counted to thirty before moving. She wanted to make sure that the quake was over before trying to work her way free. While she counted, she physically checked her condition. Her butt ached terribly from the drop that landed her on the ground. The throbbing in her left arm remained an agony, and she was sure she would have a nasty bruise on her left hip bone. At least the blisters on her feet had healed enough to be only a minor inconvenience.

"Karina! Where are you?" Joe's voice sifted through to her.

"I'm down here." Karina pushed the canvas up a little with her right hand.

"Keep talking," Joe said. "The tent has dozens of bumps in it. I can't tell which is you."

"I'll count," she said, using her right arm to push the canvas a few inches from her face. "One, two, three ..."

By the time Karina reached twelve, she heard a ripping sound behind her right ear and felt the refreshing coolness of the night air. In less than a minute, Joe cut away enough canvas to free her head and shoulders.

"Thanks, Joe. I was suffocating in—" Karina looked at Joe, but it wasn't her rescuer that caught her attention. Far above Joe, the once dark form of Mauna Loa glowed a bright red and filled the night sky. Large red-tailed comets sprang into the air, reached their apex, and streaked earthward.

"Are you hurt?" Joe asked, pulling Karina from the last restraining tent folds.

She answered without taking her eyes from Mauna Loa's fireworks display. "I hurt everywhere, but I don't think I have any major injuries. Is anyone else hurt?"

Joe guided her toward several figures sitting around a lantern someone had placed on a tarp. "None of the boys are hurt. They're searching through the collapsed tents for enough clothes for everyone. I think Megan broke a toe when she stumbled over a rock, but all of the other girls seem fine. They made it out before the tent collapsed."

Heather raced to them. "I'll take her from here. Sally wants you and Devon to see if the planes are damaged."

Karina squeezed Joe's hand. "Try to contact Martin with the radio. He has to find Penny. She's still out there somewhere."

"Hey," Heather said as Joe slipped away into the darkness. "Like, we're all making a fashion statement this evening."

In the pale glow emitted from the battery-powered lantern, Karina looked down at her attire. A large rip in her nightshirt attested to an imminent need for a new outfit. "It was too dark to find clothes."

Heather chuckled, "Don't worry about it. I didn't even bother to look for clothes. I'm wearing Paul's sweatshirt. Like, some hero, huh?"

Worry about Penny kept her from seeing any humor in their situation. "Been there myself. Where's Megan? Joe said she was hurt."

"Over there." Heather pointed to several Blue Horizons students crowded together. "Jessica's taking care of her."

Karina ambled over and saw that Jessica had taped Megan's injured toe to her other good toes. She talked briefly with each of the girls. During that time, the boys returned with an assortment of clothes.

After everyone was suitably dressed and had found socks and boots, Karina asked Joe, Heather, and Jessica to follow her to the ultralights. She used the pretext of trying to call Martin, but she had hastily formed a plan for finding Penny. Karina needed help, and she couldn't wait for Martin to return. The lava spilling down Mauna Loa flowed directly toward the valley where she had sent Martin in search of the kids. This was a major eruption. In her heart, Karina knew time was running out, and she wasn't about to stand by and do nothing.

"I don't know," Joe said. "It sounds awfully risky. Martin will have our heads."

Karina had just finished explaining her plan. She knew it was risky, but she didn't know what else to do. "I'm open to better plans, but I've got to do something. If you think it's too risky, I understand. Jessie?"

Jessica looked at her feet and then into Karina's eyes. "If Martin doesn't kill me over this, my parents will, but I'm in."

"Me too," Heather said. The tall girl smiled in a facetious manner. "I'm a natural brat rebelling against my father and authority. Like, I've got a reputation to uphold."

Karina returned Heather's smile, remembering the adventures she'd shared with Heather at Ocean Quest Academy and the truth in Heather's words. "Thanks. Joe?"

Joe didn't verbally answer. He walked over to Karina, lifted her off her feet, planted a firm kiss on her lips, and set her down. For the first time since meeting Joe, she saw tears in his eyes. Even when they had been stranded in the Amazon, Joe had never cried. His tears reminded Karina that she would be responsible for what happened from here on out.

"Thanks," she said, briefly hugging him. "The sun will rise in less than an hour. Let's hurry."

"I still think you should fly *Bluebird*." Joe held her hand. "Let me lead the ground search."

"As much as I hate to admit it," Karina said. "You're a much better pilot than I am. Besides, I want to be with Penny and Kiwi when we find them. We'll keep in touch by radio."

A voice of authority invaded the moment, calling for all Blue Horizons students to gather over at the light. Karina figured it was Sally's voice; it was too soft to be Martin's or Mr. Smithson's. She needed to get her group moving, or the rescue attempt would be over before it began. Karina knew that Sally's first priority would be to move them all back to the motel, and such a move meant that any rescue efforts from that point forward would be conducted solely by adults.

Karina motioned for Joe to get going and then led Jessica and Heather around the far end of the field. Karina hoped that the confusion of trying to get everyone organized would give her the precious minutes necessary to reach her objective: the three all-terrain vehicles (ATVs) Martin had rented to help haul equipment around.

In light provided by the rising sun, Karina saw Sally giving instructions. Her hunch had been correct. She saw the kids climb into one of the vans. As Sally turned in her direction, Karina dropped to hands and knees, using the brush for cover. She saw Heather and Jessica follow her example. A pang of guilt gave Karina a deep sense of remorse. Once before, she had broken rules and gone on an unauthorized rescue mission. Sally had also been in charge that time.

She reached the three-wheeled ATVs and climbed onto the seat of the one closest to her, the one with the radio she would need to talk with Joe. For a brief second, Karina almost changed her mind, almost ended her quest. Torn between loyalties, her determination faltered as she grappled between her desire to save the girls and not to disobey Sally again. She was about to tell Jessica and Heather to turn around when her hand brushed against the little gold cross that hung outside her T-shirt.

Karina held the cross in her hand, squeezed it tightly, and softly recited the inscription. "In Him all things are possible." It was the locket that Penny had given Karina during a particularly challenging time in her own life. The locket cemented her course of action. Without further thoughts about loyalties or consequences, she turned the ignition key, gunned the engine, and sped across the field. Over her shoulder, she saw that Jessica and Heather followed closely behind.

After twenty minutes of hard cross-country riding, Karina lost her perspective. She knew she was getting close to the lava flows. Steam and smoke drifted at her from every direction. She stopped her vehicle and reached for the handheld radio seated in a pouch on the ATV's handlebar.

"Road Runner to Path Finder, do you copy? Over." Karina used the code Joe had assigned. She scanned the early morning sky and saw the blue ultralight circling above. Joe was her safety net. From the air, he could direct them around the dangerous lava flows—at least for the few hours he had fuel to remain airborne.

"This is Path Finder," Joe's voice sprang from the radio. "Turn left and head on a course of 3-1-5 degrees. That should keep you clear of the lava and keep you on your planned course. Hurry, that lava is really moving. This has to be Mauna Loa's biggest eruption in decades. Over."

"Thanks, Path Finder," Karina said, thumbing her microphone. "Out." She turned to her partners in crime. "This way."

After a frustrating hour of course changes directed by Joe, Karina reached the location she sought—the spot where she hoped to find Penny. She shielded her eyes from the sun and was about to tell Jessica and Heather to split up and start searching the woods on foot when a voice came over the radio.

"Karina, I have you in sight. Turn your vehicles around and return to the main road immediately. Over." Martin's voice commanded.

Karina looked at the sky and spotted a second ultralight circling the area. She reached for the radio. "Martin, I'm sorry. Have you found Penny and Kiwi? Over."

"Not yet, but there are dozens of police, firemen, and park rangers searching for them," Martin said, anger filling each word. "They've already thoroughly searched that area. If the kids were there, they would have been seen. Now get back to that road. Over."

Tears of frustration filled Karina's eyes. She turned to her friends. "What do think?"

"Whatever you say," Jessica said.

Heather brushed hair from her eyes. "Like, we can't get into any more trouble than we're already in. Let's finish this."

Karina decided to thank Jessica and Heather for their trust and friendship and tell them the search was over, but she suddenly knew exactly where to find the girls.

Deciding that she couldn't abdicate the responsibility for the girls' safety to the chance that others might find them, she pressed the speak button on her radio. "Sorry, Martin. I've got one more place to look. Please forgive me. Over and out." She switched the radio to the planned alternate frequency. Joe had insisted that they would need a secret frequency when Martin found them. Karina admired Joe's wisdom and attention to detail.

"Where are we headed?" Jessica asked.

"Penny brought Kiwi out here to take pictures of the lava flow," Karina said.

"She pointed at Mauna Loa and the lava being tossed high above its main crater. "Where would Kiwi get the best picture of that?"

"The Wilderness Overlook," Jessica said. "That's where I'd go."

"Tell Joe," Heather said. "Like, he can confirm your hunch before we can get halfway there."

Karina keyed her microphone. "Joe, are you on this frequency? Over."

"Copy that, Road Runner." Joe stayed with formal radio procedure, which Karina found amusing since Joe knew Martin was already aware of their scheme. "What can I do for you? Over."

"Plot me a course to the Wilderness Overlook," Karina said. "Then head over and see if the kids are there. It's the best spot to take photos of Mauna Loa. Over."

Karina watched as Joe made a wide circle of the area. She also kept Martin's ultralight in sight. Martin was probably furious with her at the moment, and Karina was sure that their reunion would be very unpleasant. Never before had she so openly disobeyed him. If this had happened before Martin had become her guardian, Karina was sure it would mean her expulsion from Blue Horizons. She prayed Martin would go easy on Heather, Jessica, and Joe. She was prepared to take all of the blame.

"Road Runner," Joe called at the end of his route, "head back the way you came—but hurry. The lava is moving into that area, and volcanic ash is beginning to fall. Also, there are several police cars on the main road, so keep off the main trails. I'm going for a look. Be back soon. Over."

"Thanks, Joe," Karina said. "Talk with you soon. Out."

Staying away from the police and rangers would only be necessary long enough to reach the kids. After she found the girls, Karina wanted all the help she could get. Following Joe's suggestion, she worked her way over old dried lava flows and through dense brush. Jessica and Heather trailed closely behind. She also noted that Martin followed her progress.

"Rini!" Joe used Karina's nickname instead of formal procedure. "Your hunch is right on target. I've seen both Penny and Kiwi. I've already alerted Martin. He's notifying the rangers. He said to let them handle it."

Karina checked her position. She was only four or five minutes away. "No way, plot me a course to the kids."

"Turn left and follow the ridgeline. But be careful. Lava is flowing on both sides of your position. If you don't hurry, you'll be cut off," Joe said.

She turned left and gunned the ATV. Volcanic ash fell like a dry, dirty-white snow, limiting visibility to little more than a mile. As she put the radio to her mouth to thank Joe, she hit a bump and dropped it. Regretfully, she watched the radio hit hard rock and break apart. Anger welled inside her, and rough ground threatened to flip the ATV. Falling white ash limited her vision. She turned all her attention to reaching Penny.

"Karina!" Penny dashed to her as she pulled to a stop near the high rock crest called Wilderness Outlook.

She hugged the twelve-year-old to her for a moment and then shook her. "Don't ever scare me like that again. You've got everyone worried sick. Your dad is searching all over for you."

Penny looked down at her feet. "I had to help Kiwi. I thought you would understand."

Karina did understand Penny's actions. She gave her another quick hug and waved toward where Jessica and Heather waited. "Get Kiwi. We've got to get out of here."

As Penny turned to obey her last command, Karina heard the sickening sound of an ultralight engine sputtering. She searched through the ash-filled sky and saw Martin's plane circling high above and away from the falling ash. Then, to her horror, she saw Joe's plane descending. Breathlessly, she watched as the little plane dropped below her position.

"No!" Karina screamed as the ultralight crashed into heavy brush a quarter mile south of her position. "Joe!"

CHAPTER 15

On the Run

Volcanic ash blurred Karina's vision as she scrambled through the underbrush and worked her way to the crash site. The ash accumulated to a depth of nearly two inches and made the ground slippery. Breathing became torture. As rough, dry branches slapped against her face and whipped her legs, she heard only her own labored breathing and Heather's heavy footsteps. Fear pushed her on at a reckless pace.

Gasping and coughing, she stumbled downward, scrambled around a boulder, and missed a step. Karina's already bruised hip took the brunt of her fall. She yelped, rolled to her feet, and continued limping down the steep, rocky hill. The tail section of Joe's plane came into view. No matter what happened, she wouldn't stop until she reached him. She had to help Joe—if he was alive. Fortunately, she saw no smoke or any other signs of fire.

Running on legs that shook from oxygen debt and lactic acid buildup, Karina's knees buckled only yards from the crashed ultralight. She put her hands out as she fell forward and scraped her palms on coarse rocks hidden beneath the volcanic ash; she landed hard on her stomach. The impact knocked the remaining air from her tortured lungs. Crawling forward on hands and knees, tears blurred her vision, blinding her to the fact that no one sat inside the little plane's cockpit.

"Joe! Joe!" she screamed as she worked her way to the plane's shattered canopy. "Where are you?"

Adrenaline provided strength far beyond her capabilities. Karina's bloody hands pried open the left side of the badly bent canopy window frame. Wiping her eyes with the short sleeve of her T-shirt, Karina saw the bloodstained instrument panel, and her strength gave out. She sank to her knees, coughing and crying uncontrollably.

For what seemed an eternity, she placed her head against the aluminum tubing that framed the twisted seat where Joe had once piloted the doomed ultralight airplane.

She looked about frantically and yelled, "Joe! Joe! Call to me. How bad are you hurt?"

Heather grabbed her arm. "We don't have much time. You go down the hill and search. I'll head uphill."

"I suggest we all go uphill."

The familiar voice thrilled Karina. She and Heather turned as one, and Karina's emotional sobs increased until she cried uncontrollably. Tears of joy blurred her vision.

Joe hobbled from the dense brush and hugged her tightly. Heather patted Joe on the back. Karina noticed a deep gash above Joe's left eye and his bloody T-shirt. Regaining her composure, she leaned Joe against the wreckage and rummaged through the smashed plane until she found the first aid kit. She silently thanked Martin for including a first aid kit as standard equipment on each ultralight.

Thoughts of Martin turned Karina's head upward. She located his airplane circling, outside the range of falling ash. By the time Karina finished bandaging Joe's laceration and tended her own scrapes, falling ash had accumulated to a depth of more than three inches.

As Karina closed the first aid kit, Heather asked, "What now?"

"Let's get to the ATVs and get out of here," she said.

Joe shook his head. "We have to climb back to the overlook and wait for help. Before I lost my engine, I was coming in low enough to drop you a message to tell you that lava has encircled this area. The ATVs won't be any use."

"Like, great," Heather said. "How much time before the lava reaches the overlook?"

"I'm not sure," Joe said. He lifted the small emergency backpack Karina had salvaged from *Bluebird*'s wreckage. "Five hours? Maybe six, if we're lucky."

Karina coughed and cleared her throat. "Let's find a place to get out of this ash. Breathing all this acidic ash is going to kill us if the lava doesn't."

Covering her mouth with a bandana, Karina hiked slowly up the hill. Joe limped along behind her. Karina discovered that he had bumped his knee against the control panel during his crash landing. Heather came last. Besides danger from flowing lava and the persistent "ash snow" that made walking and breathing difficult, embarrassment hurried Karina along. In her desperate rush to reach Joe, she had dumped Penny and Kiwi's safety on Jessica. She sarcastically noted to herself that the day seemed to be getting better and better. If they didn't all die together before help arrived, she still had to face Martin's wrath. At least she had found Penny and Kiwi. That ought to count for something.

"Sorry," Karina offered her apology as Jessica helped her over the Wilderness Overlook's protective rail. "I should have consulted with you before running off like that."

"Forget it." Jessica turned and pulled Kiwi in front of her. "Do you want this one, or can I have her?"

While Heather helped Joe over the railing, Karina removed her bandana, knelt down, and took both of Kiwi's hands. Tears and ash stained the child's face. "Why?"

She said only one word, but it seemed to crush the little girl. Kiwi threw her arms around Karina, buried her head against Karina's chest, and bawled. The anger drained from Karina, and she held Kiwi until the child finished crying. The others moved over to the ATVs so she could be alone with Kiwi.

"I'm sorry," Kiwi sobbed. "I had to. Daddy was taking me back to the mainland. This was my only chance. Now I'm never going home again. I'm never going to see my dad or mom again. I'm so scared."

Kiwi's words tore Karina apart. She tightly hugged the little girl, unashamed at the tears rolling down her own ash-covered cheeks. Karina wanted to tell Kiwi not to cry, that everything would be all right, and that she'd have plenty of time to see her family again. But that might have been a lie, and she didn't want to give the child any false hopes. Instinct told her that Kiwi might be right.

"No matter what happens, we'll be here with you," she said. "We'll face whatever comes together."

Kiwi wiped tears from her dirty face. "Thanks, Karina. I knew you'd understand." The child buried her head against the comfort of Karina's chest, this time without tears.

Staring into a sky filled with ash, Karina no longer saw Martin's ultralight. She knew the falling ash presented a serious danger for airplane engines—ultralights or helicopters. Karina suspected that volcanic ash caused Joe's crash. She expected no immediate rescue by air.

Eventually, Joe led everyone down from the top of the overlook into the relative shelter of palm trees. They needed a plan, but no one suggested any ideas that had a chance of success. All the while, lava worked its way closer to their location. By Joe's computations, they had less than three hours before it reached them. Karina motioned for Penny and Kiwi to join the conversation.

"You know, this ash is extremely unusual for a shield volcano eruption," Kiwi said, sitting beside Karina.

"We'll talk about it in a minute," Karina said. "We're trying to figure out a plan to get us out of here."

"I think we'd better go now," Kiwi said.

"Me too," Penny agreed. "It's hard to breathe here. I don't think anyone can get to us. The lava has us surrounded, and all this ash makes flying impossible."

Karina could have throttled Penny for saying the obvious. She wanted to keep the truth of the impending danger from Kiwi until the very last minute. "Being surrounded by lava leaves us with nowhere to go. This is the safest spot for now."

"No it's not," Penny said, looking to Kiwi. "The lava tube should be safer than here. I don't think the lava will spill into it. The tube runs uphill from the entrance."

A small tremor barely halted Karina's reply. "What are you talking about?"

"The lava tube that Kiwi and I hid in," Penny said. "That's where we've been staying. It's just down the hill from here. The tube is hard to see, though. If Kiwi hadn't leaned against the bush that hides the opening, we'd never have found it."

"You mean you've been here the entire time?" Karina asked in amazement. "We thought we saw you over by the Kilauea eruption, yesterday."

Again, Penny looked to Kiwi. This time the child nodded. Penny continued, "We were over there. We knew that you'd be looking for us there, so we just went to take pictures and then came back here."

The magnitude of Penny and Kiwi's conspiracy angered Karina, pushing aside their present circumstances for the moment. She shook her finger at Penny. "You discovered that lava tube earlier this week while we were sightseeing, and you didn't tell us. You planned this runaway scheme—just in case you needed it. You wait until we get out of here. You are going to regret the day that you pulled such a stupid stunt."

Penny's sudden tears and pained expression made Karina wish that she'd kept her anger under control.

Joe came to her aid, giving her time to calm down and think. "Let's stay focused here. If we don't survive, punishment will be irrelevant. If we do survive, there will be people standing in line to hand it out."

Karina gave Joe a weak smile of gratitude and took Penny's hand. "Show us the lava tube. I'd like to get out of this ash."

Heather and Jessica added words of agreement, and they were on their way. Penny led them back to the Wilderness Overlook and down its north slope. The lava tube was so covered by brush that it would have taken a wildfire or, as in Kiwi's case, a lucky accident to find it. Even then, the opening was so small that Heather and Joe had difficulty squeezing through.

Inside the lava tube, Karina discovered how proficient Penny and Kiwi were at planning. From a supply of items more bountiful than Karina thought possible, Penny quickly provided everyone with a flashlight, extra batteries, and a chemical light stick. She also handed each person a couple of one-liter water bottles, several chocolate almond bars, and a small snack-sized can of tuna fish.

"Sorry," Penny apologized to Karina each time she handed her an item.

She ruffled Penny's hair. "I love you, you little turkey. Forget it."

"Well, campers," Joe said after everyone settled around the lava tube's narrow opening. "Here's how I see the situation. The lava is going to reach this spot in about two hours. It may close off this opening. I agree with Penny's assessment that the lava will not flow in here, at least not very far. But," Joe paused, "if it covers this opening, this lava tube could become our tomb. Nobody knows we are here. Everyone will think the lava got us."

Karina looked at the dim, black tunnel and shivered at the thought of being trapped inside without any light. She shined her flashlight up the tunnel and noted that it quickly expanded in height. Someone Kiwi's size could walk upright. The rest would have to stoop or crawl on hands and knees.

"Maybe this thing has another entrance," Karina suggested. "I say, let's explore."

As soon as she made the suggestion, Kiwi's spirits improved dramatically. Penny beamed at the idea. Jessica and Heather began gathering supplies. Only Joe made no move.

"Something wrong?" Karina asked. She eased herself down beside him. Her hip hurt badly from earlier falls, and her skinned hands made the move quite painful.

Joe shook his head. "No. I just don't have much hope for success. This lava tube has been here for a long time. If it had other openings, someone would have discovered them by now. I don't think we have much chance if the lava reaches this point. I sure botched things up this time."

Karina understood Joe's melancholy attitude. He thought they were all going to die, and he blamed himself for their present situation. She leaned against him and rested her head on his shoulder. "This is really all my fault—if you don't count Penny and Kiwi's part in it. I'm the one who talked everyone into this half-baked rescue attempt. I should have waited for Martin. I should have trusted him."

"If you hadn't come, the little kids would be facing this all alone. I just wish we had left Heather and Jessica out of it." Joe allowed his head to meet hers.

"I'm not giving up yet," Heather said, sliding down beside Joe. "Like, this was my choice. I could have said no. I wanted to be a part of it. So don't blame yourself on my part."

"That goes double for me," Jessica said. She sat down next to Karina. "You left me out of all of your other escapades: rescuing those two little girls from the flood and saving Cindy from the Amazon. I wasn't even with you during the shipwreck. Each time, I promised myself that I'd be with you next time. You couldn't have kept me from being here—no matter how it turns out."

She didn't want to cry, but Jessica's friendship and devotion hit her hard. She embraced her friend tightly, and Jessica joined her teary serenade.

"Like, I hate to interrupt this sob session," Heather said, "but it's time to go. Kiwi, you're the smallest. Lead on, my dear."

After an hour of painful, hunched over travel, the lava tube became level and opened enough for everyone to walk upright. Karina and Joe limped along, and the footing became very rough. Then another problem stopped them completely. The main lava tube branched off into three sections, two large enough to easily walk through and one that required crawling on hands and knees.

"To keep from getting lost, I suggest taking the tube to the left," Joe said. They all sat in a circle around one flashlight, saving batteries. "That way, if there is no opening at the end, all we have to do is take the next passage on our left when we exit back into this chamber. We won't forget which tube we've already explored."

Karina said, "That tube is tall enough to walk in without crawling. I think we should conserve light by using one of the chemical lights. That gives us longer battery power. We can't probe into dark places with the light sticks."

"Good thinking," Penny said, praising Karina's idea.

She patted Penny on the back. "Thanks, but don't try buttering me up. You're still in trouble."

Penny grimaced. "Of that, I'm certain."

Karina gave Penny a playful bop on top of her head and then hugged Kiwi. She worried about the child. The little girl had started the exploration very energetically and full of adventure, but Kiwi had barely spoken during the last half hour. Karina feared she might be headed for another collapse.

Five hours of traveling fully explored the two easy lava tube sections—but to no avail. All they earned for their troubles were two dead ends and long return hikes—made more difficult because of two strong earthquakes. Now, they rested before the shorter tube—their last option. While they rested, Joe and Jessica made a trip back to their original entry hole, only to report that lava had filled at least a hundred feet of the passageway. They had no choice but to explore their final option.

Karina looked down the passageway. *Please, God,* she prayed silently, *let this lead somewhere. I know it will take a miracle to get out of here. Please give us a miracle.*

Without speaking, Karina led the weary group down the narrow tube. Eventually, it opened and branched off in several more directions. She called a halt.

"According to my watch, it's almost midnight. Let's call it a night." Karina sat down and pulled Kiwi onto her lap, which hurt because of the bruises on her hip. The little girl fell asleep almost before Karina got comfortable.

Without talking, she watched the others eat some chocolate, make small talk, and fall asleep. Other than the embarrassing moments when someone had to go to the bathroom, the day's exploration had been endurable—tiring—but endurable.

Kiwi's breathing became irregular just before morning. Karina tried to get Kiwi to eat some chocolate and drink some water. After much coaxing, Kiwi ate two tiny chocolate squares and sipped some water. Then she fell back into a deep sleep. Her breathing became more stable, and Karina decided they should stay put as long as it took for Kiwi to recover.

Having made the decision for a longer rest, she made herself comfortable between Penny and Kiwi. The hard floor and her assortment of minor injuries made it difficult to sleep, but exhaustion finally led to fitful slumber.

Karina dreamed that she was running down the hill again, racing toward Joe's crashed ultralight. Again, branches continued to slap her face, each slap stinging more than the last. The branches seemed to have evil intent. Each time one landed against her face, it called out her name, teasing her.

"Karina! Wake up!" A particularly hard slap opened Karina's eyes. One slap later, she focused on her adversary—Kiwi.

"We've got to go!" Kiwi pointed down a side tunnel they had not explored. A red glow slowly moved their way.

Karina's mind cleared instantly. "Joe, get everybody moving. Lava!"

"Where did that come from?" Jessica demanded.

"Lava must have burned its way into that tube," Joe said, helping Heather to her feet. "Hurry, we don't have much time. Feel the heat?"

Blindly, Karina grabbed Penny and Kiwi. She led them down the only passageway large enough to walk through. She had forgotten food and water in her haste. Using her flashlight, Karina moved as quickly as possible without danger of tripping. Any delay might prove fatal.

After about a minute, she stopped long enough to see that Joe, Heather, and Jessica followed. They trailed a few yards behind Karina; so did the lava. If this passage didn't lead somewhere, they were doomed.

Fear drove her onward. Karina ignored Kiwi's labored breathing and Penny's cries to slow down. She hated pushing Kiwi and knew the child might collapse at any moment, but stopping promised a horrible death. Joe eventually caught her and put Kiwi on his back. Then he motioned for Karina to go.

Burning lungs and aching legs demanded rest, but the lava kept coming. Its menacing glow gave everyone the strength needed to keep moving forward as the red death encroached at a steady pace. If they didn't hit a dead end, they might have a chance. The passage began to incline slightly, and Karina guessed they had pulled at least a hundred yards ahead. She prayed the incline would slow or stop the lava.

"Stop!" Joe yelled, grabbing onto Karina's shoulder.

She stopped and looked at Joe. He pointed to the floor a few feet in front of her, and she shined her light in the indicated direction. The beam from her flashlight fell on empty space. If Joe hadn't stopped her, Karina would have walked into it. At her feet lay a new detriment, an opening at least twenty feet across—too far to jump.

"No!" Karina stomped her foot in anger. "What now?"

"Is the lava going to get us?" Penny asked.

"What's going on?" Jessica demanded.

"We've come to a large hole," Joe said. "How far are we ahead of the lava?"

"Not far enough," Kiwi said. "I can see red down the tunnel."

Lying on her stomach, Karina shined her light into the abyss. The light didn't reach the bottom. Joe and the others joined her. Lying shoulder to shoulder, she discovered that Jessica had rescued their meager supplies.

"Give me something to drop into the pit," Karina said. "Maybe we can tell how deep it is by counting how long it takes to hit bottom."

Jessica gave Karina a can of tuna, which she dropped into the opening. The sound of an object hitting water rewarded her effort.

"That didn't take long," Heather said.

"It can't be too deep," Jessica said, hopefully. "The can took less than two seconds to hit the water."

"It could still be over twenty feet," Joe said thoughtfully. "Let's drop a light stick and see what happens.

"I'll do it," Karina said. "I've got the best position."

"Hurry!" Penny urged. "The lava is getting closer. I can feel the heat."

Horror filled Karina as she frantically took Joe's light stick and dropped it into the pit. In its dull glow, Karina estimated the water to be about eight or ten feet below them. The light stick sank deep enough that its glow became a tiny speck.

With no way to estimate the water's depth and the red glow of lava drawing ever nearer, Karina determined that they had only two choices—neither of which offered much hope for survival. They could stay put and hope the lava didn't reach them, or they could jump into the water. If the water was deep enough to break their fall, if the water led to another passageway, and if there was somewhere they could stand, they just might have a chance—too many ifs. Deciding that drowning was the better way to die, Karina rose to her feet and reached out both hands, one grabbed Penny's hand and the other secured Kiwi's.

"Jump!" Karina had a vague idea that she should have been more romantic with what would probably be the last word she ever spoke. She looked upward for a last glimpse of Joe, but water closed around her before she found him—cold, deep water.

CHAPTER 16

The Darkness before Dawn

Kicking furiously, Karina worked to get Kiwi's head above the water. Penny had jerked away from her the instant they hit the water. Kiwi clung to her, not kicking to help, and it took all of her strength to reach the surface.

"Penny!" she shouted. "Penny!"

"Here," Penny called from behind her.

As Karina joined Penny, three more splashes in close succession told her that Joe and the girls had joined her desperate attempt to survive. Kiwi gained confidence, pulled away, and floated next to her. Karina reached into her pocket and pulled out her last light stick. She bent it until the inner chemical pack broke and then shook it with one hand. Soft, white light pushed back the darkness and softly illuminated the area. The light stick that Karina had dropped into the water glowed beneath her. Its tiny glow indicated a deep pool of water.

Joe called, "Swim this way."

Karina swam toward Joe's voice and found that the water got shallower. She saw Heather and Jessica with Joe; Heather stood in chest-deep water. Three kicks later, Karina's foot touched bottom. By the time she reached her friends, the water was shallow enough for everyone except Kiwi to stand.

"There seems to be a slight current," Karina said as she reached Joe. "The water is running back toward the pit. Do you think we should follow the current?"

"I think we should head upstream," Heather said. "Like, if lava begins spilling in here, it will follow the path of least resistance and take the downstream course."

"That sounds right to me," Joe said, taking Kiwi from her and setting the little girl on his shoulders. "What do you think, volcano girl?"

Karina admired the way Joe handled difficult situations. Almost without trying, he gave Kiwi comfort and made her feel important. A good frame of mind would go a long way toward helping the child's condition.

"Definitely upstream," Kiwi said with great conviction.

"How do you know upstream is the right way?" Penny asked.

"I don't, but I don't want to go where the lava will flow. Let's get moving. Hot lava will heat this water very quickly," Kiwi said. "I don't want to be boiled like a lobster."

"Me neither," Jessica agreed.

"I've got the light. I'll lead," Karina said. She worked her way around the group and assumed a leading position. "Penny, follow me. Joe, bring up the rear with Kiwi. Let us know if she gets too heavy."

"Like, yeah," Heather said, "we can all take turns carrying the volcano lady."

Karina almost felt Kiwi beaming from all the attention. The girl began a steady chatter with Joe and Penny, spreading her knowledge about volcanoes to everyone in the group.

For the first ten minutes, Karina walked through waist-deep water. Then the water level dropped to her thighs, to her knees, and finally to her ankles. At the same time, the dark black lava walls narrowed. The passageway ended in a narrow chamber; water gushed from a large hole in the wall high above her.

"This is a far as we go," Karina said.

Jessica stared at the gushing water. "Maybe we can climb out. I think I see a ledge off to the right of where the water is surging from the rock."

"Looks pretty high," Penny said.

Heather rubbed her hand against one wall. "Slick too—just our luck to have smooth lava when we need it rough for hand and foot holds."

Joe made several attempts to climb the steep walls. Each time he slipped and made no progress. "Sorry. It's not too high, maybe fifteen or sixteen feet. But it's too smooth to get started."

"What about building a human ladder?" Penny asked. "Heather can stand on Joe's shoulder, and I can climb up."

"It's worth a try," Karina agreed. "Be careful and take a flashlight."

Karina guided Joe into place and steadied him while Jessica and Penny helped Heather climb onto Joe's shoulders. Then Karina gave Penny a boost, but the weight proved too much for Joe's injured knee, and they had to abort the attempt.

After a long rest, Joe suggested he might be able to handle the weight if he lifted Jessica and Penny. He took a stance that placed his injured knee against the cave wall, and his leg didn't give way. Jessica stood on his shoulders, and Penny climbed onto Jessica's shoulders.

"I can't quite reach the ledge," Penny said. "But I think I can see light. Karina, turn off your flashlight."

Karina shoved the light stick into the back pocket of her jeans and turned off the flashlight she had used to spotlight Penny. "Can you see anything? It's all dark down here."

"Yes. There's light coming from somewhere," Penny said. Her announcement thrilled the group. "It's dim, but it's definitely light."

For almost five minutes, while Penny tried to climb onto the ledge, Joe held the combined weight, but she couldn't make the transition. In the end, Karina and Heather helped Penny climb down. Fatigue and cold, ankle-deep water chilled everyone, so Karina passed out the last of the chocolate that Jessica had saved.

"Is there anything you can latch onto if we made a rope from our clothes?" Karina asked. Kiwi shivered in her arms.

"Not that I could see," Penny said. "But we could try."

"Maybe I can handle Heather's weight long enough for Penny to climb," Joe suggested, bending his leg to test his knee.

"Do that again," Karina said. Her stomach churned with fear. She hoped her imagination was playing tricks on her. "I think the water's rising."

Everyone looked down, trying to judge any change in the water's depth. Joe spoke first. "The water is higher, two or three inches higher."

"It must have just started rising," Jessica said. "When I got down from Joe's shoulders, the water was barely over my ankles. Now it's at least three inches higher."

"Why is the water rising?" Penny whined. "Haven't we got enough problems?"

The distraught child sank against a smooth lava wall and cried. Karina handed Kiwi to Jessica and put her arms around the distraught preteen. She rubbed the child's back to warm her. The rest of the group tried to determine how fast the water was rising and what might be causing the increased water level.

"It's not fair," Penny cried. "Nothing is going right."

"We're still alive," Karina said. She thought about lying to Penny and telling her that everything would work out, that they'd find some solution, but she decided that Penny had a right to know the truth. "We've been very lucky so far. By all rights we should be dead. I won't promise you that everything is going to turn out fine; it probably won't. But don't you dare quit on me. As long as we can, we are going to survive. Now stop the tears. They don't help."

Penny took a couple of deep gulps of air and hugged Karina. "I love you."

She kissed Penny's forehead. "I love you too. Go keep Kiwi occupied while we try to find a plan to get us out of this place."

Over the next fifteen minutes, they devised numerous schemes—none of which had any real chance of success. During that time, the water rose above Karina's knees. At that rate, she figured the water would be over Kiwi's head in another hour and everyone else's in less than two.

Heather said, "Like, my guess is that lava spilled into the passageway behind us and has dammed up the stream. Heaven knows the water isn't getting any warmer, so I don't think it's coming this way."

"Great," Jessica said. "So we drown in cold water instead of in a hot spring. What's your point?"

"Like," Heather continued, "if lava has dammed the stream, can't we tread water and wait until it rises high enough to reach the ledge?"

Checking her watch, Karina quickly estimated the time it would take for water to fill the chamber. "Five to six hours—a long time to tread water."

"Not really," Heather insisted. "Look, before you came to Ocean Quest to join us for the semester we spent together, I took a course on survival swimming. I can teach you a simple technique that allows a person to float for a long period of time. Like, if you don't panic, you can tread water for hours and hours."

Karina was doubtful, but she listened with an open mind.

Heather explained the procedure. "Start by treading water. Then take a deep breath and float facedown in the water. Keep your arms at your side." She demonstrated. "When you need another breath, raise both of your arms above your her head, like doing a jumping jack exercise; only turn your palms outward instead of clapping them together." Heather extended her arms outward and pushed down on imaginary water until her hands reached the sides of her thighs. "Pushing down with your arms raises your head long enough to get another deep breath of air. Like, then all you have to do is relax with your face back in the water. Because the entire procedure uses very little energy, we should be possible to float for a very long time. I had to float for an hour in order to pass the course, and it was, like, easy. I could have floated much longer."

"Sounds like a plan," Joe said. He practiced the procedure. "What about the cold?"

"Can't help you there," Heather admitted. "Like, we trained in warm ocean water."

Karina had a sudden inspiration. "If we get cold, we can tread water. Kicking will burn up calories and warm us. When we get warm enough or too tired, we can float again."

"Best idea I've heard," Jessica said. "Can we learn it quickly?"

Heather led everyone back down the passageway until the water was deep enough to practice. In less than fifteen minutes, everyone—including Penny and Kiwi—was comfortable using the survival technique that Heather modeled.

———

Karina made a smooth transition from survival swimming to treading water. Two hours after learning the survival technique, she had been forced to begin survival swimming. Karina remembered the anxiety Penny and Cindy felt when the water first forced them to hold onto the taller kids and then begin survival swimming. After some initial panic, both little girls relaxed and even seemed to enjoy the challenge.

Karina checked the illuminated dial on her watch. A little over three hours had passed since she had been forced to float. She looked at Joe in the dull glare provided by the chemical light.

"How's it going?" Joe asked. He treaded water near where she floated with Penny.

"Fine. How are you doing, Kiwi?"

"I'm cold," came a whisper from over Joe's shoulder.

The soft, pained voice worried Karina. Joe had taken charge of Kiwi after the child gave up and stopped floating. Kiwi clung to him. Joe gave Karina a grim look and shook his head.

She worked the small waterproof flashlight from the jeans floating beside her. Jessica had pointed out that jeans would soak up water and weigh them down, so the girls and Joe had slipped off their jeans and let them float over their shoulders. The flashlight's narrow beam showed that the water needed to rise another five feet before it rose high enough for them to climb out: another two or three hours at the current rate. A terribly long time for a child in Kiwi's condition.

Kicking her bare feet back and forth to keep her head above water—her socks were in one pocket of her jeans, but her boots lay submerged ten or twelve feet below her—Karina swam over to Kiwi.

"Hey, girl. It won't be much longer. You hang in there. Penny saw light in the upper passageway. We'll be out in warm sunshine before you know it."

"How long?"

The soft voice held a note of resignation that told Karina any time would be too long. She held one hand out and managed to find a small rock to support her. Karina steadied herself and used her free hand to rub Kiwi's back.

"Not too long. Where's your camera?" Karina searched for a topic that would take Kiwi's mind away from her discomfort and focus it on something that might hold the child's attention.

"Heather has two of them; Jessica has the other," Kiwi said, her voice more firm.

"Won't the water ruin them?" Karina asked. She shifted her hand to a higher rock, looked around, and saw the other girls still using the survival swimming procedure.

"No," Kiwi assured Karina, "the disposables I use are waterproof. I chose them because I thought they might protect against heat and fumes."

Joe gallantly kept Kiwi afloat while Karina raised the child's spirits. "Hold onto me, tiger," he said. "Rest for a bit."

"What kind of pictures have you taken?" Karina asked.

"Lots of lava pictures. Some from Kilauea. More from Mauna Loa."

Karina swam nearer to Joe and Kiwi and treaded water. "Which are best?"

Kiwi paused for only a moment. "I like the lava flows from Kilauea that we took from the ridge by where we camped. Remember?"

She playfully bopped the top of Kiwi's head. "How could I forget? Shortly after taking those pictures, we had to run for our lives."

Joe shifted Kiwi's position so that she was nearer to Karina. "Hey, lava girl, what about Mauna Loa. Its eruption is much bigger."

"Much," she agreed. "I got some really nice pictures of lava being thrown high into the air. But the ash interfered with the pictures and made it hard to breathe. I was happy when Penny said that your plane was flying overhead. She thought it might be Martin. I didn't think we'd be found, though, until Karina rode up the hill."

The thought of Martin saddened Karina. She doubted that she would ever see him again. She forced the thought from her mind. "We were really lucky to have found you. Lots of rangers and police tried to find you and couldn't. Penny's dad and Martin searched all night for you guys."

"You know this was all my idea," Kiwi said. "I'm so happy that Penny came with me. I couldn't have done it without her."

"Would you have gone without Penny?" Joe asked.

"Yep," Kiwi said with conviction. "This was my last chance. It would have been scarier without Penny, but I'd still have gone." She directed her next words to Karina. "Please tell her father that she only came because I talked her into it. She shouldn't be punished too much. It's my fault."

Karina put out a hand and squeezed the child's arm. "I'll tell him. I'm sure he'll be proud that she was such a good friend, but he was awfully worried. How do you think your dad will react?"

In the dull light, Karina saw Kiwi shrug. She sniffed back tears. "Not much. He'll yell a little. But not much."

Fatigue from treading water for so long forced Karina to search for a handhold; she found none. She struggled to keep her head above water. Joe grabbed her arm and supported her until she found a small crack to slip her fingers into for support.

"The water level might be high enough for me to climb out if someone can take Kiwi," Joe said.

"Are you sure?" Karina worked to keep excitement from her voice. "I don't want to get everyone's hopes up if you can't make it."

He looked up at the ledge a few feet above. "It's worth a try."

She took two deep breaths and released her grip. "I'll get the others." She swam to Heather.

Kiwi asked, "Do you really think you can climb out?"

"We'll soon know," Joe said.

Karina tapped Heather's shoulder, and the girl immediately made the transition from survival swimming to treading water. "What's up?"

Fatigue forced Karina to grab Heather's shoulder for support. She gasped, "Joe thinks he might be able to climb out if someone can support Kiwi."

"Like, wow!" Heather exclaimed. "Let me tow you. I'll get the others."

Karina held onto Heather as she swam to Jessica and tapped her on top of the head. "Joe's going to try to climb out. Tell Penny and join us by Joe and Kiwi," Heather said.

Karina took a deep breath and let go of Heather's shoulders. "I'm okay. I can swim now. I'll try to keep Kiwi afloat. You see if you can help Joe."

Heather took charge. "Like, no way, babe. Kiwi's mine. You've been helping her for hours while all we did was rest and float. You rest. We'll take care of Kiwi and help Joe."

Karina wanted to argue, but Heather took Kiwi. Jessica swam past her and took Joe's jeans. Disgusted that she was not stronger but relieved that she didn't have to support Kiwi's weight, Karina found a hold on the wall and watched as Joe dropped beneath the surface, burst upward, and grabbed for the rim.

Joe reached the ledge, but his hands slipped. "Falling," he yelled. He splashed back into the water and surfaced, spitting out water. "Did I hit anyone?"

"We're fine," Penny said. "Are you okay? You almost made it."

The nearly successful attempt greatly raised Karina's spirits and energy level. "Everyone move back a little," she said. "Rest a bit before trying again."

Joe shook his head. "I'm okay, but everyone move aside. The ledge is pretty slippery. I might fall again."

Karina watched Joe drop beneath the surface and lunge upward. The attempt was almost successful. He clung to the ledge and got one foot up before falling.

Joe surfaced and slapped the water angrily. "Damn, just another inch!"

Jessica grabbed his arm and pulled him over by Karina. "Rest before you try again. We can wait a few minutes while you rest."

He looked at Karina and shrugged.

She smiled. Joe *never* used bad language. "You'll get us out of here," Karina said. "You always come to the rescue."

Heather agreed, "Like, yeah. You're our hero." She moved Kiwi from her back and held the child in front of her. "Right, volcano girl?"

"Yep. Definitely a hero," Kiwi said weakly. She shivered.

Joe turned to Karina. "One more try. Then I'll tread water for a while and let the water level rise a little higher." Determination radiated through each word.

Karina used her free arm to pull him close to her. She kissed his cheek. "For luck."

Joe swam to the wall directly beneath the ledge and felt along it for handholds. He placed his hands on the wall and dropped beneath the surface. Lunging upward, Joe got both elbows atop the ledge and then one leg. With a deep grunt, he hoisted himself from the water. Cheers erupted among the remaining swimmers.

"Toss me my jeans," he called down. "I can lower them to you to use as a rope. It's less than three feet."

Jessica tossed Joe his jeans. He lowered one pant leg to Karina and held onto the other. Penny climbed first. Then Karina sent Jessica. After Jessica, Heather tossed the rest of the clothes to Joe. Lying on his stomach with Jessica holding his legs, Joe reached down, grasped Kiwi's arms, and lifted the little girl for Penny to pull onto the ledge. Karina heaved a sigh of relief as Kiwi slid over the rim.

"You next," Heather said.

Karina protested, "No. You go. I should be last."

Heather moved into position to boost Karina to Joe's waiting arms. "Like, I'm heavier. Joe won't be able to lift me by himself. You and Jessica lie across Joe's legs. I'm strong enough to climb out once I get going."

Exhaustion prevented Karina from arguing. Heather was certainly stronger. At five feet ten inches, Heather was also several inches taller than Karina. Firm hands pushed her up to Joe's waiting arms.

"Welcome aboard," he said as Karina rolled to safety. "I sent Penny and Kiwi toward the light with strict instructions not to go anywhere without us."

Moments later Karina and Jessica pulled Heather from the water. Then Karina led everyone on a search for a path to the surface.

"Oh my! Look at that," Jessica said. Her voice echoed the amazement everyone felt.

Through a four-foot high opening in the lava tube that led to the outside world, Karina witnessed a fantastic sight—a sight that held the group spellbound and hypnotized Kiwi. Karina sat with her back against a smooth section of rock wall; Kiwi sat on her lap. The pool of water she had climbed from was only fifty yards behind her. The lava tube opening was wide enough that all of them could sit in the opening and look out.

Kiwi smiled up at Karina. "This is a *major* eruption."

Rivers of lava flowed down from Mauna Loa. Some thick, dark-red flows inched their way down the steep mountain slope; other bright-red flows ran downhill at the pace of molasses on a warm summer day, while a few bright red and white flows raced past the slower lava. All of the flows mixed together in the steep valley below, pooled, and began a magnificent crusade toward the ocean.

Karina estimated the combined flowing mass to be six or seven feet high. The lava obliterated everything in its path. Fields of tall grass and small trees burst into flames and burned ahead of the flow, announcing the indiscriminate killer's presence to all living creatures unlucky enough not to be somewhere else.

Exhausted and hungry, everyone sat and watched the volcano's amazing show unfolding before them, a new epoch in the history of Mauna Loa's eruptions. Kiwi's weight on her lap had put Karina's legs to sleep. Penny's head rested on Karina's left shoulder, and Joe sat on her right. Across from Karina, separated by a stream of spring water, Heather and Jessica slumped together.

Tired beyond all thoughts about rescue or what additional steps were necessary to assure their survival, eyes remained glued on the lava flows. Wandering through the lava tube—and their desperate rush from the encroaching lava inside the tube—had positioned them on a steep hillside about a mile from Mauna Loa's flowing lava. At least cold and heat were no longer a problem. The outside air warmed them, while cool air inside the lava tube kept heat from becoming a problem.

Karina reached down and cupped her hand into the stream and drank freely from the spring water. The spring had filled the passageway from which they had escaped and now flowed backward, out from the opening and onto the hillside beyond. She knew untreated water might contain microorganisms that could cause illness later, but dehydration was her immediate problem. No one spoke of food. Having none, everyone pushed the thought aside and ignored empty feelings that would soon become painful.

As the sun traversed the evening sky, even the grandeur of an erupting volcano couldn't ward off exhausted sleep. Karina was the last to succumb. Kiwi had kept up a steady conversation that lasted long after the others nestled down to sleep. Kiwi's excitement and increased energy level encouraged Karina. Maybe the child would survive this experience to see her family again. Thoughts of rescue filled Karina, and peaceful dreams brought her more comfort than leaning against hard rock should provide.

Looking out into a star-filled night sky, Kiwi sat cuddled against Karina's right side. Penny and Jessica lay hunched together on

Karina's left, sleeping soundly. After a serious discussion about the dangers of hiking barefoot through the night in search of help, Joe and Heather had climbed the steep hillside above the lava tube opening and departed in search of rescue.

"Karina, look!" Kiwi pointed to a high arching ember of lava. "A lava bomb. That's a lava bomb."

"What's a lava bomb?" Karina asked, feigning more enthusiasm than she felt.

"Lava bombs are pieces of lava thrown into the air that are larger than the size of a walnut," Kiwi happily explained. "Pieces thrown into the air that are pea-sized are called cinders, and anything smaller than that is called ash."

"Martin needs to hire you to teach his volcano course," Karina said, praising Kiwi's knowledge. "If I pass my final exam, I'll have you to thank."

Kiwi shifted around and hugged her tightly. Then she assumed a more comfortable position, snuggling against Karina. "I wish I could. Even with all the pain and fear, this has been the greatest experience of my life." Karina gently rubbed the child's arms. "My last wish would never have been fulfilled without you and Penny. Please tell Daddy that I love him and Mom and all my family."

The conversation's serious tone caught Karina by surprise. She paused to collect her thoughts, hugging Kiwi tightly to her. "You'll see your dad again very soon now. Joe and Heather will have help here before you know it, maybe before morning. We're safe from the lava flows. It's just a matter of time before help arrives."

"I hope you're right, but I feel funny. I think I'm dying," Kiwi said softly.

Karina fought hard not to gasp. She remembered Martin telling her during a first aid class that when a child told you that he or she was dying, the child probably was dying. She hugged Kiwi tightly and spoke softly in the child's right ear, carefully choosing her words. "Kiwi, I'm very happy to have been with you during this experience. I'm sure that your father will be delighted that your wish has been fulfilled. But I want you to make every effort to see him again. Try to give him a chance to share in your last wish."

"I'll try," Kiwi said. "Look! Three of them!"

Pleased with the distraction, Karina looked to where the child pointed out a string of lava bombs sailing skyward. For long hours, she held Kiwi and watched Mauna Loa's continuing eruption, which Kiwi said was its largest eruption in hundreds of years.

Shortly after two o'clock in the morning, Kiwi's breathing became erratic, and the child began asking questions for which Karina had no sure answer.

"Will I go to heaven?" Kiwi asked. "My daddy said I would because I believe in God, but we didn't go to church much."

Karina looked toward Jessica and Penny for support, but both girls lay clumped together in exhausted sleep. Reaching into the past to a conversation she'd once had with Cindy after Cindy's father had died, Karina tried to comfort the child. "Joe should probably answer this question. He is more knowledgeable in such matters than I am."

"Joe's not here." Kiwi leaned her head against Karina's shoulder.

Karina paused to collect her thoughts. "Cindy once asked me the same question after her father died. They hadn't been faithful in their church attendance either. My parents also died when I was young, and we didn't attend church very often."

Kiwi wiggled around until Karina looked into her dark brown eyes. The child waited expectantly.

"I told Cindy that I knew her father was in heaven. I believe my parents are there. Don't ask me why I believe this, but I do."

"I've not been very good," Kiwi said. "Think God will want me?"

Karina patted the girl's leg. "Joe once explained to me that it's not what we do that counts; it is what God's done for us. I'm sure that when you die, you'll go to heaven. You'll see my parents, and Cindy's father will be waiting for you." She tickled and teased Kiwi. "But if God doesn't want you, he can certainly send you back to me."

The child laughed and tickled Karina back. After several minutes of quiet wrestling, a breathless Kiwi lay against Karina. A deep trembling of the ground and a massive blob of bright lava hurtling into the sky turned Kiwi's attention back to Mauna Loa. "God must be powerful. Thanks, Karina."

She waited for Kiwi to say more, but the child remained silent. Mauna Loa took center stage by throwing tons of lava high into the air. Even though Karina had seen enough hot lava to last her a lifetime, the sight was too impressive to look anywhere else. Bonded by the moment, Karina and Kiwi watched silently, happy with the love and compassion each shared.

Fear kept Karina awake long after Kiwi fell asleep—fear that Kiwi would not be alive when she awoke, as had happened while she comforted Cindy's dying father. Kiwi breathed easily, but her breathing remained uneven, with some pauses long enough to worry Karina that Kiwi wouldn't breathe again. Her thoughts went back to Missouri and the cave. Her stomach tightened, and her hands became cool and clammy. Karina wasn't sure she could handle another child dying in her presence. She prayed that she would be spared such punishment.

The end came with the rising sun. Long pauses between each breath told Karina that Kiwi's time was at hand. Briefly, she thought about trying to wake the child, to encourage her to keep fighting. But she decided that would not be fair. It was far better for Kiwi to leave this world in peaceful slumber rather than with the panicked realization that her life was about to end.

Kiwi took two deep breaths and remained still. Karina kissed her good-bye. "Sleep well, honey."

Silent tears ran shamelessly down Karina's cheeks as she hugged Kiwi's silent form and rocked her back and forth. Sunlight beamed down from the rising sun, and she noted that even Mauna Loa mourned the moment, for the mighty volcano ceased its rumbling, and lava no longer shot into the sky. A strange calmness settled on Karina, unlike the panic she had felt at Philip's death. She lifted her eyes to the sky and prayed.

Her heart told her Kiwi was safe and happy. A peace filled Karina that she'd not felt since the tragic cave rescue. Carefully shifting Kiwi to the cave floor, Karina lay next to the child, and worries of how to tell everyone about Kiwi's last moments faded slowly into nothingness.

CHAPTER 17

The New Dawn

Opening her eyes to bright sunlight, Karina sighed and hugged her pillow. Events from the last few days pressed down upon her—being rescued less than an hour after Kiwi died, frantically comforting Penny, painfully breaking the news to Kiwi's father, and attending Kiwi's funeral service.

Karina rolled over onto her stomach and looked at the empty bed across from her. Jessica had already risen. A clock radio sitting on the small table between the beds told Karina that it would soon be her time of reckoning. She slipped back the sheet, moved into the bathroom, started the shower, and nursed the handles until a hot stream sprayed against the shower curtain.

Inside the warm spray, Karina cried again. She didn't cry because of what Martin might decide to do with her. Unlike previous times when her future hung in the balance, Martin was now her guardian. She would not be sent away. Her tears were for Joe, Jessica, and Heather. Joe and Jessica were in serious danger of being expelled from Blue Horizons. Heather was only at Blue Horizons for the summer semester, but Martin's report back to Ocean Quest Academy might get Heather dismissed as well. She was already on probation at Ocean Quest for earlier disobedience.

Rotating slowly in the warm shower, Karina also cried for Penny. The child had barely spoken to anyone since Kiwi's death. Penny remained angry with Karina for not waking her when she knew Kiwi was dying. At least Dr. Winfield had argued in Karina's favor on that point. He had also thanked her over and over for keeping Penny safe. Karina stopped crying as she remembered Dr. Winfield gently taking Penny into his arms and carrying her away.

Memories of Kiwi's funeral service at the chapel made Karina proud of her guardian—it had been Kiwi's request that her body be cremated. Martin had arranged for all of Kiwi's family to fly to Hawaii for the service. He had personally paid for their airfares, hotel rooms, and meals. If she figured correctly, Martin would soon decide her fate and the fate of her friends.

A knock on the bathroom door cut short Karina's reflections. She turned off the shower, grabbed a large bath towel, and wrapped it around her. She inched open the bathroom door. Jessica stood on the other side.

"Martin is ready," Jessica said. "He wants to speak with all of us—but one at a time. I'm first. Wish me luck; my parents are here. I may not have time to say good-bye."

Karina stepped from the bathroom and hugged her best friend, ignoring the fact that she was still wet and Jessica was dressed in her formal school uniform. "Tell Martin it was all my fault. He knows it was my idea."

Jessica lightly pushed Karina away and shook her head. "It may have been your idea, but it was my decision. I'm ready for any punishment that Martin gives me. I only hope he doesn't expel me. I'd rather not leave Blue Horizons under such circumstances."

Karina knew that Jessica had more than Martin to worry about; she also had to worry about her parents. They were furious with her and threatened to remove her from Blue Horizons. Not able to find any words of comfort or wisdom, Karina gave Jessica another quick hug and walked her to the door.

A short time later she stood outside Martin's motel room. She hesitated momentarily, adjusted her tie, smoothed out her skirt, and straightened her blazer. She lightly knocked on the heavy wood door.

"It's open," Martin said in response to Karina's soft knock.

Taking a deep breath to summon courage, she entered. He motioned for her to sit on one of the chairs arranged around a small table. Karina took a seat, sat up straight, and looked directly into Martin's eyes.

"Sir," she began, "it was all my fault. I'm responsible for the loss of the ATVs and *Bluebird*. I used my friendship with Heather, Jessica, and Joe to convince them to join me. Please don't hold them accountable for my actions."

Martin rose from behind the table and sat in a chair beside Karina. "That's very noble of you, Karina. But you can't take responsibility for the decisions of others." He put a hand on her shoulder. "You seem to have an uncanny knack for disobeying rules and then having your decisions prove you right."

Feeling the warmth from Martin's firm grasp, Karina decided to push further. "I'm not sure what you mean, but it is very important to me that most of the blame be mine. Punish me any way you like. But please don't send my friends away. They wouldn't be in a position to be expelled if it weren't for me."

For a long time, Martin didn't speak. Then he got up and paced back and forth, an action that made Karina extremely nervous. She patted the carpet with the toe of her shoe, while her fingers nervously tapped on the seat of the metal chair.

Martin stopped pacing, walked to the bed, and opened a briefcase. He pulled an envelope from a stack of papers. He handed Karina the envelope. "Before we go any further, read this."

Karina opened the envelope and began reading, which led to another bout of crying. Inside the envelope was a note addressed to Karina from Kiwi. It had been written the night Kiwi and Penny had run away. As she read Kiwi's final request, she sobbed and forgot about her own situation.

Dear Karina,

Thank you for the fun I had surfing and skin diving and the volcanic eruption I saw on the ridge. Penny and I are sneaking out to see another eruption (please don't be mad). I have another favor to ask. Last night I had a bad time. If I die before leaving Hawaii (I think I will), please spread my ashes into the wind from the Mauna Kea Observatory. From there I can always be with my volcanoes.

Always your friend,
Kiwi

P.S. Please don't be mad at Penny!

Martin sat beside Karina and waited until she stopped crying. Then he enlightened her about the fate of her friends. "Before we discuss your part in this affair, let me tell you what disciplinary actions have already been imposed.

"Heather will remain with us until we finish here in Hawaii—another two weeks. She will return to Ocean Quest Academy for the fall semester. Her father sent a rather substantial check to cover the cost of the equipment that was lost. I've sent it back; I consider that loss to be your responsibility. While Heather remains with us, she is restricted to her quarters every evening and may not venture out without Sally or me to accompany her. In other words, she's grounded."

Karina's spirits rose.

"Joe is also grounded," Martin continued. "Not only to his room, but from flying. However, he will be accepted back at Blue Horizons in the fall for his senior year."

Karina winced. Being grounded meant that Joe would have to wait to get his private pilot's license.

"Jessica is grounded for the remainder of the summer semester; however, her parents may decide to take her with them tonight when they fly back to the mainland, and she may not be returning to Blue Horizons in the fall."

Karina stood to speak, but Martin raised his hand for silence. "The decision is not mine to make. Her parents have the final say as to her future at Blue Horizons. They will join us this afternoon; we'll learn then what has been decided."

Karina nodded and sat down. "Will Kiwi's family be there?"

"They changed their airplane tickets so that they could attend, but they must depart for the airport shortly afterward. Kiwi's mother and father didn't want to miss this special moment with those who helped grant Kiwi her last wish." Martin took her hands in his. "Now, as to your situation. If you hadn't disobeyed, Penny may have died alongside Kiwi—alone and very frightened. Their bodies may never have been found. I speak for *everyone* in expressing our sincere gratitude for saving the girls from such a painful death. However, I can't punish the others and excuse your behavior. You will share in the grounding your classmates have received, and you will work off the cost of the lost equipment."

"How?" Karina asked. "I don't even have a part-time job."

"Blue Horizons has received a donation of $25 million to expand its capacity," Martin said. "Next semester we will have more staff members, more students, and a second focus besides flying. Mountaineering will be added to our curriculum. To pay off your debt, you will play houseparent to a group of four thirteen-year-old girls, including Victoria Lee—the girl you pulled from the ocean. Add keeping an eye on Cindy to your list of responsibilities, and I'm sure you'll agree that you will have paid back every dollar before the year is out."

"Houseparent? Me?" Karina realized that Martin had just taken away most of her free time for an entire year. "Can't you just whip me instead?"

Martin laughed at Karina's suggestion. "You don't get off that easy. Every time you disobey me and risk your life, I lose years off mine. If I have to suffer, so do you." He looked into her eyes and spoke in a more serious tone. "You have marvelous instincts, react quickly in an emergency, and impulsively come to correct decisions. In the years that I've worked in the military and on rescue teams, I've known others with such character traits. Many have died in the performance of their duties. I want you to understand that one of these days, you might not be so lucky. You have already survived more extreme situations than are allowed most people. Do you understand what I'm saying?"

Karina reflected on Martin's words and wisdom. She knew how lucky she was to be alive. She also realized how much helping others meant to her and decided that she'd better get a grip on her impulsiveness, or she'd likely follow in the footsteps of the—many—Martin had spoken about. She bit her lip and solemnly nodded her understanding.

Martin hugged her. "Good. Let's get ready for the afternoon. Are you ready?"

The question sent Karina back to her motel room. Kiwi's final request would take some preparation and push Karina to her emotional limit.

The brisk, cool wind outside the Mauna Kea Observatory blew Karina's hair in front of her face as she held the prayer she had painstakingly written and rewritten. Standing nine thousand feet above sea level gave her a magnificent view of the big island of Hawaii and the surrounding ocean. She viewed the results of Mauna Loa's recent eruption. The volcano had stopped erupting the day Kiwi died. Since then, it had been silent except for a puff of steam now and then. Karina turned her back to her audience and paused to gain control of her emotions. She couldn't speak without crying.

"Are you all right?" Jessica asked, putting an arm around Karina.

She nodded and turned back to finish what she had started. Sally and most of Karina's classmates stood in a semicircle in front of her. Joe, Heather, and Jessica stood at her left side. Immediately to her right stood Martin, Jessica's parents, Dr. and Mrs. Winfield, Penny, and Cindy. Beside them stood Kiwi's family.

"It was Kiwi's last wish that I spread her ashes to the wind at the observatory here on Mauna Kea so that she may forever observe the volcanoes she loved so dearly. But first, I'd like to read a prayer that I wrote for Kiwi." She opened the folded piece of paper and read:

Dear God, thank you for the wonderful times we've had swimming and playing, surfing and sightseeing. Thank you that we got to know a special girl named Kiwi, whose love of volcanoes nearly drove us all mad.

Bless Kiwi now and give her rest in your heavenly arms. Hold the loved ones she held dear in the knowledge of her joy to rest so high above the sea for eternity. She can now watch volcanoes erupt without fear or harm.

Let Kiwi be happy and laugh much every day. As she has filled our hearts with love and peace, help us to remember her enthusiasm and dedication and let her spirit uplift us as we each go our own way.

Dear Lord, as our own lives draw to an end, give us the strength and courage that Kiwi had. Help us to know that she waits high above and bring us together again through your holy Grace. Amen.

Karina paused to force back tears. Then she knelt down and picked up the small urn at her feet. She worked the lid free, walked several steps forward to a spot overlooking the valley, and tossed Kiwi's ashes high into the outgoing wind.

"Good-bye from all of us, Kiwi. May you forever rest in peace."

The wind lifted Kiwi's ashes and carried them high into the air. No one spoke to break the somber moment. Sally and Mr. Smithson took the Blue Horizons group back to the motel. Dr. and Mrs. Winfield took charge of Cindy. Then Kiwi's father approached.

He solemnly shook Karina's hand. "I can't tell you how much we appreciate you and your friends being with Kiwi at the end. Knowing she was in the arms of someone who cared for her makes her passing so much easier to bear." He paused and wiped a tear from his face. "We will always be in your debt."

Karina squeezed the tall black man's hands, and he smiled back at her. She marveled that he had the same pearly-white teeth and chin structure that Kiwi had. "No, sir," she said. "I will always be in Kiwi's debt. She was such an inspiration to me, and I truly believe that God sent her to me to help me through a hard time in my life."

Kiwi's father thanked Karina again for her prayer and then departed with his family for the airport. After a lengthy discussion with Jessica, her parents also left. Martin allowed Karina, Joe, Jessica, Heather, and Penny to remain behind. He waited for them in the car so that they might have a few moments alone to console each other and share final memories.

Penny took Karina's hand. "Kiwi's happy now. I know she is," Penny said. "I'm sorry that I was angry with you. I was really mad at myself that I had fallen asleep and had not been there for her."

Tears prevented Karina from answering, and Joe put an arm around her. She squeezed Penny's hand, gaining enough control to speak. "I'm just emotional. Kiwi is happy. I know that."

"And we're still a team," Jessica said, taking Karina's free hand and squeezing it tightly. "My parents said I could stay at Blue Horizons."

Karina broke free from Penny and Joe and flung her arms around Jessica. "What changed their minds? What happened?"

"I owe it all to Martin," Jessica said. "My parents and I fought all morning. Mom hugged me, then slapped me, and then hugged me." Jessica pulled out from Karina's grasp and wiped a tear from the corner of her eye. "She acted that way because she thought I had died. Then Dad told me I couldn't stay at Blue Horizons. I argued and begged and cried, but it didn't do any good. I was packing to leave when Martin knocked on our door." Jessica smiled at Karina. "You must have been writing your prayer. When Martin explained how we had saved Penny's life and comforted Kiwi until she died, my parents were so proud of me. Being here and listening to your prayer changed Dad's mind. He relented and said I could stay."

"That's great." Heather patted Jessica on the back. "Like, this team really needs a tall, rich kid to keep an eye on them, so I'm staying for the fall semester."

"Really?" Karina couldn't believe her ears.

"Yep," Heather said. "After Martin told me I could finish the semester, I called Ocean Quest Academy. It was okay with them if Martin agreed. An hour before coming up here, I asked him. He said he'd be honored. Like, look out world; I'm ready to fly—if I can get over my fear of heights."

The mention of flying reminded Karina that Joe's punishment included being grounded. She looked at him, raised her eyebrows, and shrugged.

Joe smiled a return. "Being earthbound for a few weeks isn't the end of the world. It'll give me some time to study for the FAA written exam. Events *beyond my control* have kept me a bit busy lately and forced me to ignore my studies."

Joe's humor brought laughter. Everyone shivered in the cool wind. As the group took a final look in the direction that the wind had carried Kiwi's ashes, Penny took Karina's hand and whispered into her ear.

"That is an absolutely fantastic idea," Karina said, giving Penny a hug. "Let's ask Martin."

"What's fantastic?" Joe asked.

"Like, let us in on it," Heather said.

"Remember," Jessica added, "friends forever."

Karina looked to Penny, who nodded her consent. "Penny suggested a name for the new ultralight trainer that will replace *Bluebird.* How about *Mauna Kiwi?*"

"Sounds great to me." Joe hoisted Penny onto his back and headed toward the parking lot.

Heather took Karina's left hand, and Jessica grabbed her right. Walking toward Martin's car, Heather asked the group, "Like, do you think we can learn to climb mountains without creating a major crisis?"

"Not with my record," Karina giggled. "We'll probably all fall into a crevasse."

"As long as we're together," Jessica said. "Together, we can handle anything."

Hands locked in those of her friends, Karina felt at peace with all that had happened during the emotionally demanding summer session. She wasn't sure what the future held, but she knew she would not face it alone.

"To future adventures," Karina said. She firmly squeezed her friends' hands and raised them above her head. "Together."